BALL DON'T LIE

MATT de la PEÑA

BALL DON'T LIE

EMBER

Text copyright © 2005 by Matt de la Peña
Cover art copyright © 2005 by Alex Williamson

All rights reserved. Published in the United States by Ember, an imprint of Random House Children's Books, a division of Random House, Inc., New York. Originally published in hardcover in the United States by Delacorte Press, an imprint of Random House Children's Books, New York, in 2005.

Ember and the colophon are trademarks of Random House, Inc.

Visit us on the Web! www.randomhouse.com/teens

Educators and librarians, for a variety of teaching tools, visit us at www.randomhouse.com/teachers

The Library of Congress has cataloged the hardcover edition of this work as follows:
Peña, Matt de la.
Ball don't lie / Matt de la Peña. — 1st ed.
p. cm.
Summary: Seventeen-year-old Sticky lives to play basketball at school and Lincoln Rec Center in Los Angeles and is headed for the pros, but he is unaware of the many dangers—including his own past—that threaten his dream.
ISBN 978-0-385-73232-1 (trade) — ISBN 978-0-385-90258-8 (glb) —
ISBN 978-0-307-43316-9 (ebook)
[1. Basketball—Fiction. 2. Obsessive-compulsive disorder—Fiction.
3. Foster home care—Fiction. 4. Race relations—Fiction.
5. Los Angeles (Calif.)—Fiction.] I. Title: Ball do not lie. II. Title.
PZ7.P3725Bal 2005
[Fic]—dc22
2004018057

ISBN 978-0-385-73425-7 (tr. pbk.)

RL: 6.0

Printed in the United States of America

17 16 15 14 13 12 11

First Ember Edition 2011

For Al and Roni de la Peña

Dreadlock Man,

with his fierce fists and suspect jump shot, sets his stuff ($1.45 sandals, key to bike lock, extra T-shirt) on the bleachers and holds his hands out for the ball. It's ten in the morning and Lincoln Rec has just opened. Sticky's at the free-throw line working out his routine, while all the regulars come swaggering in. *Come on, little man,* Dreadlock Man says. *Give up the rock.*

Sticky throws an around-the-back, no-look dime. Watches Dreadlock Man rise into the air with his awful form—calves tightening, dreads scattering, eyes poised on the goal—and let go of a sorry-looking line drive. Before he comes back down to the dusty old hardwood, he yells out: *Peanut Butter!* Says it every time he takes a jumper. *Peanut*

Butter! That's what he wants everyone to call him, but nobody does.

When the ball ricochets off the side of the backboard, entirely missing the rim, he says what any man would say: *Hey, yo, Stick, let me get one more.*

Hawk passes through the door, from sunny day into old dark gym. A big black man. Wears bright wraparound shades and baggy shorts, the new Jordans on his size-sixteen feet. Hawk has a little money to his name. He's one of the few Lincoln Rec ballers who does. Some of the regulars say he made a few movies a couple years back. A stunt double maybe or security on the set. If you look quickly, get a fast profile shot, you might think he looks like someone.

Hey, yo, Dreadlock Man, he says, megaphoning a hand around his mouth. *I got five says you brick that shot.* The whole side of his shaved head flexes as he chews hard at his gum.

Dreadlock Man takes a couple awkward dribbles and rises again. *Peanut Butter!* This time his ball arcs through the air without backspin. A Phil Niekro knuckleball that thuds off the back of the rim and drops into Sticky's waiting hands.

Damn, Dreadlock Man, your shot's straight broke. Hawk falls into the bleachers laughing, goes to lace up his new sneaks.

Other dudes come strutting into the gym. Slapping hands. Slinging their bags onto the bleachers and talking trash.

Sticky high-dribbles to the other end of the court, spins in an acrobatic reverse. He points up at an invisible crowd.

2

Dreadlock Man watches, hands on hips. Yells out: *Come on, Stick, we tryin to shoot down here.*

A couple other balls get tossed into the rotation. Everybody shooting short set-shots to get warm, stretching out stiff shoulders and legs. Most of these cats are just out of bed. A couple have pulled themselves off a piece of cardboard on court two, having spent the night where all the homeless stay.

Lincoln Rec functions both as a great place to hoop and a small-time homeless shelter.

Sometimes things overlap.

Sticky comes dribbling down from the other side of the court with his left hand. He goes right up to Dante, who's just walked in carrying a duffel bag, the best player in the gym, and shoots a soft twenty-footer over his outstretched hand. Dante and Sticky watch the ball smack both sides of the rim and bounce off toward the east sideline.

Go get that brick, Stick, Dante says. *Bring it back my way so you could watch a real shooter.*

Dante played ball overseas for six or seven seasons; he's slick with both the rock and his mouth. Some cats say, *Watch it, man,* to newcomers, *dude will beat you two times.* Then they sit back and clown those who brush off their warning:

Told ya, dawg. Didn't I tell him, Big J, when he walked his sorry ass in here?

Yeah, I heard it, OP. I was sitting right there when you said it.

Dante's skin shines black as night, and his hair is scarecrow wild. The devil's growth fingers out from his chin.

Sticky skips a bounce pass to Dante, who pats it around his back a little, through his legs some, close to the ground

3

with his tips like a magician, and then fires up a twenty-five-footer that nestles in the gut of the net. *You see how I play the strings, young Stick?* He laughs a little and nods his head: *Just like that, baby boy. That's string music.*

Dante struts off the court with hip-hop rhythm, brushes past a businessman (who's stopped in to watch these black guys play: arms folded, subtle smile) and lies down near the bleachers to stretch his thirty-seven-year-old back.

This is Lincoln Rec on a Thursday, midsummer.

It's the best place in L.A. to ball. Some sports mag even did a cover story about it a few years back. Gym manager Jimmy's gold-tooth smile spread right across pages seventy-two and seventy-three. The article talked about how one court houses the homeless and the other accommodates the fearless. How Michael Cage sometimes shows up. Cliff Levingston. Eddie Johnson. Bill Walton was quoted saying: "It's the sweetest run in all of Southern California." The gym is in the middle of a pretty good-sized park, adjacent to some museums and business offices. The place gets so dark that when you've been in there a while and you go to peek your head outside to check your car, your eyes freeze up and hide like you've just stared in the sun.

Games go to eleven straight up. No win by two here. Fouls are called by the offense. The ball they use is dead weight. The leather has soaked up so much sweat from so many different dudes over the years, it takes a lot of legs just to get it up to the rim.

Other than that, there's a constant sour smell in the air, a NO DUNKING sign that *nobody* pays attention to, and an un-

4

written rule that all who step foot through the gym doors with the intention of getting on the court better come with their A-game. "If you're gonna run with the big dogs," the article reads, "you can't pee like a puppy."

Sticky does what he does every day. He stands on the free-throw line with his ball. Simple as that. It doesn't matter who says what to him, if a ball caroms out his way, or nothing: He's not moving. He puts his rock between his knees and goes to tuck his shirt in. Pulls his shirt back out and retucks. Pulls it out and retucks. Ball between his knees, watching everybody shoot warm-up jumpers. Pulls out and retucks. Pulls out and retucks. There are eighteen, nineteen guys by this time—shooting around, running a quick game of twenty-one to get loose—this is the only way Sticky can make sure he finds himself balling in the first game. Pulls his shirt out and retucks. Pulls out and retucks. He's seventeen and white; these guys are men. Even though his game has improved from here to the 405, and most regulars swear they'd make room on their squad, there's still that thought in the back of his head that he might not get picked up.

He can't kick the aftertaste of that first month he started showing up, way back before he was a sophomore. It's only been a year and some change, but any baller would swear it's been longer. He'd cruise into the gym wearing all his state-issued gear, a bottle of tap water and bag of granola in his backpack, and the kid wouldn't get in one game all day. He'd just sit up in the bleachers like the thirteenth man, feeling like a scrub, headphones on his ears and basketball in his hands, figuring out on the sly who he could take. Absorbing the rhythms of squeaking sneaks and slapping hands, mouths left running all day and the rap of body against body in the paint.

Shoot em up! Dante yells from the side, touching his toes with both hands.

And here's Sticky, already on the free-throw line with his ball. Simple fifteen-footer. Shot ninety-two percent this past season on JV. Ninety-four percent in league. He bounces twice with the left, wipes right-hand sweat off on his sock and cradles the ball. Same deal, different day. Pulls in a deep breath, runs an index finger across his bead necklace three times (just like that, peeking up at the rim: one, two, three). Middle finger in the groove of his rock, thumb between the felt-penned 7 and F. Shot's up and it rips through the bottom of the net.

First two who knock down free throws are captains. Sticky's got first pick.

OP follows and misses way short.

Hawk has one go in and out.

Dallas shoots an air ball. *I just got here, man. My first shot.*

Finally Trey gets a generous bounce and the ball rolls in.

I got Dante, Sticky says.

All right then, Trey says, *gimme Slim. . . .*

I Almost Forgot

to tell you about Sticky. . . .

How he keeps his raisin-brown hair cropped close. Faded up on the sides with some fancy-ass clippers he snatched from Macy's. How he's long and thin like somebody's stick-figure sketch, scissored off lined paper and Scotch-taped to a basketball court. How he goes everywhere with his duct-taped Walkman cranked up—loud rips of Jay-Z and Tupac before hoops, old-school Alexander O'Neal when it's time to chill. Sometimes the right-side phone goes out for a sec, but the kid knows just where to slap to get it going again. Only time he pulls the headphones off is when he's about to hoop or get with some little honey.

Sticky places the deck and phones in his bag, along with

his flea-bitten ball, and zips up. Then he slides his stuff under the first bleacher. Slides it back out and back in. Back out and back in. Back out and back in. When something in the process fits just right he wraps the straps around the side support three times and ties up.

There's twelve bucks in that bag, and Sticky knows to watch it all day. Some pretty shady dudes roll through Lincoln Rec. Guys that'll thumb through stray bags when everybody's head is in the game, looking like rats in a trash bag for something quick to jack. A watch or earring. A fat gold chain. Somebody's hard-earned twelve bucks.

Some guys would steal from their best friend's bag if it came right down to it.

Sticky scrounged up all that cash this past week at the Third Street Promenade, after extended sessions of hardcore hoop. He panhandled with a bowl like back when he was a kid. Same spot and everything.

Hard-earned currency.

Twelve bucks to buy the stuffed bear he spotted in some old lady's card shop about a week ago. His girl Anh-thu's sixteenth birthday is today and he's set on hooking it up right. Figures he'll put the gold bracelet he's planning on swiping from a department store on one of the little brown bear's arms. Give it to her first thing tonight when they meet.

But check it out, Sticky would never steal from an old lady's card shop, he's got morals about things like that. Some gold from a department store, though? That's ripe for the taking.

He has the exact gold bracelet all picked out and everything. Saleslady called it a snake because of the way it wraps around itself. So slick and shiny and it never kinks. *You could crumple it all up in your hand,* the lady said, spinning and pulling at it in her palm. *And it still won't kink. See?*

Sticky spied it a few days back after his boy Sin sat him down and told him how it goes. *Dude, you gotta score your girl a gift,* he said as they rolled through Foot Locker, lifting new hoop shoes off the rack, checking them from every angle and then sticking them back up. *Not somethin all dumb, either. It's like this: if you tryin to get with some little lady, but you ain't sure, flowers are cool. Candy. But if you hangin with her consistently, you gotta step up big.*

He looked Sticky right in the eyes when he said it, a pair of the new Iversons hanging in his right hand. *There's no gettin around it, man. It's mandatory.*

A couple minutes later Sticky spotted the snake in Macy's and stopped Sin cold. *This is it, dude,* he said, running his fingers along the glass set up to keep grubby hands away. *This is the one I gotta get her.*

Sin stepped up next to him, squinted his eyes to get a better look. *All right,* he said, nodding. *OK.*

Yeah, she's gonna dig this, Sticky said. *I just got this feelin about it.*

Sin touched the glass, and Sticky called the lady over.

Lift the bracelet, pay for the bear: He's had it all worked out like this for almost a full week.

It's been a crazy hot summer in Los Angeles. Hot and dry. Like a tray of crackers just pulled from the oven. Like the whole city was pulled up by the roots and set down in the Mojave. Overheated cars line the freeway shoulder.

Abandoned. The parking lot in front of the gym is an afternoon mirage. The sun pushing its hot rays so deep into the newly laid pavement, it feels like you're walking on grainy-black bread dough. Packs of businessmen slip two fingers between their throat and collar on the lunchtime march back from their cars, waiting for a cool breeze that never shows up. After midday games, all the guys jockey for the water fountain like a group of camels looking for a two-week fix.

Some of the old-timers go on and on about this global warming thing people are talking about, how all the concrete and packed freeways are going to be the end of this crazy city. *Feel like I'm in hell today,* Old-man Perkins says to no one in particular. *Man, I done felt like this almost every day this summer.*

You said it, OP, Slim says as a ball falls into his hands. He banks one in off the glass and holds his hands out for the change. *Already told you I'm out. I'm gonna go back where I got most my peoples, up in Carolina. Soon as I get my last check, poof, I'm yesterday's news.*

Others sit in front of the huge gym fan and pass around cold beer in a water bottle. Jimmy posted a sign that says NO ALCOHOL right above the entrance, did it just this summer, but a little beer in a water bottle doesn't bother him much. Not when the gym's as stuffy as it is today. Not when a guy can break a sweat just talking. Everybody's mouths cracked and full of cotton.

The blazing sunlight sneaks in through the slightly propped door. About seven or eight feet of warped rectangle glare that the team shooting at the south bucket has to deal with all game. But there's no getting around it. Gym policy. Jimmy tells everyone it's something handed down to him, something his boss made completely clear, door has to stay open all day. Guys sitting out who know the deal stand in the door out of courtesy. And it helps. Sometimes Jimmy himself stands there, arms folded, watching the games. Sticky tells everybody he can figure out what time it is by looking at the way the rectangle is folding up on itself.

Check ball, Old-man Perkins yells.

Yeah, y'all, it's already two games down, man. Johnson counts all the guys, one at a time, with a slow index finger. *Three games down, matter a fact.*

Sticky ties the drawstrings on his shorts, waiting for the first ten to walk out onto the court so they can get things started. He unties his drawstring and ties again. Unties and ties. He's a thin 6' 3" at the top of the key, with skinny legs poking out of old hoop shorts. A fat homemade tattoo on his left shoulder, BABY, and deep brown eyes that pierce through anyone who catches his stare.

He unties and ties again.

Sticky's face is chiseled and tan. He doesn't talk much, but when he smiles all the girls seem to like what he's saying.

Unties and ties.

A couple uneven scars map his face. One that zigs and zags above his right eye from a knife (got cornered in an alley back in Long Beach and wouldn't give up his three bucks. Slash). Another circles up behind his left ear. The skin charred and purple about the size of a pencil eraser. He says he has no idea how he got that one.

Finally Dante slips off his platinum watch and tosses it into his bag. Shady characters know Dante's platinum is off-limits. His fists come down hard, anybody will tell you.

There are silent understandings in even the most messed-up settings. A delicate balance. He stands up and struts out onto the long dusty court. *Let the runs begin,* he says, and gives daps to Dallas. He straightens out his tucked-in shirt and starts in on Trey. *You didn't ask for all this, did you, Trey-daddy? To have to come out here and try to check a big baller like myself?*

Trey pushes out an uncomfortable laugh, wipes hands on his shorts. He looks down at his shoes and kicks his heel into the floor a couple times. *We'll see what up, D,* he says, and pushes out another laugh.

Dante makes ten and everybody matches up on defense. Rob snatches the ball out of New York's hands and bounces it hard off the ground with both hands. Power dribble. *I got white boy,* he says, and shoves the ball into Sticky's chest, glaring.

Rob is: faded Malcolm X T-shirt covering faded yellow skin. Thick gold rope and dookie yellow cornrows. *I'm gonna slap the handcuffs on you, white boy.*

Slim, you match up with Dallas, Trey says, pointing to Dallas on the wing. *Big Mac, you d-up New York.* He rolls up and slaps Big Mac on his big butt. *Keep this reboundin fool off the boards.*

I got this light-in-the-ass cat, Big Mac says, and throws a couple playful jabs into New York's ribs.

I got Dante, Trey says. *Y'all help out in the middle when he drives.*

Rob spits on the ground, runs his sneaks through for grip. He turns to Sticky and holds his hands out for the check.

Sticky tosses a bounce pass into his waiting hands. Rob

spins around with the ball on his hip. *Y'all good?* he says to his squad. But just as he is about to check the ball in play, Slim throws his hands in the air.

Hold up, hold up, Rob. I got a rock in my shoe. Slim jogs over to the bleachers and starts unlacing his shoe.

Before anybody can start in on Slim, Crazy Ray staggers up to the sideline from the homeless court. *You lazy sons a bitches,* he says. *Look at ya. Don't know nuthin about no god-damn game of basketball. A bunch a gang-bangin thugs is all you is.* Ray's words spew out forty proof, and he points an old bony finger at everybody on the court. Like he does every day. A dark green plastic bag, outdoor size, wrapped around his thin upper body. Hanging down like a dress. He takes a few more unbalanced steps until he's standing at half-court. Armholes cut out on both sides. Pulled over a dull orange T-shirt.

Halloween in late July.

His black face mashes up and he yells: *Ain't like it was back in my day. We had respect for the game.*

Everybody starts in on Ray to get off the court.

Go on, old man, get back over where you belong.

Ain't nobody tryin to hear about no 1940.

Somebody get that decrepit, cryin-ass bum off the court.

I got em, I got em, Dallas says, hustling over to Ray. *Let's go, old man, come on.* He takes hold of both arms and backs him up slow.

Ray shakes a fist over Dallas's shoulder as he retreats. *Y'all got no heart,* he says in a weaker voice. *No heart.* And then the tears start rolling down his cheeks. Big heavy tears that launch off his quivering chin. The second he wipes all the wet away with a big right hand, six or seven more make the dive.

Same script, different day.

Dallas settles the Crazy Ray situation whenever it pops up. Most of the time it's just once a day. He'll walk out onto the court each morning with the same rap, get pulled off by Dallas and break down as he shouts a last line or two. But some days the old cat has a little more energy and comes staggering out again before closing. When most guys have taken off and all that's left are a couple ragged games of three-on-three.

Sticky spits on his right hand, watching. Lifts his right foot up and wipes the dust off his sole. Spits and wipes. Spits and wipes. He's watching Dallas handle Crazy Ray, but he's thinking about that smooth-looking gold bracelet. Figuring out the different ways he can go about snatching it. Trying to picture Anh-thu's face when he drops it on her tonight. Never thought he'd actually be excited to get a girl a gift. But Anh-thu's different. Anh-thu's his lady.

He spits again and wipes his right sole. Spits and wipes. Does the same thing again and again and then starts in on the left. Spits and wipes.

Spits and wipes.

Spits and wipes.

Dante watches the whole deal from a few feet away, says to him: *Hey, yo, Stick,* as Slim jogs back out onto the court claiming he's cool now, he's ready. *Yo, Stick, for real, what the hell you doin over there?*

There's This Whole

thing where Sticky sets a cup down fifteen, twenty times when nobody's looking. Thirty times. Until the heavy base meets the garage-sale coffee table with just the right feel. One of the dudes who lives with him in his current foster home, the only other white kid, calls him "Sticky Two Times."

A couple years back, a friend's mom went to pick her boy and Sticky up from a park when thick gray clouds opened up and drenched everything in sight. Heavy drops slapped against the blacktop, streaked down the metal backboard, gathered at the ends of the ragged chain net. The mom sat with her wagon running as her boy jumped into the front seat all wet. But Sticky couldn't leave until he hit the perfect shot. No rim. He kept shooting it over and over.

Come on, Stick! his buddy yelled out the window.

Middle finger in the groove, thumb between the 7 and F. Another shot went through but grazed iron.

Middle finger in the groove, thumb between the 7 and F. Shot bounced off the back rim and caromed out toward the sideline.

Please, son, the woman pleaded, *you've got to get out of this rain!* She sat on her horn.

Sticky kept chasing down his ball, though, carrying it back out to the arc to try again. Couldn't stop. He swallowed down hard at the lump in his throat. His chest burned. The salty rain dripped off his hanging bottom lip, ran down his neck and into his soaked tank top. He squinted his eyes and spit.

There was the crashing sound of thunder.

Let's just go, Mom, the boy said. *Sticky's foster place is only a couple blocks down.* Another shot floated through the air again and rimmed out. *I told you how he is. We'll be here all night.*

Sticky ran to get another rebound, clawing at the skin on his forearm, elbowing himself in the stomach.

We can't just leave him here, the mother said. *God-damn it!*

Back even further, when Sticky was six and still lived with his mom in Long Beach, he already had this weird thing with change.

Baby would get them both on a bus going out to Santa Monica on certain weekends. When the government check she picked up every two weeks didn't stretch far enough. She'd set him up in the middle of the Third Street Promenade with a big white bowl. She'd dress him in dirty rags and rub dirt into his paper-thin cheeks, put a construction-paper sign around his neck that said: MY BOY NEEDS MONEY TO EAT.

This is back before he could ride a two-wheeler.

Back when Baby was still calling him Travis.

An older lady might tilt her head when she saw him there, sitting Indian style next to the freshly trimmed acacia, make that cooing sound older women make. She might go straight to her change purse and fish out a few quarters. Drop them in the bowl one at a time.

A guy in a too-cool suit might pimp by and look back over his shoulder. Reach into deep pockets for a dime or nickel and lob it the couple feet underhand. He'd slap hands with a fellow suit-buddy if the coin went straight in.

And every time Sticky got a new coin he would pull it out and toss it back in. Pull out and toss back in. He'd keep doing it again and again until something in the sound felt right.

Pull out and toss back in.

Pull out and toss back in.

It annoyed Baby on certain days. When there was nothing in her blood and all she could do was scowl. She'd slap at his hand and snarl. *Jesus Christ! Leave the money alone!*

And he'd stop. Like a good boy. But the urge to reach back in the bowl was torture. A thousand drips on the forehead, tied up. He'd stare at it. Heart racing. Everything around him shutting down. It was just his body and the bowl. And his trembling hands.

Another woman would walk by and pat Sticky on the head. *Oh, here, honey.* Toss a quarter in.

Now he was behind. Two quarters in wrong. Or one quarter and one nickel. Two dimes. He'd look up at Baby standing above him.

She'd glare down. *Please, for the sake of my sanity, leave the goddamn change alone.*

Back to the bowl. Everything crashing in. His limbs warming. Eyes burning.

Everything else in the world turning off.

Third Street Promenade

is blowing up. A hundred shopping bags swing-ing in rhythm. Marching, marching, marching. Plastic people with plastic hair, pushing and shoving. Plastic world. Stop in the middle of traffic on a cell phone. *Dana, I'm like already here. I'm just outside Crate & Barrel.* A near pileup just outside Gap Kids.

There are stairs and elevators in Santa Monica Place. An escalator shooting up to the third floor with blinking lights. There are open doors and red Sale signs. This-is-who-we-are music oozing out of every mall shop.

Can I help you?

Is there something in particular you're looking for?

Hi, my name is David.

My name is Veronica.

I'm Stuart, if you have any questions don't hesitate to ask.

Anh-thu and Laura are sitting in the middle of the food court, finishing up teriyaki bowls. Their first break in a marathon day. Everything in Millers Outpost is at least twenty percent off. The super-sale table is knocked down fifty percent. Since the doors first swung open at eight-thirty, Millers has been madness. Hundreds of hands pulling out shirts, unsnapping snaps, unzipping zippers, reaching into pockets, unfolding and throwing back, holding up against a body in the mirror and spinning around. Anh-thu's on until nine this evening. Even if it is her birthday. Laura's scheduled to leave at nine, too. Both have been dreading this sale for weeks.

The food court is slammed throughout the day during the summer. European tourists with shiny cameras and black socks, folding greasy slices of pizza. Japanese business-men looking every blonde up and down, staring them around a corner or up an escalator. Quarter Pounders with a knife and fork. A mother and daughter shoveling Chinese into open mouths. Leaning over plastic plates with mouth-fuls of chow mein. Cutting through excess noodle with bright white teeth and lifting smiling faces to one another. Fancy bags full at their feet. Groups of bored kids run in packs between the crowded tables. From the valley. From the South Bay. From East L.A. and West L.A. and Culver City.

The lines at each food stop extend out into the walkway like crooked trails of ants.

Anh-thu pinches a piece of broccoli with her chopsticks, slips it into her mouth. She notices a group of Mexican guys

20

staring as she chews. One of the guys flips out a long tongue and wiggles it around. His friends laugh and throw playful punches at each other.

Hey, Laura, Anh-thu says, *your friends are trying to get your attention.*

Laura swings her head around. Gets the same tongue wiggle from the same guy. *Hey, why don't you go hang out at the junior high!* she yells, and turns back around.

The guys all laugh at their boy. *Ahhh, she punked you, man.*

She's clowning.

Laura pulls a piece of fat from her mouth with two fingers, wraps it in a white napkin. *Why guys gotta do that shit, Annie? What they think, we gonna go right over there and give em some?*

Anh-thu forces a smile and picks up her drink. She focuses on a piece of rice that has tumbled onto the table between the Styrofoam bowl and her cotton tank top. She rubs a hand across her cramping stomach and sucks her Coke through a straw.

What's the matter, girl? Laura says.

Nothing.

Nah, I could tell when somethin be wrong with you, Annie. Your lips go all tight in a circle. She points to Anh-thu's lips, tries to make her own into the same shape as an example.

Anh-thu frowns. *I don't know,* she says. *It's nothing.*

What, you can't tell your girl nothin no more?

It's stupid, Laura. . . . I mean, I'm stupid.

Hey, heina! the Mexican guy yells. *Yo!*

Laura doesn't bother turning around this time, gives an

over-the-shoulder flip-off. *Pendejos. Anyways, go on with what you was saying, girl.*

Forget it. It's nothing. Anh-thu moves the food around in her bowl, grabs hold of a piece of chicken, lets it go.

Anh-thu's half Vietnamese. She's tall and thin with straight black hair falling down a pretty brown back. Green eyes like two tiny mirrors when the sun's in a certain spot in the sky. Sticky tells her she's his jujube when they meet at night in the park. Jujube like the candy she's always chewing on between classes at school. And when somebody asks how to say her name right, he tells them: *You know, Anh-thu. Like, not on one, but on two. Anh-thu.*

They've been hanging together almost a year now and everybody says they match good together.

The crew pull out chairs and stand up cool. They leave dirty trays on dirty tables and walk smooth slow toward the girls. White wife-beaters and baggy khakis hanging off skinny bodies. Fifteen-year-old gangsta style. Hair slicked. Earrings and tats. Gold chains.

Anh-thu sees them coming but pretends she doesn't.

Laura pulls out a mini mirror from her bag, checks her made-up face from different angles. Long lashes and penciled-in eyebrows. Thick cherry lips. Fake mole. She lightly pats each cheek with powder.

The guy with the tongue leads his boys to their table. *Hey, homegirl,* he says, *ain't no need for no attitude.*

Laura brings a frown up to him slow. Puts her stuff away.

For real, he says. *We gotta just start over and shit.* He smooths out four or five peach-fuzz mustache hairs and looks at Anh-thu. He leans his hands on the table and turns back to Laura. *We about to go smoke some a this chronic right now.* He peeks a baggy partially out of his pocket, looks around the mall for somebody spying his petty crime. *You down?*

The crew hang back a little, hands deep in pockets. One kicks a cigarette butt across the black and white tile. It comes to a spinning stop under a table of businesswomen.

Laura turns to Anh-thu with wide eyes, then back to the guy. *First of all, dude, that tongue thing you did was rude. Like the biggest turnoff. Secondly, you and your friends look like you're in junior high and we both in college.* She motions between herself and Anh-thu. *And lastly, we got serious boyfriends who go to UCLA.* Having said all that, Laura tilts her head a little to the side and smiles. *So, uh, probably not.*

The guy's sneaky little smile runs away. He pulls his hands off the table and smooths his stash again. Looks at his boys and pulls up his sagging pants. *You got an attitude, you know that? Better watch it before someone puts their foot in your mouth.*

One of the other guys pulls a small knife from his pocket and flips open the blade.

Anh-thu moves her eyes off the guy and stares down at the table.

Laura slides her bag over to Anh-thu, pulls her chair out and stands up. She gets right up in the tongue guy's grill with her finger. *Yo, why you coming over to me and my girl's table anyway, man? Somebody invite you?*

It's OK, Anh-thu says. *Laura, we'll just move somewhere else.*

Screw that, Annie. Laura kicks her chair over on its side.

Everybody around them turns to look. Veins push out on her forehead. Teeth lock. When the guy takes a baby step back, she takes one forward. *Nobody said for this punk to come over here.*

She turns to Anh-thu. *We ask them over here?*

Anh-thu shakes her head quick and folds her arms. Laura puts her palms in the air and tells the guy: *Nobody wants you over here, man.*

Crazy broad! the guy says. He turns to his boys and backs up. *Look at this crazy psycho broad, yo!*

Laura puts her palm in his face and shakes her head. *Weak little cholo.*

The guy with the knife moves forward, toward Laura. His boy spots the blade and stops him short. *Be cool, yo,* he says. *Not here.*

Anh-thu watches the guy fold the knife back up and drop it in his pocket. Watches him put his hands in his pockets too, then take them back out.

Go play your little games with kids your own age, Laura says, setting her chair back upright. She sits down slowly, keeps an eye on them the whole time.

The tongue guy tries to get all hard again. Mad-dogs a couple seconds. He runs a hand through his greasy hair and motions to his boys. *Come on, man, forget about this psycho-broad, let's roll.* And they start off.

He looks back halfway through the food court and yells so everybody can hear: *Yo, that's a crazy bitch over there!* He points at the girls' table.

Everybody drops their small talk again and turns to look. All the bangers glare back at different times. They strut through the food court, chains swinging beside thighs, into the center of the mall and out of sight.

Fakers! Laura yells out. Everybody turns toward her again, and she breaks into laughter.

Anh-thu forces another smile and smooths her hair behind each ear. *I didn't know what they were gonna do,* she says.

Don't worry, Annie. They wasn't nothin but posers. I could tell you that right now. Laura touches Anh-thu's arm. *You see his face, though, girl? You see how serious he got when I told em what's up?* She imitates his look and then bends over laughing.

Anh-thu puts her chopsticks back in her bowl, sifts around for a piece of broccoli.

A few Japanese men at the table in front of them spin around straight-faced. Their thick ties stuffed inside stiff white dress shirts while they eat. Laura looks up at them and puts on her serious face, tells them: *Sorry.*

When they turn back she starts laughing again.

She slows down and picks up her fork. Moves a strand of curly brown hair out of her face with the back of her hand. *Like we was gonna go smoke out with them fools.*

Anh-thu pinches a piece of broccoli and slips it into her mouth. She pulls at her bra through her tank top.

Laura shovels a forkful of rice into her mouth and puts her fork down. As she chews, she reaches into her bag and pulls out a small wrapped gift. Sets it up on the table. Anh-thu places her chopsticks in her bowl and wipes her mouth. She rolls her eyes. *Laura, you didn't have to get me something.*

It's your sweet sixteen, of course I'm gonna get you

somethin. Laura pushes the gift across the shiny plastic table. *You my girl, ain't you?*

Anh-thu picks up the gift and slips her hand under one of the folds. She pulls it apart by the tape without ripping the red and blue paper. Laura watches, smiling and sitting on her hands. Anh-thu folds the paper back up nice and sets it to the side. Pulls the box open and carefully peels the tissue paper. *Oh, my God, Laura, this frame's totally beautiful.* She reaches over the table and hugs Laura. *I love it.*

Happy birthday, Annie.

They let go and Anh-thu holds the frame up: sparkling black plastic with white roses in the upper right corner. Laura takes it from Anh-thu and turns it around. *It's one of them ones you can put like twenty pictures in. See?* She pulls out the bottom lever and the sample picture is replaced by another.

Anh-thu takes it back and pulls the bottom out. Pictures switch places again. *That's so cool,* she says. *I've never seen one of these.* Pulls the bottom again. Pictures switch.

Laura picks up her fork, moves the rice and vegetables around until she uncovers a piece of chicken. She stabs and slides it into her mouth. *I was thinking you could have a bunch of pictures of you and Sticky in there,* she says with her mouth full. *You guys are so cute together.*

Anh-thu holds the frame to the side before putting it back in the box. She puts the folded paper on top and then closes the box back up. *If we had any.* She unzips her backpack, puts the box inside and zips it closed. *You know, I don't even have one picture of us together? We went in that booth outside Sam Goody like a month ago, but Sticky says he lost them all.* She looks inside her bowl and pushes it to the side.

Laura smiles at a group of white guys walking by. One of them looks back over his shoulder. *Yum, he looks good,* she says. *He's a total UCLA guy, you can tell by the way he dresses.* Laura always talks about landing a guy from UCLA. On weekends she and her two cousins use fake IDs to get into Westwood bars and flirt with the best-looking Bruins.

She stares in their direction until they round a corner, out of sight. *What was you sayin again, Annie? Oh, yeah, you guys don't got no pictures. Take a camera tonight. Just get one of them disposable ones.*

Anh-thu folds her fingers and lifts her head to think. *I could do that.*

What are you guys doing, anyway? Laura looks up at Anh-thu and frowns. *Sticky better take you somewhere.*

He won't tell me. Just said to meet him at the Colorado entrance at nine. He says he has everything figured out.

Anh-thu stares blankly at the table for a few seconds and then rubs her eyes with the back of her hands. All this talk about Sticky and now her eyes are glassy. She crosses her legs and folds up her napkin.

For real, what's the matter? Laura says. She puts her fork down and dabs at her lips.

I might have messed up.

How?

I might have messed up bad, Laura, Anh-thu says, and holds a folded napkin against her closed eyes.

What are you talkin about, girl?

Anh-thu lowers her head. A heavy tear starts down her right cheek and she wipes it with the napkin.

Oh, my God, Annie. Laura shoves her bowl from in front of her. Walks around the table and sits next to Anh-thu.

27

It's just somethin I gotta deal with.

You don't wanna talk?

Anh-thu shakes her head.

Laura reaches into her purse and pulls out a pack of cigarettes. Slips one out, puts it between her lips and flicks on a
lighter. She pulls in the smoke. Exhales. *You don't wanna
talk, all right,* she says. *But maybe I could help.*

They both sit quiet. Anh-thu balls her napkin up and
tosses it in her bowl. Laura stares at the table and smokes.

Anh-thu looks down at her watch. *Oh, my God,* she says,
it's already past eleven-thirty.

Laura stabs her cigarette into her bowl and grabs her bag
strap. *Sergio's gonna kill us,* she says.

Anh-thu fumbles with her backpack zipper, opens up and
pulls out her Millers name tag. Pins it on her shirt. She dabs
at her eyes one last time with another napkin as they push
away from their chairs and throw their bowls in the trash.

Laura stops Anh-thu before they leave, holds her by the
shoulders. *I'm serious, Annie, you wanna talk, I'm here.*

I know, Anh-thu says. *I appreciate it.*

Ain't nobody supposed to be sad on they birthday, Laura
says. *For real.*

They both take off running through the food court, in
the same direction the Mexican guys had gone, dodging
packs of people on their way back to Millers.

Nobody Knew Anything

about Sticky turning seventeen. Except his foster lady, Georgia, who put three candles in a Hostess Cup Cake that morning before going to work.

This was back on the day of the big play-off game, four months ago. Anh-thu didn't know. Sticky's foster siblings didn't know. Coach Reynolds, who finally subbed him into the game with only seven minutes remaining in the third quarter, he didn't have a clue.

Georgia set the Cup Cake on the edge of the coffee table next to where Sticky sleeps, out on the green and brown couch in the living room. Pieces of dull orange foam bulging through thin rips in the worn fabric, swelling up between his arms and legs.

And Sticky didn't exactly offer up any info himself. Almost made it through the entire day without saying a word. The only time it was even mentioned was when Sticky, Dave, and Sin were spread-eagled against a cop car, getting searched for weapons. Hands on the roof, feet wide, as a pissed-off, out-of-breath cop patted them down one at a time.

Three sets of eyes on the jagged pavement.

The cop with the radio came walking around the front of the car with a grin on his face, shaking his head. *Hey, listen to this one,* he said, tapping his partner on the shoulder with the radio antenna.

Dave and Sin looked at Sticky all confused after the cop said what he said.

It's your birthday today? Dave said.

Sticky shrugged.

For real? Sin said.

But that's as far as it went. Nobody felt like singing happy birthday to you, cuffed in the back of some cop car on the way to the station.

Sticky Swipes Gear

like he shoots hoops. Shuts off his mind and rolls instinct. Every move in a department store is a Sports-Center highlight:

You go in with an empty Double Gulp cup and walk out drinking your favorite new shirt through a straw.

You try on those new Nikes with a hat pulled low, walk around Fragrances three, four times to check the feel, and cruise right out of the store. Get your sprint on if the high-pitched alarm starts screaming.

You walk past the register and out the front doors with three new shirts draped over the shoulder. In front of every-one. Bar codes dangling like fish in a cotton waterfall. If the blue-hair behind the counter says, *Excuse me, sir, have you*

31

paid for that? (which they never do, because they don't really give a damn either) you say, *No, I'm OK, ma'am. I'm OK, sir.* Maybe add a quick *It's all taken care of,* like you know exactly what you're doing. And you do. Then you cruise out calm like some suit guy with a heavy wallet.

It's the same high that's floating around a hoop court. Lift a product and don't give up a dime.

Makes you feel alive.

Take, for example, the day Sticky met Anh-thu in Millers Outpost last summer. He dropped in thinking layer scam (go in wearing your baggiest jeans, pull six or seven pants off the rack and hop into an empty dressing room. Leave the two best pair on under jeans, dump the rest in the sales-chick's arms and roll out cool). But when Sticky was busy sifting through the overstocked rack, beats jumping through Walkman headphones, pulling a pair of khakis off the rack and putting them back, pulling off and putting back, pulling and putting, Anh-thu came up on his blind side.

Can I help you find something? she said, tapping him on the shoulder.

Sticky jumped two feet.

Even when you shoplift with a slow heart, somebody's voice behind you can sound like a pair of heavy handcuffs rattling. Sticky turned around thinking undercover security, but what he found was Anh-thu.

Something clicked.

He knew the face, dark-type skin in the center of long black hair. Straight. Yeah, he'd seen her before, coming in or out of the caf, standing with her girls outside econ class, but never up close like this. Where he could see the green in her eyes. To be straight up, his stomach dropped. All he could do was stare. It was like the time his cart strained up to the highest peak on Space Mountain during some big foster outing to Disneyland. He could feel it in his stomach: Something crazy was about to go down.

Um, hel-lo, Anh-thu said, waving a hand in front of his daydream face. *Can I help you?*

Sticky hadn't been with too many ladies up to that point. You have to understand that. Some of the sluttier chicks at school, like Angelica and Chloe. A rich white girl everybody called Grand Slam (cause one, her dad owned a local Denny's, and two, if you paid her a little attention, three, four days in a row, you were bound to take a trip around the bases) who used to buy Sticky lunch at school every Friday when the caf came through with pizza. There were a couple episodes with girls he lived with in previous foster homes. Sneak in each other's room after lights-out. But he never felt anything special with any of them. It was just something you were supposed to do, like cheating on tests and drinking forties with the boys.

Yeah, Sticky said, shaking out of it. *I need some new pants.*

You have to realize, Sticky was a baller first and foremost. There wasn't any time for chicks. He was too busy working on the Iverson crossover, or trying to sneak the rock over the rim with two hands-behind-the-back and call it a reverse.

Fire one off before a big game and legs go to rubber by halftime.

Come on, Anh-thu said. *We just got this cool new line of Bugle Boys. I'll show you.*

Anh-thu, on the other hand, she's always had a pack of

dudes on her heels. Blacks, whites, Mexicans, Asians—even grown men who come in shopping for their kids scribble down digits on a business card, try and slip it to her while she rings them up at the register. It's been this way since she moved to L.A. from Modesto. Her pops, who refuses to speak English in their house, has tried everything: ten o'clock curfews, big brother chaperoning her Saturday nights, checking skirt length with a ruler before letting her leave the house for school. But it's all hopeless. The more he tries, the more they blow up her cell phone.

American boys, he always mumbles in disgust.

Here, how do you like these? Anh-thu said, holding up a pair of khakis with white stitching. *What size are we looking for? Yeah, these will look way cool on you.*

In the dressing room Sticky experienced his first episode of shoplifting jitters. He stared at the pants like they were a pile of undercover cop bait.

He took off his baggy jeans and slipped the first Bugle Boy khakis over his boxers. Snapped, unsnapped, and snapped again. Perfect fit in the mirror. Kinda smooth, too. Unsnapped and snapped. Unsnapped and snapped. Unsnapped and snapped. He spun around to check the sag. Belt loops hung just below the boxer label, like they're supposed to. Unsnapped and snapped. Unsnapped and snapped. Slipped on the second pair, a little lighter shade with deeper pockets. But they were cool too.

How we doing in there? Anh-thu said through the door. *You need a different size or anything?*

Nah, Sticky said.

He sat down on the bench and spent a few seconds looking at his face in the mirror. The scars. The dark brown eyes and long eyelashes. The closely cut brown hair. He had a pretty face, according to his old foster friend, Maria. *You're a boy with a pretty face,* she'd always tease him. He looked away from the mirror.

He could still see Anh-thu in his head, and he didn't know what to do about it. He could still smell her smell through the door. Something wasn't right in his stomach.

The kid was shook.

He went to slip his jeans over the khakis but stopped himself cold. Tried again but couldn't come through. It wasn't fear so much, that maybe this girl was secretly keeping a head count of all his items. Nothing like that. And he dug the pants all right. Needed some khakis for school and everything. But he couldn't finish the play. There'd be no stealing this time. Do the right thing out of respect to this super-pretty Vietnamese girl. The one that had his mind doing some crazy jig.

He stripped and zipped up his jeans alone. He even folded the Bugle Boys up super nice to give back.

When he broke out of the dressing room, holding a pile of pants in his arms, he found Anh-thu helping some other buster. A black kid from the varsity football squad, one of the starting defensive backs. He watched the guy's mouth move as he walked up on them. Anh-thu bent over to let out a laugh.

I smacked the crap outta my puppy, the guy said, working the scene. *He's gotta learn about that. I shoved his nose right in my ripped-up shirt and told him, No, little Pepper! You can't be messin up my gear like that.*

Anh-thu seemed all jazzed by what the guy was saying so Sticky hung back. On the sly he spied the defensive back lightly touching Anh-thu on the shoulder, Anh-thu looking up into the guy's face with her full attention.

Sticky decided to say screw it and turned to take off.

But just as he was about to set the pile down and flee the scene, Anh-thu dropped the hammer on the defensive back. *You know,* she said, *it sounds fun and everything, but I have a boyfriend.*

The guy smiled big, pushed out a laugh. *For real?* he said. He put the flashy shirt back up on the rack.

But thanks for asking.

Who's the lucky Jack?

Anh-thu turned around and pointed at Sticky. *Him!*

Sticky did a double take on Anh-thu's finger pointing at him. He looked over his shoulder. Nobody.

Well, man, the guy said, putting his hand up on a shelf of folded white T-shirts, then taking it off and slipping it into his pocket. *My moms probably has the pot roast all ready. I should probably, you know . . . I'll most likely just come in sometime next week to pick up that shirt.*

Sounds good, Anh-thu said. *Oh, and try to keep your puppy away from your clothes.*

The guy worked up another laugh. *Yeah, we'll see,* he said, and made his move for the exit.

Anh-thu walked over to Sticky with a big embarrassed smile on her face. *I'm sorry I did that,* she said, taking the pile of pants out of Sticky's hands. *I didn't know what else to say. It just totally popped in my head.*

Sticky stuck hands in his pockets, real cool-like, and looked to the floor. He brought his head up to check those green eyes again but quickly cut away. He leaned against a shelf of white cotton V-necks and said: *Them pants wasn't really my thing.*

Anh-thu laughed a little and fingered one of the price tags. *It's OK,* she said. *They make us try to sell these. Maybe some other pants, though? You might like our Anchor Blue stuff, they're super-baggy and comfortable.*

Sticky pulled his hands from his pockets. He locked them up behind his back for a sec, linked fingers, then stuck both hands back in his pockets. *Nah,* he said.

Yeah, forget it. Anh-thu put the pants on a pile of T-shirts and pulled her long black hair behind her ears. *You know, I go on break in like ten minutes, you wanna get some hot chocolate or something? Down in the food court?* She smoothed loose hair behind both her ears.

Sticky tapped his right foot against the bottom of the shelf a couple times and looked up at her. *Nah, I can't,* he said.

Then he walked out of the store.

Current Foster Lady,

Georgia, pulled up to Sticky's foster care pad in almost the same meat-and-potato minivan as his previous lady, Mrs. Smith. Same dull white paint job and sloping hood. Same snail-like movement across the crumbling road.

Could have been a déjà vu situation if it wasn't for Georgia's bumper-to-bumper sports stripe. Red.

Sticky was sixteen, and he promised the old Mexican director he'd try harder this time.

He spied her through the game room window: creeping along the curb out front, double-checking a scribbled-down address. She was in the middle of the road and two or three cars had to swing into the other lane to make the pass. He spied her screwing up a simple parallel park, shutting off that familiar minivan-engine hum, stepping out (fat arms and fat legs poking out of a two-man-tent-like summer dress), and slamming the door shut behind her.

She stood there duck-footed and stared up at his run-down foster care pad, the place where she'd agreed to take on another kid only two weeks previous.

Add a fifth to her pack of strays. Three hundred and sixty dollars a month per stray from the state.

Do the math.

Sticky spied all this through the game room window while at the same time kicking Counselor Julius's ass in foosball again.

Earlier that morning, Julius had laid down the challenge. *Let's run a quick game, Stick,* he said, his dark blue Duke cap pulled cool-like crooked over his smooth black face. All the residents shoveled spoonfuls of cereal into their mouths. Warehouse-size sacks lying between them, generic flakes spilling onto the table. *For old times' sake.*

Sticky took one last bite before he set the spoon in his bowl. He pulled the spoon out and set it back in. Pulled out and set back in. Pulled out and set back in. Julius knew the routine and rolled his eyes.

Pulled out and set back in.

Pulled out and set back in.

When the dull tap of metal on plastic sounded like Sticky thought it should, he hustled over to the foosball table and grabbed two of the worn-out handles.

Back in those days, Sticky spent all his free time playing foosball. Couldn't get enough. The other residents said he took it way too far. Always spinning the handles around. Always pulling and pushing the rusting arms, stopping the ball on a dime and firing it into the box. Aerial shots, crank shots, simple bank shots off either wall, snake shots where a heavy spin shoots the colorful ball out like a rainbow across the blue face of the game. All this even if there was nobody on the other side to play to eleven.

You're obsessed with a stupid game, Maria always said, on nights she'd sneak into his room after lights-out. She'd look him right in the eyes after they messed around in his bed for a while, tell him: *I don't get it, why play a game when you can talk to a real person?*

Sticky would pick at the calluses on the insides of his fingers. Shrug her off. Sometimes he'd peel a callus off completely and toss it in her lap.

But if anybody needed to find Sticky in his foster care pad, all they had to do was follow these simple directions: move straight through the living room, past the always shouting TV, hang a sharp left before the long dark hall, swing on through the kitchen, past the locked-up counselors' office and into the tight-quarter game room. That was where he'd be. After chores. After lunch. Before lights-out. Sometimes even in the middle of the night, when he'd sneak out of his room to duct-tape a defenseman he dreamed was starting to crack.

And maybe Maria had it right, maybe he was obsessed with playing a dumb game, but when he beat somebody good, got them all flustered and defeated, the blood ran through his veins all smooth like melted butter. Warm and fast. The rush of heat moving along his skin giving him a reason to spring out of bed in the morning.

It wasn't so much the foosball he was addicted to anyway, it was the beating people.

He'd beat the old Mexican director, who rolled in with boxes full of frozen foods twice a week. The director, who'd already sent him off with a packed bag three separate times, only to eventually have him returned like a shirt that didn't fit. A pair of pants. He'd beat all the residents at least twice a day, including Maria, who he'd play with one hand behind his back. He'd beat any new buster that got dropped off before they had time to unpack their bag. He'd beat the night watch. He'd beat the college girls who showed up to give presentations about sexually transmitted diseases. But the sweetest wins of all came against Counselor Julius. With all his hooting and hollering whenever he scored a goal. His intense facial expressions, all eyebrows and teeth. Sticky knew once he got Julius to the table, he'd have somebody to beat for hours.

Julius would get so pissed at all the losing, he'd end up dragging Sticky down to a local park with the scuffed-up house basketball. This was back before Sticky could even dribble with his left hand. Julius strutting out onto the blacktop in his Scottie Pippen jersey and new Air Jordans. His fake diamond earrings. Sticky with his standard white T-shirt issued by the state. Standard old blue jeans, ripped in the knees by the resident who'd handed them down. Sorry-looking white Wilson low-tops.

Julius would kick Sticky's butt in one-on-one, game after game. Back him up in the post. Block his shots. Swipe the ball when he dribbled. The whole time talking trash. The whole time giving Sticky this new game to fixate on. To obsess about. To do over and over and over until he got good. A reason to dribble back down on solo missions. Every day.

41

Return to the scene of the crime, where Julius had kept in on him until foosball frustration faded from his mind.

With all those jumpers Sticky shot by himself, sometimes long after the moon replaced the sun above the backboard, it wasn't long before he was getting Julius in hoops, too.

Then Counselor Julius had nowhere to turn.

All right, Stick, Julius said, cupping the white ball in his hands and blowing on it. *One more foosball game before this lady shows up, and I swear to God I'm gonna get you this time.*
We'll see.

But you know the routine, how one game turns into ten and before you know it, Sticky's two points away from taking thirteen straight.

He ran off the first seven or eight in a flash, mixed in a couple shutouts. And then a frustrated Counselor Julius came up with the idea of switching sides. Sticky went from whipping Julius with his back to the window, to whipping him facing it. Like that. And to top it all off, Sticky didn't even give his full attention to that thirteenth game. He had one eye on the action and the other spying this new foster lady making her way up the driveway.

Georgia finally got to the door and knocked three times hard. Julius, playing the part of responsible counselor, abandoned foosball. *That's her, Stick,* he said, pulling his hands from the handles and straightening his cap. He reached back and took one last whack, but Sticky blocked the shot with a quick shift of his goalie.

You lucky, too, Julius said, *I was about to catch my rhythm.* He hustled to the front door.

Julius pulled the heavy door open and painted on his best smile. *Hello, ma'am,* he said, shaking her hand. *I'm Julius. If you'll just follow me into the office, I'll have you sign a few things. It won't take long.*

That's him, right? the woman said, pointing through the game room door at Sticky.

Yes, ma'am, Travis Reichard. That's his given name. But he goes by Sticky around here.

Oh, that name, the lady said in a voice so Sticky couldn't hear. She moved under the game room door frame. *We'll have to do something about that awful name.*

Like I said, ma'am, real name is Travis. I'm not even sure how he got the name Sticky.

She watched Sticky slap the ball around a couple more times and then piped up: *Hello, Travis.* She spoke in a long and drawn-out voice, as if Sticky was retarded. *How are you today?*

There were a few awkward seconds of dead air.

Tell the lady hi, Julius said. *Where's your manners, big guy?*

Sticky put his head up, then his hand up. *But my name's Sticky,* he said, and went back to hitting the ball around.

Counselor Julius smiled.

Georgia smiled.

We're gonna give you a fine place to live, she said. *Me and my husband. I think you'll be very happy in our home.*

Minivans and this same opening line, *Our happy home . . .* There must be a book these ladies check out from the county library.

She stood watching Sticky a couple more seconds, then turned and followed Julius into the office, to get the details worked out.

It's Tied Sevens

and Sticky's handling the rock up top. Back and forth with the left hand. In front of his glazed body. Rhythm pats. Type of dribbles that get you in the groove to cut and slash, body loose and quick to make somebody look like a fool.

Rob's weight is on the back of his heels on defense. Waiting.

The face rattles off truth in situations like this. Fear flickering in Rob's wide eyes: Get too close and Sticky zips by for a layin, give too much room and Sticky sticks a jumper in his eye. Too many possibilities when the man with the ball gets to say which way and when, how fast and for how long. And you can multiply all that by ten if the guy can play. Get busted on in front of everybody. Get dragged all game by the skinny white kid everybody talks about.

All the loudmouths on the sideline are at full attention.

Sticky jab-steps right and pulls back, keeps his dribble.

Rob retreats.

Sticky is: through the legs, around the back, playing hoops with a yo-yo. Walk the dog when everybody calls for a trick. Hold the ball too long.

He is: stolen Nike shoes, stolen mesh shorts, ankle socks. Back and forth handling the ball, knees bent, his eyes in Rob's eyes. Piss off the old purists who cry for a return to fundamentals. The ones who've lost so much vision they're blind to the dance of it all. The spin move like a skirt lifting pirouette on callused toes. The dip. Jump shot splashing through the net like a perfect dismount.

There's spirituality here. On this court. With these guys. Holding this ball.

Dallas clears out of the lane. *Go on, Stick,* he says, pointing to the open lane, backpedaling. *Take him, boy*.

Sticky is: in neutral down a mountain hill without sound. There's no little voice saying where to go or how. Everything is in slow motion:

You could go to that one nasty spin when the defender's vulnerable.

Could cross somebody over and pull up for the short midrange jumper.

Could skip an around-the-back pass to a cutter for the cram.

Could spin the rock around the right side of this clown and cut around the left, meet up on the other side for a slick-looking finger roll.

You could shoot from twenty-four feet out. From twenty-five feet out.

You could knock it in off the glass.

Could bust it straight through.

Or you could just hold the rock at your side for a quick sec, watch everybody watching you. . . .

Every pair of eyes is watching as Sticky makes his move on Rob—goes through his legs to the right, hesitates, the ball spinning like a top in the palm of his hand, weightless, stutter-steps one way (Rob's feet go right, body left, have a nice trip), crosses him back the other way and blasts to the basket, dropping a sweet little no-look dime to Dante when the big man comes over to help.

Dante rises up uncontested and flushes in a two-hand jam.

That's on you, New York says in Big Mac's face.

Eight-seven! Dallas yells out on the way back downcourt. *Good guys!*

Everybody on the side goes crazy, falling all over each other. Laughing and frowning at the same time. *Goddamn, Rob,* Old-man Perkins says, his fist raised to his lips. *That white boy just took you. I ain't gonna lie.*

He clowned you! Johnson hollers, slapping five with Old-man Perkins and then taking a couple steps onto the court.

Dante points at Sticky on the way back down the court. *Good look, boy.*

That kid's got a bag full of highlights, don't he, J? Old-man Perkins says, falling back onto the dull bleachers. Between somebody's carved-in initials. *Goddamn, he got a bag a highlights.*

And Dante just flushes it through, OP, Johnson says back. *He don't barely even touch the rim when he dunks. Straight through like Dominique use to do for the Hawks.*

And that's the thing about this game. Go back on your heels and somebody's gonna spin you around. Break you down. Shake left and have you falling all over yourself. Walk down the lane for two or drop a highlight on you. It's all about the oohs and aahs from the sidelines. Turn heads. Do something that makes them stand up and slap fives, something that has them still talking on the way out, when Jimmy shuts and locks the doors to go home for the night.

Everybody from Dreadlock Man to all the three-piece suits who roll in during their lunch hour, even Rob (though he would never give up the information), they all watch a little harder when Sticky gets the ball on the wing. There's something natural about the kid. Something authentic. Simple pass to the post comes in a wraparound no-look. Sticky either comes out with some spectacular mouth-dropping demonstration or he messes up. Nothing in between. But when he hooks up something slick, some Pistol Pete hide-the-ball trick shot during a game, and this happens more often than not, everybody on the sideline falls all over each other slapping bleachers and providing commentary:

That white boy can ball, huh, Heavy?

I said the whole time he could play, KP.

I mean, he can ball, *though.*

He don't play like no regular white boy, that's why.

Trey pops out on the wing and Slim hits him with a chest pass. He sizes up Dante, jab-steps at him. Big Mac comes out of the post and sets a 280-pound screen. Trey slides right and Dante struggles to get through. Enough time to fire up a long jump shot. But the ball hits the front of the rim and pops straight up.

Dallas springs up to get it, high-dribbles back the other way. He gets trapped in the corner and throws out a desperation hook pass that Dante somehow tracks down. Everybody's out of position when Dante starts left, switches right and buries a fifteen-foot jumper over Trey's outstretched hand.

Nine-seven, Dallas yells out.

Sticky picks up Rob as he dribbles down the court. Payback is in Rob's eyes. Sideline comments can get under your skin. Especially when the white boy you hate is doing all the damage. He isolates Sticky on the left wing, dribbling with his back to the basket. *Clear out, Slim,* he yells. *I got a mouse in the house.*

Sticky gets low and pushes with his legs. He's down forty pounds and a stack of strength. And Rob always takes him into the post. Throws his big butt into Sticky's middle and takes up the slack. Slaps hands away when they come onto the small of his back.

Rob starts baseline, brings up his head, stutters his steps and pushes the ball in front of his body toward the middle of the court. Sticky retreats on defense and keeps his position. Rob spins quickly back toward the baseline but loses the ball. It leaks out toward the sideline, where Sticky is quick to scoop it up and head the other way.

He races downcourt toward the bucket for an uncontested flush. But just as he's about to take his two and a half steps—guys on the sidelines laughing at Rob lying on the ground, Dante and Dallas jogging behind the play—Rob goes to his knees and yells out, *Foul!* The sound of his deep voice echoing throughout the gym.

Foul!

Everybody on the sidelines goes crazy:

Nah, Rob, white boy ripped you clean!

That's an embarrassment call!

You weak, Rob!

Dallas runs clear around the court with his hands on his head. *Oh, hell no!* he keeps yelling. *Hell no!*

Rob gets to a squatting position and looks down the court. *That's my ball! My ball!*

Sticky sits on the ball under the far basket while everybody yells at everybody else. Dante holds his hands out for the rock and tells him: *It wasn't no foul, boy.*

I didn't touch em, Sticky says.

Come on, Dante says, and helps Sticky up. Takes the ball and tucks it under his arm.

Sticky shakes his head and stands alongside Dante. *I won't even get three games cause of this dude.*

What you gotta do, boy? Dante shoots a look down the other end of the court where the argument is building.

It's my girl's birthday.

What I tell you about messin with them tricks, Dante says, and starts walking toward the commotion.

It'll mess with my game, Sticky says, following Dante.

That's right.

I just gotta handle something, though, Sticky says.

49

Dante laughs and shakes his head. He steps into the middle of the argument and yells over everybody: *That's a bitch-ass call, Rob!*

What, I can't get a call? Rob says.

Shoot for ball, man, Johnson says from the sideline. *Gotta shoot for that one.*

We ain't shootin for nuthin! Trey yells. *My man made a call.*

Respect the man's call! someone else yells from the side.

Y'all know that wasn't no foul, Dallas says.

And nobody backs down in situations like these. There's too much at stake. Fifteen guys swelling up the sidelines means the team that loses will be waiting three games minimum. Street ball debates are part of the game; sometimes it's the team with the biggest mouths that holds court all day.

Carlos, a five-foot toothless Mexican, rolls off his bag on the homeless court and walks up to the pack. *There is no foul here,* he says with a heavy accent, pointing at Rob. *I watch and this is very bad call.*

Get off my court, Rob says, puffing up. *Before somebody knocks your little midget-ass out.*

This is bad call. Carlos walks to the side a bit, doesn't look Rob in the eyes. *No way, your ball. This is very much bad call.*

I ain't playin, Rob says. He clenches his fists, takes a few steps forward.

The few businessmen eating lunch near the door drop their forks. These guys show up to see one of two things: a nasty dunk or a big-time altercation. And with Rob in Carlos's face and Slim pulling Trey away from Dallas, with everybody yelling stuff out at the same time, they have their altercation.

It's twelve-thirty on a Thursday. Pale businessmen watching black bodies posture and toss threats. The guys on the sidelines are black. The motionless bodies scattered across the homeless court are black. The two boys reaching skinny arms up the mouth of the soda machine are black. The Mexicans are black. Even Sticky, with his flashy passes and through-the-legs-around-the-back strut, is black.

Pale businessmen will take this story and hold everyone's attention back in the office. They'll all congregate around somebody's desk. The water cooler. In the men's room. *It's so wild, man. You have to go check it out sometime.*

Fat Chuck comes down out of the bleachers with his sagging gray sweats. An overweight, always-smelling-like-tequila mulatto who shows up almost every day to watch but never plays. He goes right up to Rob and tries to talk reason. *Come on now, guys.* He places his hand on Rob's left bicep. *Now you know Jimmy gonna come runnin out his office if you all keep it up.*

Rob pulls his arm out of Chuck's grasp. Glares. He turns his attention to the pack that's moving to the other side of the court. *You ain't gettin that,* he says. *It's my rock. I ain't movin one step from here.*

Fat Chuck backs up and watches him.

I Could Tell

you a lot about this game. . . .

How a dark gym like Lincoln Rec is a different world. Full of theft and dunk, smooth jumpers and fragile egos. Full of its own funky politics and stratification. Music bleeding out of old rattling speakers from open to close. Old rhythm and blues. Stevie Wonder. Aretha Franklin. Funk. Motown. Marvin Gaye. Sometimes Jimmy gets talked into hard-core rap on weekends. Or Trey sneaks in his three-year-old demo tape.

Always music.

There are fat rats that scurry through the lane on game point. Beady eyes on the man with the ball. There are roaches congregating under the bleachers.

There is so much dust on the slick floor that sometimes a guy will go to stop and slide right out of the gym. Every time there's a break in the action, ten guys put palm to sole for grip.

There are a hundred different ways of talking and a thousand uses of the word *motherfucker*.

There are no women.

In the winter there are so many homeless bodies spread out across court two you can hardly see the floor. There are leaks when it rains. Rusted pots are set out to collect heavy drops. Sometimes a guy will track in mud and delay the games. Jimmy sets out a twenty-five-dollar heater and everybody puts their hands up to it before they play.

In the summer you can hear the foundation cracking. The walls, the ceiling. Like the old gym is stretching out its stiff arms and legs.

There are faded bloodstains and tooth marks in the wood. Arguments that end with a gun being pulled. Like a year ago when Old-man Perkins couldn't get his call one crowded Saturday. Guy laughed right in his face. Perkins calmly walked over to the sideline and pulled a forty-five out of a gym bag. *Now, whose ball is it?* he said, holding the gun limp at his side. Drips of sweat running down his wrinkled forehead.

Your ball, old man, the guy said, backing up with his hands in the air.

And everybody shows up for a different reason. A potpourri of ballers:

Some guys come because they're regulars. Used to seeing all the fellas on a daily basis.

Some show for the first time on a tip from a friend. Try their skills in the best pickup around to see if they can hang.

A couple NBA cats roll through when it's their off-season.

Some jokers walk through the doors looking for nothing more than a sweat. They come in wearing wet suit–looking wraps around bulging stomachs. Keep love handles away without hopping on a treadmill. They get run out of the gym after one game.

Some guys come to drop rainbow jumpers from deep.

Some come to throw their bodies around down low. To bang with the big boys.

Some guys pull in every day because they love talking trash. Barbershop talk in high-tops. They always have something to say when they score. They have something to say when anybody scores.

Some guys show up because they have nothing better to do.

Some guys come because they didn't play much in college. Get the sour taste out of their mouth by busting somebody up.

Some cause they didn't play much in high school.

Some guys show up drunk. High. Tweaking.

Some of the best ballers roll in wearing a work shirt and jeans. Some of the worst have top-of-the-line sneakers, top-of-the-line gym shorts, the most effective and smooth-looking knee braces. Basketball runway show.

Some guys come to dunk on somebody. They come to hype up all the loudmouths on the sideline with a rim-rocking two-hand bash.

Some don't mind being one of the loudmouths that gets

hyped when the guy who comes to dunk on somebody, dunks on somebody.

Sticky shows up cause the game's his life and the guys are like family.

Some guys stay behind when the gym closes, curl up on their spot on court two with the rest of the homeless.

Some come to score enough junk to soothe junky bones. Chronic. Ups. Downs. Meth. Crack. X. Or to score shiny watches. Gold bracelets. Platinum hoop earrings. Heavy ropes.

Some come to sell.

Some feel like they're part of something. Like a book club or church.

Some show up because they just got off work. Doing all-night security or hustling on the streets.

Sometimes a cop is guarding a robber. Everybody has a joke when that happens.

Some guys roll in because they're addicted to competition. Gotta beat somebody in something to get happy.

Some cause it's the only place in the world they get respect. The only place they have any real control.

But no matter who they are, or why they come, every one of them squints their eyes when they step foot out of the dark gym and back into the bright world that waits outside.

Baby Dressed Up

sexy on Friday and Saturday nights after dinner. All through the time Mico was hanging around the apartment.

She'd high-heel through the bedroom door frame like a movie star, creeping slow-motion like a cat sneaking up on a mouse. Black skirt riding high, slits on both sides. Or the sequined pink deal with the silver zipper down the front. Legs shooting out six laps around the track when she plopped down on the couch with makeup and a mirror.

Sticky couldn't take six-year-old eyes off his mom when she dressed like that.

On the way out the door one Saturday night, the day Mico moved all his stuff in, Baby butterfly-kissed Sticky on the cheek. Like she always did. Fluttering eyelashes that tickled his skin. *Mommy's gotta go to work now,* she said. *My little Sticky Boy.* She squeezed his shoulders and smiled so big her eyes almost shut. And no matter how uneasy Sticky was about staying with some random guy again, he couldn't help himself: when she smiled, he smiled. Even if they were just playing it as a game, see who could keep a straight face longest, he was always the first to fold.

Bye, Baby, Sticky whispered when she hugged him.

Bye-bye, little boy. She touched a finger to his nose. *My little dirt-faced Sticky Boy.*

She went over to Mico and kissed him all over his face. *I'm so glad you're here, Mico. Little Sticky Boy is too.* She stood back and put her hands on her hips. *This is just going to work out so great. You'll see.*

Just go make us some money, Mico said. *Then it'll be all good.* He glanced over at the fridge and pointed. *You gonna bring over that six-pack before you leave?*

Baby hopped over to the fridge like a bunny, giggling. She opened the door and reached her hands in for the beer.

Mico and Baby were a six-month team. They counted twenties every Sunday morning while Sticky watched cartoons. Mico had connections on the street, made sure Baby was safe and took his cut. Baby liked eating good meals and getting her hair done at a salon. She also liked having a man in the house. A big strong man with a confident walk. If it had been up to her, Mico would have stayed a lot longer than the six months. Even if he did punch her in the mouth once when she'd talked back. Even if when he got super-high he sometimes thought it was funny to toss empty beer cans at her sleeping boy.

But Mico ran off with a girl even younger and prettier than Baby. Took off in the middle of the night and left half his stuff.

Back before Mico showed up it was just Baby and Sticky living together. Eating tuna out of a can or noodles with butter. Cold hot dogs. Both walking around the dim, run-down apartment with bare feet. Plates of ceiling paint would flake off at night, float to the ground like little flying saucers. There were trails of ants. Roaches. Daddy longlegs sleeping in every corner. Dust balls spinning across the dull kitchen tile when a gust of wind came through the rusty screen.

Baby didn't work, and Sticky didn't go to school.

They slept together on a broken futon bed in the middle of the room. Their apartment in a shady part of Long Beach. Rumbling trains would wake them throughout the night. A loud earthquake of power rattling their thin windows.

During the day, Baby was either dancing around the place on her toes or sobbing under the covers. There was nothing in between. She either rolled up a magazine like a mike and sang with her favorite radio songs, or she sat in the open window with tears streaming down her face, saying: *I swear um gonna do it this time. I swear to God um gonna jump.* She'd look down at the sidewalk with both hands white-knuckled against the window frame. *You'll be better off without your crazy mom.*

Before falling asleep each night, Baby would tell Sticky stories about his dad. And every night he was a different person. An actor. A construction worker. The head of some prestigious company overseas. Sticky would snuggle in close to Baby, shut his eyes and try to picture it all in his head.

Some nights his dad loved sports. Lettered in everything back in high school. During big games on TV, he would sit Baby down and explain all the rules. Other nights he hated the violence of football, preferred sinking into a comfortable chair with a thick Russian novel. Sipping gin and puffing a cigar.

Sometimes he'd sailed across the Pacific in record time. Battled high winds and monster whitecaps. No lifejacket. Then she'd turn it all around a week later, say the man's only real fear in the world was the Lord's dark oceans.

A lot of times she told Sticky his dad was dead. Shot down in a foreign country. The medals still in a box back in Virginia. Or he was taken out during a big-time drug bust while working for the FBI. One time he'd died when his car spun out of control and launched off the Golden Gate Bridge. Sticky would picture the car flipping over, again and again, then the giant splash.

But other nights Baby would claim his dad had placed a call that very day. That he was thinking about swinging by for a quick visit.

The story Sticky really believed, though, was the one Baby told most often. His dad was a country-western singer she'd met only once. *He had the voice of an angel,* she'd say all dramatic, staring into the flickering light hanging from the ceiling. *And those boots, little boy. When you get old enough you have to buy yourself a pair of boots.*

Sticky had this story memorized. How when his dad

came out to L.A. from Virginia, to try to make the jump into movies, Baby packed Sticky up and followed her singer out by bus. How she and Sticky stayed six months at a YMCA in East L.A., shared a bathroom with the entire third floor. How at night she would put him in an old TV box so he wouldn't crawl away. Cover him with two or three pillowcases from the Salvation Army. All that effort and her singer didn't return even one of her phone calls. Didn't answer even one of her letters.

Sticky believed this story because Baby would lower her eyes when she told it. She'd get all quiet and stare at the floor.

Baby stood at the door waving before she left. She did a twirl and waved some more. Mico shook his head and turned to the TV. He pulled a can from the plastic rings. Sticky watched Baby and laughed.

She laughed with Sticky as she waved. Got on one knee and began blowing dramatic kisses.

Don't I look pretty, Mico? she said, standing up, resting a hand on her twenty-four-year-old hip and spinning around like a fashion model. Subtly covering her birthmark cheek with her free hand. *Don't you think I'll be the prettiest one on the block?*

You probably blowin a big score with all this messin around, Mico said.

Baby made a face, and Sticky laughed.

That afternoon Sticky had watched Mico show up with a pickup truck full of his stuff. Watched him take load after load into the apartment and dump it. As Mico brought stuff in, Baby took Sticky's stuff out of their one bedroom and piled it up next to the TV.

This will be so great for you, she said as Sticky watched her. *Every boy needs a daddy. Hey, maybe he'll wanna throw the football around if you ask him.* She skipped back into the room singing with a B-52 song playing on the clock radio.

In a few minutes she skipped back out with Sticky's pillow, his two blankets folded. *We're gonna be a real family now,* she told him.

Soon as Baby was out the door, Sticky ducked into a corner of the living room and sat with his back against the wall.

He stood up and sat back down again.

Back up and back down.

Back up and back down.

Back up and back down.

Mico looked over and Sticky stopped. They sized each other up for a sec, then Mico tipped his beer and went back to the TV. Sticky went up and down a half dozen more times until it felt right. When he sat for good he wrapped both arms around his knees and spied the room: Mico's jacket hanging off the kitchen table like a leather waterfall. The bedroom door, closed for the first time ever. Keep Out. Mico kicking his feet up on the table and picking something from his teeth.

Sticky shifted around a bit. He pulled his legs in tighter and rested his chin on his knees.

Why you so quiet, kid? Mico said. He took a healthy pinch of something out of his black smoke box and started rolling it up like a cigarette. *Come sit up here with me and I'll show you how you roll em.* He licked the Zig-Zag and pulled a lighter out of his pocket. Aimed and sucked in. He held the smoke in and talked at the same time. *All the little kids in your school would be impressed*. He looked at Sticky and let the thick gray smoke snake through his lips.

Sticky looked down and picked at the rug between his feet.

What, you ain't wanna be the big man on campus? He pulled in another long drag and held it. *Couple years, man . . . You gonna start chasin the ladies.*

Mico cracked open a can of beer and scooped up the remote. He blew the smoke through his wide nostrils and took a long swig. Flipped through channels.

Sticky kept his mouth closed. He stared at Mico's sharp brown face. His nappy black hair down to the shoulders. The green words and pictures scribbled up and down both muscled arms. The way he sank into the couch and rested his beer can between his legs.

Your time's gonna come, Mico said, flipping through channels. *Grab one a them little cheerleaders and pull her behind the lockers.* He pulled in a drag and blew it out. *Them's the best days of your life, kid. Chasin after the fine girls. Even the not-so-fine ones.*

Mico laughed and turned his head to look at Sticky. *I was a equal-opportunity type of dude.*

Sticky watched Mico tilt the can against his mouth again. Watched his lips work the can like a baby with a bottle. The front of his neck driving up and down as he swallowed.

That night, Mico stayed up late watching late-night comics and *I Love Lucy* reruns. He talked on the phone with a deep voice and kicked his dirty boots up on the end of the couch.

Sticky tried to stay awake too. Gave everything to keep heavy lids from sliding down tired eyes. He went back and forth between the TV and Mico. Watched guests wave to a cheering crowd before taking a seat next to Leno, and Mico crumple up empty beer can after empty beer can. Watched singer Bette Midler extend her free hand out whenever she went after a high note, watched Mico flick cigarette ashes onto one of Baby's beauty magazines. Sticky listened to Lucy's jokes and Mico's laugh. Ricky's heavy accent and the long, deep belches Mico blew up at the ceiling.

The longer Sticky watched Mico, the more he warmed up to him. He liked how Mico laughed at everything. A deep manly laugh. And he was so big and strong. Like he could beat most people in a fight. Sticky pictured Mico walking with him down the street to the market. He pictured everybody making room as they walked past, not wanting any trouble.

At one point Sticky even thought: *Maybe this guy could be my dad.*

The later it got, though, the more Sticky lost the battle with his tired eyes. And soon he drifted into sleep.

Sticky woke up an hour later with Mico tapping him on the forehead.

What? he yelled, shooting to his feet. *What?* His blurry eyes darting around the room.

Mico pulled a cigarette from his mouth, let it hang between two fingers. *You should go to sleep, kid.* He unfolded one of Sticky's blankets and spread it out on the rug. *Sleep on this,* he said, pointing to the blanket.

Sticky walked over to the blanket and went to his knees. Mico tossed another blanket on his lap and walked to the fridge. He reached in and pulled out another beer, cracked it open.

Sticky smoothed the blanket over his legs, went to lay his head down but realized he didn't have his pillow.

Pillow's over there, Mico said, pointing toward the table. He tilted the can back and sucked down a few swigs. He leaned his elbows on the blotchy counter and looked all around the tiny apartment. His eyes drooped, head swayed. He laughed and shook his head, then stumbled back to his spot on the couch.

Sticky was up fast. He grabbed the pillow with one hand and pulled it behind him. But as he passed the table, his pillow knocked Mico's black smoke box to the ground. The box tumbled and landed upside down. Clumps of pot scattering everywhere.

What the hell you doin? Mico yelled, quickly reaching for the box, turning it right side up.

Sorry, Sticky said, nervously trying to pick the crumpled green out of the thick, dark rug.

Mico crushed his cigarette into Baby's magazine and got down on his knees. He pushed Sticky's little hands away and sifted through the rug himself, trying to rescue some of the bigger clumps. *Man, I just bought this shit.*

I'm sorry, Sticky said.

Mico quickly realized it was useless, that most of his stuff had been swallowed by long tentacles of rug, and then he flipped.

He jumped up and gripped Sticky by the ear. Shoved his nose into the rug and told him: *Sorry don't do nothin for me now, do it?* He pushed Sticky's face into the rug so hard that his cheeks and lips smashed. *See that? Huh? I just bought all that weed yesterday.*

I'm sorry, Sticky said. *I'm sorry.*

Mico jerked Sticky's head again and let go.

Sticky sat up quick like he'd just been held under water. Almost drowned. He sucked air through his nose. Fought the lump in his throat, swallowed at it a couple times and made a frown out of his eyebrows.

Mico stuck a finger in Sticky's face, told him: *I'm gonna tell you how this is gonna go, kid.* He took a few deep breaths, trying to calm down. *Now that I'm stayin here, we go by my rules. I don't care how it went with your moms. All that's over. From now on we go by my rules.*

He pulled a new cigarette out of his pack and lit it. Sucked in hard and threw the pack back onto the table. *Now, I ain't never had to mess with no kid before, but I'm gonna do like my pops did with me. When I messed up, my pops whipped me good.*

Mico pulled in another drag and blew it to the side of Sticky's red face. *That's how my pops made me a man. Now, if I'm gonna stay here in this crappy apartment* . . . He circled his finger around the room. *If I gotta live like this, man, you damn for sure we doin things my way.*

He held the cigarette in his left hand, reached around with his right and scratched his shoulder blade. Transferred the cigarette back into his right hand. *I'm gonna make you grow up to be a man.*

Mico reached out quick and grabbed the back of Sticky's head, pushed his face into the couch. He held Sticky's head still with a strong left hand and stuck the burning cigarette against the thin skin behind his left ear.

The sizzle on skin made Sticky swallow everything. Gasping and sucking. Choking. Pushing with his hands to get away. He was sucking in all the pain and dry-heaving through his mouth and nose.

Mico held his head tight, screwed the embers in.

The skin melting and dripping. The smell like burning rags. Everything snapping and cracking and breaking in his ear.

He held the cigarette there until Sticky's charred skin pulled every last bit of the red out.

Warm piss ran down Sticky's jeans. Darkened the faded blue denim. Pooled on the rug in front of his bare curled toes.

Sometimes I Think

if I don't make it to the NBA I'll kill myself. I know it don't sound so good when I say it, Annie, but that's how I feel. There ain't nothin else I wanna do. Just play ball. I mean, I hear them people talkin bout how hard it is to make it and all that, but I know I could do it. Dallas says if I keep workin on my game I got a good chance. Slim, too. They said I got the intangibles. Old-man Perkins says if he was startin up a squad from scratch he'd be lookin for a point guard just like me. Someone who could score points and get assists.

It's like this, Annie, God puts us here for a reason. We all born with somethin we could do good, but it's up to us to make sure we use it. That's why I play ball so much. I ain't gonna lie, I think God put me here to play ball. And when I go to pray at *night, I pray so I could get better and better. That's why I grew so much last year. That's why I could shoot so good. It ain't just me doin it.*

This lady I used to stay with told me all about what could happen when you pray. And she was true. I know she was now.

Last week I was walkin back from Lincoln Rec, you know, and I just started thinkin about all this. It was after I had one a my best days ever. I couldn't miss a jumper, my dribbles were super tight, I was swipin the ball left and right from everybody. I remember right where I was when I started thinkin about it: corner of Washington and Grand View, right outside the Foster's Freeze where this crazy white dude was strummin his guitar. I remember it was gettin all dark and there wasn't too many cars out. I sat down at the bus stop there and thought about it. I couldn't believe what's happenin to me. How good I could ball now. How I can take almost any guy I play against now. And I know it ain't just me, Annie, but God, too. I know I couldn't ball like that just by myself.

Do you understand what a sweet life they got in the NBA? They got fat bank accounts and big-ass houses. They got three, four cars each. BMWs and Expeditions. Range Rovers. And all they gotta do is just play ball all day.

They get paid to play ball, Annie. That's crazy.

Sometimes when I'm sitting in class I picture what it would be like if I got there. The announcer sayin my name over the P.A., the crowd holding up signs, me chillin out back at the hotel after a big game, watchin some highlight I did on SportsCenter. When I'm walkin through the airport people pointin at me and sayin, "Is that Sticky Reichard? Nah, for real, is that Sticky Reichard?"

When I think about that too much, my stomach starts gettin all messed up.

I know it don't sound good, Annie, but I think if I couldn't make it I wouldn't wanna be around no more. Cause it's all I got in my life, you know? Playin ball. It's all I got in the whole world. And if I couldn't make it, I woulda been wrong all this time about God's plan.

But you ain't gotta worry about all that, girl. Cause I swear to you, man, one day I'm gonna make it to the NBA. . . .

Francine Was All

smiles when she drove up to Sticky's foster care pad in her old-school Volkswagen van. Bumper stickers about Greenpeace and the Dodgers. Christian fish. Shiny black cross hanging like a pendulum from the rearview mirror.

Francine was the first of the foster ladies.

She had long red-gray hair and freckles. A silver cross dangling from her fragile neck. She showed up for Sticky three days after he turned nine.

The night before the pickup, all the counselors horseshoed around Sticky in the TV room. Told him how lucky he was.

This is a perfect match, Counselor Jenny said, and everybody agreed.

She picked you out of everyone, Counselor Amy said.

Sticky yanked his socks up and scrunched them back down. Yanked up and scrunched down.

Yeah, how often does somebody looking to adopt pick a nine-year-old? Jenny said, looking to the old Mexican director for the facts. *Most are looking for babies, right?*

It's rare, the director said.

She must think Sticky's pretty special, Jenny said.

Amy stroked Sticky's hair and smiled at him. *Plus you're such a tough little guy,* she said. She looked to Jenny, told her: *He didn't even cry when he first came here. Most kids do, you know.* She made a playful face to Sticky. *Do you even have tear ducts in those eyes, mister tough guy?*

But it's OK to cry, Sticky, Jenny said. *In fact, it's healthy to cry. It can make you feel better.*

Turned out Francine's husband had passed away, leaving her alone in their big house in Pasadena. All three of her own kids had grown up and graduated college. Moved away. She told the adoption agency that such a big lonely house should be shared with a child. *What better way for an old lady like me to give back?* she said, after pulling out Sticky's picture from a stack of thirty. *What could be better than giving a child like him an opportunity?*

And Francine wasn't just blowing smoke, she gave the situation everything she had. Hooked up three meals a day in the kitchen, told Sunday school stories by Sticky's bed until he fell asleep at night. She took him to movies and museums and amusement parks. Held up multiplication flash cards when she found out he bombed a math test. Every afternoon she'd be there to pick Sticky up from school, her van pulled along the curb just like any other kid's mom.

One Friday after school, Sticky pulled open the van door and spotted a wrapped package sitting on the passenger seat. *What's this?* he said.

It's for you, Francine said.

Sticky stood there a sec, ran through possible holidays in his head. He picked the box up and set it back down. *But it ain't my birthday or nothin.*

I know that, Francine said, and she laughed. *It's just because I like you. Now, go on and open it.*

Sticky climbed into the seat and ripped through the baseball wrapping paper. Tossed it to his feet. He opened the box and pulled out a brand-new black suede jacket, held it out in front of his excited face.

Francine took her hands off the wheel, folded them in her lap. Her face was frozen in a smile.

Sticky reached back in the box, pulled out a white collared shirt and a pair of black pants.

You have to have nice clothes where we're going tonight, Francine said.

They drove straight to Santa Monica from the school. Sat in heavy traffic on the 110 with everybody else. Traffic on the 10 West. They listened to talk radio and the sound of cars gassing and breaking. The smell of exhaust floated in through their open windows.

When Francine finally pulled off the 10 at Lincoln, she headed west on Broadway. They inched through Third Street

Promenade foot traffic and cars waiting to pull into parking garages. Out the window Sticky spied the exact spot he used to beg for change with Baby. Pictured himself holding out the white bowl and making the sad face Baby taught him. The felt-penned sign around his neck blowing into his face when the wind picked up. Pictured Baby right behind him, sitting Indian style and humming to herself.

Here we are, Francine said as she pulled up to the Loews Hotel lobby, shut off the engine and handed the keys to the valet guy. *This is the place.*

Up in the fancy room, Francine came out of the bathroom wearing a long black dress and lipstick. High heels. Long silver earrings that dangled over her bare freckled shoulders. She helped Sticky tuck his new shirt into his new pants. Held the jacket out so he could put one arm in and then the other.

When Sticky was all set she took out a blow-dryer and ran a brush through her wet hair. *We're going to eat at a place called Ivy at the Shore,* she shouted over the hot air. *It's a really nice place. My husband took me there for every one of our anniversaries.* She flipped off the blow-dryer and set it down. She spun around in the mirror and then turned her attention to Sticky. *Now I'm taking you.*

At dinner Francine taught Sticky about table manners: where to place the napkin in his lap, where to keep hands and elbows, how to hold the menu, which fork to use and at what time. Sticky sat stiff and listened to everything she said.

In the dim light, and with his new gear, he wondered if he looked like he belonged. Or could people tell it was his first time inside a restaurant. Ever. That it felt like a foreign country to him.

He watched a boy sitting three tables down wearing a tie. Watched the way the boy talked to adults and ordered for himself, the way he sipped soup from a spoon and dabbed at his mouth with a napkin. Every move seemed so natural. Sticky swore to himself right then and there that when he got older, had money of his own, he'd be eating at places like this every single night.

Before the food came out Francine reached over and took Sticky's hands. She closed her eyes and began a prayer: *Thank you, Lord, for this wonderful night, thank you for bringing Sticky and me into one another's lives. Lord, one day Sticky, too, will come to you. . . .*

As Francine went on, Sticky kept his eyes open. He watched the wrinkles in her chin stretch and fall as she spoke, her eyelids twitch. She always talked to him about God. Read Bible passages each morning while he wolfed down eggs and toast. She told him about Jesus and heaven, how to lead life like a true Christian. He could never figure out what to make of all that talk, but he liked that her words were aimed at him and nobody else.

Just as Francine released Sticky's hands and opened her eyes, the waitress set down their plates.

Let's eat, Francine said.

But a year into things, Francine was diagnosed with cancer. Told she had to undergo immediate and intensive treatment just to have a chance at pulling through.

Her daughter flew in from New York two days after they found out, drove the van when they took Sticky back to his foster care pad.

They dropped him off late at night.

This is only temporary, Francine said outside the van, tears running down her face. Her daughter stayed inside the van, left the motor running. *I promise,* Francine said. *The Lord will make sure of it.* Her face was outlined by a glowing sliver of moon and Sticky felt bad for her. *When I get better I'm going to rush back here and take you home.*

And as she stared at him, Sticky thought it was true what she was saying. This lady. She would come back for him.

They looked at each other for a while, neither of them moving or saying a word. Then Francine smiled through her tears and took both of his hands in hers. She kneeled so they were eye-level and told him: *I love you, Sticky.*

She hugged him tight.

Sticky didn't cry when her old Volkswagen van pulled out of the driveway and into the street. The old Mexican director's hand on his shoulder. The cold wind on the back of his neck. *Is this when you're supposed to cry?* he wondered as the van moved slowly down the long, busy road and mixed with other taillights. *Is this when you're supposed to feel sad and cry?* Because his eyes were as dry as a Santa Ana.

Francine died three months later in a hospital just outside Manhattan. Sticky found out when he overheard some counselors whispering in the office.

When he heard it for a second time later that week, a big sit-down kinda conversation with the old Mexican director, he acted like he didn't know.

Jimmy Comes Running

out the office when he hears all the racket.
Everyb-b-b-b-body g-g-g-get out! he says, and points at
the door.

Nobody notices.

He moves up to the core of the pack, invisible. Takes
quick strained breaths.

Jimmy is: eyes the size of golf balls in thick Coke-bottle
glasses, overgrown crop that starts a thumb's width from his
bushy eyebrows, old beat-up flea-bitten sweatshirt zipped
up to the throat: ARMY FOOTBALL. He yanks the rock from
Trey's grasp and stomps his foot on the ground, yells: *I s-s-s-
s-said, everyb-b-b-b-body out!*

Ballers stop dead and turn to check him this time.

Jimmy's already shut Lincoln Rec down twice this summer. Stood by the soda machine with his arms crossed while everybody grabbed their stuff and filed out slow. First time after Big Mac blasted some first-timer in the mouth and wouldn't stop kicking after he hit the ground. Guy's teeth went through his bottom lip. Blood all over the low post area. The second time when Old-man Perkins pulled a gun and dudes hit the ground, ducked behind bleachers. But Jimmy's bluffed on a handful of other occasions. When arguments build up like volcanoes and everybody blows at once. A chorus of over-the-top cursing and street ball threatening.

We ain't done nuthin, New York yells.

Nah, Rob says. *I ain't movin one step.*

G-g-g-g-get out! Jimmy says again, swinging an arm through the air and almost knocking off his glasses. He straightens himself out, adds: *N-N-N-N-NOW!*

Aah, come on, Jimmy, Dallas says.

It don't gotta be like all that, Johnson says.

Old-man Perkins jumps off the bleachers and throws somebody's towel onto the court. *I ain't even played one game yet.*

Dante walks up cool as a cat and puts a hand on Jimmy's shoulder. *Just a simple misunderstanding, Jimmy,* he says. *We about to shoot for it right now, as a matter of fact.* He looks in Jimmy's magnified eyes and smiles white teeth.

Jimmy takes a deep breath to slow himself down. He looks back at Dante and shakes his head. *You kn-kn-kn-kn-know th-th-this ain't r-right, D-D-D.*

I know it, Jimmy. I know it. The question is: What are we gonna do about it now?

All the c-c-c-c-cursin and h-h-h-h-h-h-hollerin. Jimmy

squints his eyes and scrunches up his face to get all the words out.

You know how brothers be actin sometimes, Dante tells him.

Jimmy puts a hand on a hip and looks around at all the guys' faces. Shakes his head, disgusted. *B-b-b-but th-th-they's imp-p-p-portant off-ff-ff-ff-ff-ffices next door,* he says, and points at the east wall.

I know it, Jimmy. I know about all that. Dante reaches in slowly, takes the ball from Jimmy's hands and bounces it a couple times off the hardwood. He palms the ball with his left hand and fingers his beard with the right. *But we about to settle all this jazz right now.*

Dante spins around and yells out: *Hey, yo, Rob!*

What? Rob yells back, sitting at half-court with his legs sticking straight out, weight on the palms of his hands behind him.

You made a call, shoot for it. Dante rolls the ball to Rob.

Rob gets up slow, dribbles a few times and struts to the top of the key. *Messed up I gotta shoot,* he mumbles under his breath. *White boy tries to tackle me and now I gotta shoot for it.*

Rob's the light-skinned black dude who preaches nonstop, up in the bleachers after games, about Marcus Garvey and Malcolm X. About going back to Africa and taking back from the "white devil." All that passionate preaching and the very next day he'll bring in a white chick to watch him play.

He steps up to the top of the key and takes a couple more bounces. Wipes hands on shorts and lofts up a high-arcing knuckleball that gets a good bounce on the rim and rolls in.

Water! he says, and holds his right-hand follow-through in the air so everyone can check it. *My rock!*

You right, baby, Dante says. *Your rock.*

Ball don't lie, Trey says. He picks the ball up and sticks it in New York's face. New York slaps it out of his hands.

What's the count? Slim says.

Anybody got the score? Dallas says.

My jumper's like water, Rob says.

This is very bad call, Carlos says, and he gradually retreats back to his spot on the homeless court.

New York stares at Rob and laughs. *Worst call I ever seen,* he says. He shakes his head and walks toward the baseline.

Shut up and check ball, Rob says.

Dante puts his hand on Jimmy's shoulder again and spins him back toward the office. *See, it's all good, Jimmy. My main man in charge. Boss man. Check it, we about to play straight up now. Some good old-fashion ball and no more quarrelin.* He walks Jimmy as far as the bleachers, pats him on his back and lets him go.

Jimmy takes a few steps and turns around. *N-n-no more qu-qu-qu-qu-qu-qu-quarrelin, though, D-D-D-D,* he says, shaking his finger.

We done with all that, Jimmy, Dante says, with his hands in the air. *Good old-fashion ball from now on. The way Dr. James Naismith intended it to be played all them years ago when he invented the game.*

Jimmy stands nodding his head at Dante for a few seconds. Then he turns around and walks into his office, reaches a hand back and pulls the door shut behind him.

On the Way

back to Millers, just a week after he met Anh-thu
there last summer, Sticky made himself a promise: A dude
like him wasn't leaving Millers empty-handed a second time.

He worked it all out in the back of a dark Number 3 bus.
Next to some old lady who smelled like a wet sandbox. He
came up with what route to take and how to keep his head in
the game. Told himself over and over in his head: *Just stay
cool, man, stay cool.*

But it wasn't even a question, this trip he was jacking
some khakis.

He busted in the open doors all business, stupid pop
songs turned way too loud. The smell of cheap sample
colognes. He steered straight up to the Anchor Blues and

started searching for three or four pairs he could pull into a dressing room.

Walkman turned low enough this time to hear footsteps behind his back.

Hey, Anh-thu said, coming at him from the side. *You're back.* She was excited to see him.

Sticky gave her a nod.

She put her elbows on the metal rack and watched Sticky's mad search. *You need some help?* she said.

Sticky shook her off. Pulled out one pair, checked tags twice (price and size) and then stuck them back on the rack. When the sticking-back sound didn't sound right, he pulled them off and stuck them back again. Pulled them off and stuck them back. He started to panic inside. Started sweating. Last thing he wanted to do in front of this pretty girl was act all retarded. But he couldn't stop himself. He pulled them off and stuck them back again.

Pulled them off and stuck them back.

Pulled them off and stuck them back.

Pulled them off and stuck them back.

Anh-thu didn't understand what was happening, but she had to do something. She ignored Sticky's refusal for help and stuck her hands in the mix. Right next to his. Acted like she didn't even notice Sticky's repetition. She pulled out a pair herself, looked at them, then stuck them back on the rack.

Sticky eventually got his cool back and they worked together, side by side.

Listen, Anh-thu said as they continued going through the rack. *I have to apologize about last week. About saying you*

81

were my boyfriend. I just didn't know what I could say at the time.

I ain't worried about it, Sticky said.

I just didn't want you to think I was weird. A pair of pants slipped off the hanger and dropped to the floor. Anh-thu picked them up and smoothed out the creases. *I've seen you around school and stuff, though. You're in Mrs. Edelson's econ for third period, right?*

Sticky nodded, held a pair of khakis up to his jeans.

I have her right after you. I've seen you walking out when I'm walking in.

Sticky kept his eyes on the cotton, told her: *She boring.*

Tell me about it. And she's super scatterbrained. People say she puts vodka in her orange juice every morning. Anh-thu moved in closer to Sticky. She sifted through the pants shoulder to shoulder with him. *Thirty-four in the light ones, right?*

Sticky nodded.

Plus I've seen you play basketball, too.

And that was what did it, man. Sticky dropped his hands from the search and looked right at her. This green-eyed girl with long black hair. This perfect face floating through his head all week between runs at Lincoln Rec. Just like that: Anh-thu mentions one thing about hoops and Sticky's at full attention.

Yeah, you're number seven on JV, she said. She smiled when she saw she had Sticky's attention. *I totally go to all the games. Unless I have to work or something. I love basketball.*

You check out our games? Sticky said, dropping his cool for a couple beats. Trying to picture her up in the stands and him shooting free throws with the game on the line.

Yeah, and you're the best one on the team. You make all the points. She made a face and put her hands on her hips. *Hey, just cause I'm a girl doesn't mean I don't know what's up.*

Nah, I didn't say all that.

Anh-thu pulled a thirty-four off the rack and held it out. *Is this kinda what you're looking for?*

Sticky took the pants. *Yeah, these are smooth.*

She pulled keys from her pocket and motioned for Sticky to follow.

They weaved in and out of intense late-night shoppers, through racks of shirts, hats, socks, freshly dressed mannequins, and slipped into the dressing room area, where Anh-thu unlocked one of the doors and let Sticky in. *Let me know if you need another size or anything,* she said.

She smiled big and closed the door behind her.

Sticky planted himself on the bench and stared at the pair of khakis. Not even a dime in his pockets. This girl had been to games, man. She knew his jersey number. And she was fine. Smelled good too. Sticky sat there awhile, in the dressing room, thinking about Anh-thu and the pair of pants in his lap.

Finally, he walked out of the dressing room without trying them on. He handed the khakis off to Anh-thu and told her: *These didn't really fit too good.*

Really? Anh-thu said. *You wanna try a different size?*

Nah, Sticky said. He scratched his head, leaned against a shelf of shirts, and when it wobbled, stood up straight again. *I don't think I want em no more.*

They stood next to each other in silence for a few seconds. Anh-thu folded the pants up perfect, let them fall loose and started folding all over. She watched Sticky out of the corner of her eye.

Sticky pulled a T-shirt off the rack, stood staring at the design for a little bit and then pulled out a different one.

Anh-thu put the pants on a hanger and hung them on the wrong rack. She turned and fished out Sticky's eyes, cleared her throat. *I don't know what you have to do or whatever, but I was gonna walk through the promenade after work. Before I catch the bus home.* She reached down and adjusted the strap on one of her flip-flops. *I don't know, maybe you'd wanna go with me. I mean, if you're going that way or something?*

Sticky shrugged his shoulders and buried his hands in his pockets. *That's cool,* he said, keeping away from her eyes.

Great, Anh-thu said. *Let me check out.*

They moved through the packed mall without saying a word. Through the food court and into the well-lit promenade. Waited for the green Walk sign with everybody else, and then walked across Broadway.

They strolled past Hear Music, Borders, the new Rip Curl store, the movie theater with its two-story list of films and times. They walked through a crowd that had gathered around a guy finger-picking his guitar and singing a James Taylor cover.

The night air was cool. The moon glowed through a thin patch of clouds. Sometimes Sticky would think up a question to ask, about classes or kids they both knew from school, but they all seemed dumb so he kept them to himself.

They passed Urban Outfitters and Mario's Pizza, the

glass walls of World Gym and the long curving line coming out of Starbucks. A young black kid dressed in an all-glitter suit busted fancy dance steps to Michael Jackson's greatest hits. He had only one glove on and everything. People cheered. Anh-thu kept pulling her hair behind her ears, out of her face, only to have it slip forward again.

Sticky's hand accidentally brushed against Anh-thu's a couple times, so he stuck it in his pocket. There was a subtle squeak coming from one of his Nikes, so he tried to step soft with that foot to make it go away.

It was across a crowded Santa Monica Boulevard and then west on Arizona. Sticky led the way and Anh-thu followed. They crossed Ocean Street to the beach side and had to high-step through a pack of Venice Beach overflows pounding bongos. They stopped at the bridge that goes over the PCH to the sand. Leaned elbows against the wood railing and stared out at the ocean.

I have to admit one thing to you, Anh-thu said, breaking a long silence.

OK, Sticky said.

Just so you know, my girlfriends made something up when we watched your games. The wind was strong and Anh-thu had to keep pushing her hair out of her face. *They kinda pretended like you and me were together. Like boyfriend-girlfriend. I'm sure it's cause I always talk about what a great player you are. And cause I told em I thought you were cute.* She pulled a rubber band from her pocket and put it in her mouth. Gathered her hair for a ponytail and double-wrapped. *I guess that's why I came up to you in the store like that.*

I never seen you at no games.

You're probably just concentrating. Like you're supposed to.

Sticky tossed a piece of ice plant over the cliff. *We're first place in league.*

I know.

And I'm getting called up to varsity for play-offs. Coach said he'd get me some time, too. I know it's ways off, but I can't wait.

I'll totally be going to the play-offs, Anh-thu said, and pushed Sticky, all jazzed. *My girlfriend Laura and me already talked about it. But I didn't know you were gonna be playing too. That's so cool.*

Her face went straight and she said: *Hey, why didn't you go with me to get hot chocolate last time?*

Sticky put his hands in his pockets and shrugged his shoulders. He didn't feel like getting into the whole thing about him never having money. He barely knew this girl.

Cars whizzed by on the PCH below. A trail of red lights going north, white coming south. All the different motors blending like the hum Baby used to make pushing around her broken-down vacuum. Sometimes a group of people would walk by on their way to the beach. Swinging bags full of blankets and wine. They'd disappear around the bend for a few minutes and then come out smaller on the other side of the bridge. In the distance the Santa Monica Ferris wheel was still spinning tourists around and around. Little arms and legs poking out of old-style seats. There were the faint smells of popcorn and dying seaweed in the air. The muted sound of waves rolling in across the sand.

When Sticky didn't say anything for a while, Anh-thu

wondered if he was getting bored. *Maybe I should let you go,* she said, straightening up. *I have to catch the bus anyway.*

They looked at each other for an awkward second. Sticky opened his mouth to say something but decided to keep it put away.

My dad gets worried when I take the bus too late.

Sticky made the move when Anh-thu looked to the ground. Stuck his face in hers. Touched his lips on her lips and wrapped hands around her back.

Anh-thu pressed against the railing and placed her soft hands on his face.

They looked at each other. Anh-thu giggled a little. She reached for his hand.

Sticky led her down to where the bridge starts and helped her climb over the railing. *I can't believe we're doing this,* she said as they crept along a narrow stretch of cliff and ducked underneath the bridge, out of sight.

There were abandoned fast-food bags at their feet. Styrofoam cups. A soiled blanket. Pieces of cardboard. Beer bottles that had settled in a ditch by one of the thick concrete pillars. Sticky kissed Anh-thu again. They tugged at each other's clothes.

What are we doing? Anh-thu said whenever they separated to deal with a stubborn button or snap.

They sat on the dirt, half dressed.

Sticky reached a hand up her blouse. Anh-thu fumbled with Sticky's zipper. No layer scam meant no khakis underneath. No stop in the action because of a crime.

There were voices of people walking over their heads. Spanish. English. French and Japanese. Someone dropped a glass and the shattering sound echoed under the bridge. When one of their feet slipped a little, slid across the loose dirt, a small cloud of dust would rise up into the bottom of the bridge and separate.

Then it was over. Sticky stood up quick and pulled his jeans over himself. Zipped up. Anh-thu straightened her skirt and stood up too. They both put themselves back together in silence.

OK, I think I have to go now, Anh-thu said, giggling. *I have to catch the bus.*

Sticky stepped over two faded Pepsi cans and an abandoned flannel. He got in close to Anh-thu, looked right in her eyes and pulled the loose rubber band from her hair. Anh-thu's black hair spilled down her shirt, covered her name tag. When she leaned her head back and shook her hair out, Sticky got a weird feeling in his stomach. Like everything was the way it was supposed to be: the cool breeze, the sound of the highway and the beach, the bridge and cliff covering them like they were in their own little world. He'd never had this feeling before. *You wanna be my girl?* he said, slipping his hands into his pockets.

Anh-thu looked right back into Sticky's eyes, caught her lips breaking into a smile and made her face go straight. *Yes,* she said. *I totally do.* She reached up and put her hands on the back of Sticky's head. Went up on her toes and kissed his cheek. She looked up into his eyes and let herself smile this time.

I should really go, she said.

I'll walk you to the bus stop, Sticky said.

When they climbed back onto the bridge Sticky put his

headphones on without sound. Walked slow through the homeless bodies curled up on the grass. Anh-thu picked a little yellow flower from a bush and put it behind her ear. She walked a little ahead of Sticky up to the crosswalk that would take them back into the promenade, pushed the button.

Damn, Sticky said to himself, *I guess I didn't get me no pants.*

He stared at the flower stem sticking out the back of Anh-thu's long black hair and felt happy.

Cheerleaders Screamed Out

chants and posed with blue and white pom-poms, whipped thin arms and legs around like little windup toys. The football squad leaned in close to the action on the court, sprayed venom and pointed bench-press fingers in the other team's faces. The ten-piece band broke into hype-up-the-crowd tunes the second a ref's whistle stopped play.

Sticky's seventeenth birthday may have ended in a crowded holding cell, but it kicked off in a sold-out forty-year-old high school gym.

Dominguez Hills rolled into town with twenty-two wins and a bus full of hype. Players filling out purple jerseys like men. "Too much experience," all the papers said. "Too many athletes. Two of their starters already committed to big-time

90

colleges." All this and it was Venice High's first play-off game in five years.

Sticky was the hotshot sophomore who gets called up from JV for play-offs. The outsider at the end of the bench with his warm-ups still buttoned all the way.

The kid pinched out of the huddle during time-outs.

Players called up don't see much run in the play-offs. It's a pat on the back just being on the bench. Sticker on the helmet. But all that went out the window in the middle of the third quarter, when Dominguez Hills went up by twelve. Coach Reynolds shook his head at every face he scanned on the bench. When he got to Sticky he pointed a shaky finger, told him: *Get the hell in there, kid.* Grabbed Sticky under the arm and damn-near threw his ass toward the scorer's table. *Run the point.*

Sticky jogged to the table and pulled off his warm-up jacket, tossed it behind the bench. He reached over and picked it back up, threw it down. Picked it up and threw it down.

Picked it up and threw it down.

Picked it up and threw it down.

It was a crazy time to have an episode, with all the varsity guys on the bench, watching, but he knew all he had to do was get on the court. That was when everything would disappear.

It took three or four more tries before he got the perfect toss. Then he slid a hand across both soles for grip.

The buzzer sounded and the ref waved Sticky into the game.

Reynolds put a hand on his shoulder and yelled something,

but Sticky didn't hear a word. He didn't hear anything, in fact. Not his coach. Not the crowd. Not the announcer calling his name out over the loudspeaker or his teammates telling him who to take on defense. He strutted out onto the stage with nothing but a blank mind.

When the ref whistled the ball back in play, Sticky made like it was just another street ball game down at Lincoln Rec.

See, I have this theory about hoops. About what makes one dude smooth under pressure and another fold.

Sticky picked off a cross-court pass right off the bat, high-dribbled down the sideline like Deion Sanders and stuck a deep three-pointer.

The crowd rustled.

The more a player thinks about the game—what setting they're in, who they're running against, what folks will say depending on whether or not they hook up a decent showing—the more messed up that player is gonna play. It's unnatural.

Sticky ripped the other squad's point guard clean, like he was wrapped and on a shelf at half-court, took three quick dribbles and dropped in a sweet one-handed finger roll over the rim. His face broke a smile on the way back downcourt. He pointed to the crowd and pumped his fists.

He was like a showman at the circus.

The guy in the cage with the whip.

Go ahead and pick out the smartest dude in the house, and I'll promise you he's the most weak-minded baller. All that analyzing. Examining. Calculating. Man, you gotta stay clear out there. There's no time for reflection when you need reaction to a situation.

The crowd started catching on to this new guy up from JV. Running the squad. Flashy passes and slick attacks on the bucket. Slashing and bombing away. Hoops on autopilot.

Sure, the game with refs is supposed to be different from the game on the street. More under control. Less razzle-dazzle. Fundamentals like they teach in clinics all across the country. How to play hoops for $425 per week. But Sticky plays with the same flavor no matter what the setting.

Every time you turned around in the second half, the announcer was calling Sticky's name over the loudspeaker: *STICKYYYYYYY REICHARD FOR ANOTHER TWO. COUNT IT.*

White space.

Then the whine of the school band's trumpet, a couple thuds from the bass drum. The crowd stepping up its volume another notch. The weight of all the energy testing the old gym's tired bleachers.

And some movie writer couldn't have made it up any better. The way it all came down in the end. With eleven seconds left, Dominguez Hills' star guard was at the free-throw line shooting two. Score tied 85–85. Crowd booming. Band banging through sets during a time-out Reynolds called to ice the shooter.

No matter what, Reynolds yelled over screeching horns. The whole squad was huddled around him with blank faces, ready to gobble up whatever he fed them. *No matter what, if he makes them or misses them, we call time out.*

When the kid stepped up to the line, the crowd was so out of control, stomping their feet and screaming, the rim actually started vibrating. The bottom of the net started flipping back and forth. The ref handed the kid the rock and he went into his routine: three dribbles, tuck the ball under the chin, deep breath. He lofted the first one up soft and it fell through.

The crowd died.

Just like that. Ball hits nylon, no more noise. Like someone in the control room flipped a switch. Dominguez Hills 86, Venice 85.

Purple jerseys went up and slapped their guy on the back, told him: *One more, baby. One more.*

The crowd topped out for the second free throw. Feet pounded bleachers like a tank rolling through. Both teams snuck over-the-shoulder glances at the wave of screaming fans. Felt deep vibrations swim through the floor and into their shoes, scale up weary legs and unfold in the pit of their stomachs.

Three dribbles, tuck the ball under the chin, deep breath. Kid lofted up another soft one, but this time it rattled around the rim and fell out. Venice's starting center, Sinclair, ripped down the board with two hands and made a quick T around the ball. *Time out, ref! Time out!*

Down one, nine seconds to play.

No time to analyze.

Venice huddled around Coach Reynolds again. A pocket of concentration. All the guys gave everything to ignore the cries of the crowd, the thumping of the band.

Reynolds reached for his stick of chalk and stared at the ground. All eyes were glued to a blank chalkboard. *All right, here's what we do!* he yelled, but then he fell silent again.

The crowd locked into a rhythm of sound. Two stomps

and a clap. All at once. Boom boom clap. Boom boom clap. Sticky stood pinched out of the huddle with a water bottle, squirting an arc of tap into his mouth and trying to listen.

Reynolds reached through the huddle for Sticky's arm. Pulled him into the middle of everything.

Sinclair, Reynolds said, just as the buzzer sounded. End of time-out. End of brainstorm. *You inbound to Sticky. Sticky, you penetrate and look for the open man. Nothing's there, pull up for the shot.*

Everybody looked at Sticky all crazy as they broke the huddle and stepped back onto the floor. Coach put the rock in the hands of a JV kid. A sophomore. Skinny white boy who didn't even have a name on the back of his jersey.

Sinclair put a big mitt on Sticky's head. *Come on, young-ster. Make something happen out there.*

Spread the court, Reynolds yelled, following his team halfway out onto the hardwood. He reached out for Sticky's shoulder but missed. *Don't do nothing stupid, kid!*

And a sold-out gym fell silent for Sticky.

The ref blew his whistle and handed the ball to Sinclair. The movements of the crowd without sound. Every kid on the court in super-slo-mo. Ticks of the clock farther and farther away. He jab-stepped at his defender and broke for the ball. Hands out. Sinclair whipped a pass in to him and the seconds started rolling:

Nine seconds on the clock . . . eight seconds. And, see, this is what you do . . .

You size up the purple jersey in your face, man. Some num-ber 23-be-like-Mike black face with straight teeth. Braces. Beads of sweat dribbling down his forehead. Baby Afro. The triangle of small moles on his right cheek, calling out. Down in defensive stance like basketball camp demonstration says.

Scared eyes.

Seven seconds . . . six seconds.

All your guys clear out. Give space so you can break it down. Do your thing. Lay out crazy beats cause you're the man on the mix. Official game ball leather is soft in your hands, man, like Anh-thu's smooth face up in the crowd, watching. Cup it between your fingers and forearm and feel alive.

Aware.

Necessary.

Cause, man, this is your jam they're waiting for. And this is your world they're waiting in.

See Sinclair trailing the play, his big high-top sneakers like fists against a soundproof wall.

See your path to the promised land. Without looking. Left side of the lane, where a dozen possibilities flash through your head. See your red carpet. See your yellow brick road. Hesitate. Get a split-second survey.

Feel the electricity, man, of two thousand faces burning on YOU. Four thousand eyes in the back pocket of YOUR hoop shorts.

Revel in it.

Five seconds . . . four seconds. Take off with your head down. . . .

Know the statues around you. Guys' empty faces.

Know the power in your legs and feet. The spring in your step.

Know the ticking of the clock.

Know what purple jerseys will do before they do it. It's in the way they lean.

Know the six inches of open lane that will be cut off by which guy and at what point.

Know your coach's crinkled leather face on the sideline. The ref with the whistle in his mouth, backpedaling.

Know your defender's wide eyes as a pathway to his mind.

Know your body inside and out. That it will do exactly as it's told.

Know the ball in your hands as you put it on the floor.

Know your third move before you make your first.

Know quickness.

Know stopping on a dime.

Know nothing.

Three seconds. When you blast past the slo-mo purple jersey with straight teeth, pouring out of a jar thick like syrup, the biggest purple jersey leaves his guy to cut you off. Like you knew he would. Like a stray dog after a fake toss.

You stutter-step around his tree-trunk legs and cross over.

You feel the brush of another purple jersey, like a rush of wind across your left side. But you dance by that, too. When your Nikes get in the paint, you lift into the air with the ball cupped like a football. Like a running back going over the top at the goal line. Dirty work before an end-zone shuffle.

You feel the weight of everybody in the gym holding their breath. Out of their seats and balanced on flexed toes. Bodies frozen and useless.

Purple jersey arms swing like they might block your shot, but here's the thing: It ain't nothing but a street ball game to you. Down at Lincoln Rec. Old-man Perkins in the bleachers. Fat Chuck. Dante and his rainbow jumpers. Everybody talking trash and cheating on the score. It ain't nothing but a game to eleven with two full squads on the sideline, waiting.

Defender arms swing, but they don't get nothing.

Hands full of empty air.

And when you got them all committed like that, exposed and in the air, that's when you pull it out of your pocket. That's when you break out the around-the-back flip, no-look style, to a wide-open Reggie. Purple arms get sucked back down by gravity, and your guy Reggie is laying it up off the glass for the game winner.

And it's nothing but that white-space thing again.

Sticky watched his coach leap up and down like a clown. Watched him hold back the assistant coaches with an arm bar. He watched the guys on his bench grab each other around the waist and point into the crowd. Slap fives and pump fists. He watched the biggest Dominguez Hills player in-bound the ball to their star guard. Watched him loft up a weak three-quarter-court prayer. Watched the way their bench crumbled when the ball fell twenty feet short as time expired.

All this. It happens for you in silence.

The final buzzer went off and the home crowd erupted. Everybody stomping their feet and yelling for the other team to get the hell out of the gym. Slapping hands with whoever stood on the right or left. As the band sounded off, all the guys on the bench sprang into the air, charged the court and dog-piled on Reggie. A pile of Venice hoops at midcourt. Sticky stood next to them, breathing fast, putting his hand on one of their shoulders, then taking it off.

A group of Venice football players charged the court with lettermen's jackets on. They ripped big banners off the walls and paraded around the court, holding them high above their heads. Everybody on the Dominguez Hills squad sat still on their bench, watched Venice celebrate. Some had white towels spilling off lowered heads.

Coach Reynolds pulled Sticky aside in the middle of all the mayhem. *Shoulda had you up here all year, son,* he said, trying to catch his breath. Twenty-three years on a sideline in his leather-black face. He palmed the back of Sticky's sweaty head and shook it around. *Goddamn, boy! That was one hell of a pass you just made!*

Fat Jay, the squad's big backup center, and Sinclair picked Reggie up and carried him into the stands. *Reggie's good for the game winner!* Fat Jay kept chanting. *Good for the game winner! Sent em on their way!*

Dave and Sin, Sticky's boys from the JV team, ran up into the stands after Sticky and jumped all over him. *MVP!* they kept yelling. *MVP!*

The school's longtime gym custodian, Manuel, came up and hugged Sticky. A small old Mexican man with a chewed-up beard. *One of the best wins I've ever seen,* he said, letting go of Sticky and wiping his face with a towel. Sticky used to walk with Manuel while he mopped the floor before JV practices and games. Listened to him talk about old-time hoops: Jerry West and Pistol Pete. Dr. J., Magic and Bird. Sticky reached out for Manuel's hand in the middle of the celebration, shook it firm. Manuel would let Sticky hang in the gym solo on weeknights. And Sticky appreciated it. He'd spend hours working on his shooting and ball handling. Manuel would play dumb, pretend he didn't hear a basketball tapping the hardwood or rattling the rim when he closed it down for the night. And they'd never spoken a word of it, even to each other. But this handshake, Sticky thought, this was saying it all.

Yo, Stick, Dave said. *Let's roll. We gotta celebrate.*

Come on, Sin said.

Cool, Sticky said. He let go of Manuel's hand and looked him in the eyes. He nodded.

One of the best wins ever, Manuel said again, then he made his way back down the bleachers, weaving through the thick packs of hyped-up students, and stood by his cart.

Anh-thu and her friend Laura were standing at the end of the bleachers. Sticky signaled for Dave and Sin to hold on and he hustled over to her.

Oh, my God! Laura said. *You were amazing!*

Thanks, Sticky said.

Anh-thu stood staring at Sticky, a huge smile painted on her face.

Sticky kissed her cheek, told her: *It was a good game, huh?*

Oh, my God, it was the best game ever! Anh-thu said. She covered her face with her free hand, looked at the ground. *Oh, my God, I can't stop smiling.*

Come on, Stick! Sin yelled out from near the gym exit.

MVP! Dave yelled, cupping his hand around his mouth. *MVP!*

Go on, Anh-thu said. *Celebrate with your boys. But call me tonight.* And when Sticky nodded, she snuck him a quick little hug.

The fellas all hopped in Sin's '67 Impala after Sticky grabbed his bag from the locker room. Dave was about 6' 6" so he rode shotgun. Sticky slid in back and pulled his jeans on over his hoop shorts. Pulled a clean sweatshirt on right over his sweaty jersey. He leaned forward and they all talked over each other about the comeback.

Sin turned down his reggae beats. *You see their coach's face, man? When we locked em up at eighty? Serious, you see that dude's look?*

Dave and Sticky laughed and pounded the roof.

Dave slapped a hand onto Sin's shoulder, said: *Nah, man, you see him throw his hands in the air when Stick took dude three straight times? He didn't know who the hell Stick was.*

Sin said: *Wasn't no scouting report on no number seven.*

Dave spun around to Sticky. *They didn't even know who you was, Stick.*

Sin pounded his steering wheel and yelled a grown man's yell: *Hell yeah!* Veins rising in his neck. He cranked up his beats again, so loud the whole car vibrated. Then he peeled out of the school parking lot, laying on the horn a few times with the heel of his hand, and headed north toward Santa Monica.

The Fellas All

started for the JV squad (Sticky, Dave and Sin) before Sticky got called up to varsity for the play-offs.

Sticky ran the point, led the team in both scoring and assists (25.9 ppg, 5.6 apg). Sin and Dave operated down low, controlled things in the paint.

Sin's a muscular first-generation Puerto Rican American who was also the star running back on the JV football squad. He's dark skinned with blue eyes. Not an ounce of body fat. The ladies tend to go wherever he's going.

Dave's a tall, skinny white kid from deep Venice. A section of the neighborhood people used to call Ghost Town due to the number of unsolved shootings. Everybody thinks he's a shade crazy because he's always mumbling to himself.

He lives in a one-bedroom apartment on Fifth with his mom and three sisters. Man of the house.

Things got off to a rough start when Sticky first came in at the beginning of the school year. Sin and Dave tried to be cool after open gyms, talked to him about the team and the coach and the best-looking cheerleaders, but Sticky wouldn't look anybody in the eye. It was his third school in two years, and he wasn't sure these punks by the beach were worth his time.

Sure, he showed up every time the coaches opened the gym. He listened when they went over pick-and-rolls, various zone defenses, and the half-court trap. He ran the sprints hard during conditioning. Never once complained. He even showed up for the big fund-raiser on Main Street, washed and dried cars all day like everybody else. But he never said a word to any of his new teammates. No jokes. No boasting. No talk of the past. He simply kept his mouth shut, his head down.

Sin finally grabbed Sticky by the neck before the first official practice of the season. They were in the locker room and Sticky'd gone up without saying a word and shut off Sin's reggae. He flipped it to his favorite hip-hop station and went back to lacing up his kicks. Sin froze, beanie in hand. He looked at a couple guys on the team, confused. They shrugged.

Yo, go put my tape back on, Sin said.

Sticky didn't look up.

Yo! Sin yelled this time. *Go put my damn tape back on!*

When Sticky didn't answer him that time, Sin stood up and walked toward him. See, there's one thing most people don't know about Puerto Ricans. You don't mess with their music. When Sin was halfway to Sticky he tossed his beanie to the side and charged.

Sticky sensed it was coming and fired one of his Nikes. Sin ducked and grabbed for Sticky's neck.

Sticky reached back and threw a series of wild punches, none of which landed, and then threw an elbow that caught Sin in the side of his shaved head. Sin grabbed Sticky's arms and put him in a tight headlock. They wrestled around on the floor, clawing at each other's faces, until the coaches came running in and pulled Sin off. Separated the two teammates.

What the hell's going on? Coach Reynolds demanded.

What are you doing? Coach Wilkins said.

Sticky and Sin didn't answer, they just stared at each other with fire in their eyes. The right side of Sticky's face was all scratched up and red. Both of their chests were moving in and out quick. Their fists were still clenched.

That was when the coaches pulled Sin into their office and explained about Sticky. How he had just moved into some house off Rose with five other strays. How it was the fourth foster home he'd lived in since the age of seven. Coach Wilkins, the JV coach, leaned forward and rested his elbows on his knees. *So cut the kid some slack, big guy,* he said. *You can do that, right?*

Sin shifted around in his chair, touched his fingers to a red spot on his cheek, checked them for blood. Nothing.

Coach Reynolds opened up a file he pulled from his desk drawer and cleared his throat. *Listen, I know there are some major discipline issues we're facing with this kid.* He thumbed through some of the paperwork. Scanned one of the pages with his finger. *But he gives y'all a legitimate point guard.*

He's gonna make your life so much easier, Sin, Coach Wilkins said. *His penetration will lead to easy buckets for you. Plus the kid can shoot the lights out. He's gonna stretch defenses out and you and Dave will have a goddamn field day inside.*

Listen, son, Coach Reynolds said. *I want you to cut this stuff out right now, OK? Just squash it.* He leaned back in his chair, worked a toothpick in between his teeth. *In fact, I don't wanna hear nothing else about you two ever again.* He looked over at Coach Wilkins. *Right, Coach?*

Right, Coach Wilkins said.

Sin shifted around in his chair, touched his fingers to the red spot on his cheek again. Nothing.

Coach Reynolds folded up the file and put it back in his desk drawer. Coach Wilkins lifted a whistle from the floor and put it around his neck.

Sin looked to Coach Wilkins, said: *All I'm saying, Coach, is that he ain't got no respect, and if he keeps on—*

What I'm saying, Sin, Coach Reynolds interrupted, pulling the toothpick from his mouth. *Is we don't need you adding fuel to the fire. Got it?*

Got it, Sin said.

Good, Coach Reynolds said.

Now go stretch out, Coach Wilkins said. *We'll start practice in five minutes.*

After that first practice Sin waited for Sticky in the parking lot. He didn't say one word to him until after he knocked him to the pavement with an overhand right to the ear.

That's right, boy! he said, pouncing on Sticky.

In the scramble, Sticky kept yelling out: *I'll kill you, man! I'll kill you!* He tried as hard as he could to roll over and get up, but Sin was too strong.

Sin put a knee in Sticky's chest and stared down at him with this wild look in his eyes. Told him: *I don't give a shit how many foster homes you been in. And you can believe that.*

After a few more minutes, Sticky stopped struggling and let his eyes come up to Sin's. In them he saw two tiny reflections of himself. Then he turned his head and let all his muscles relax.

It was over.

Carmen Rolled Up

to Sticky's foster care pad in a beat-up Chevy Nova with the backseat ripped out. The passenger seat was piled high with roses, tulips and daises. Sunflowers. Sticky was twelve.

Carmen was Sticky's second foster lady, and she was much younger than Francine. Prettier, too. She stepped out of the car wearing cutoff jean shorts and a tight black half-shirt. Her wavy brown hair was pulled back in a ponytail except for the wispy bangs that framed her dark brown eyes. As Carmen walked up the driveway, Counselor Amy said she looked like a movie star. Counselor Jenny argued she looked more like a runway model. But throughout the whole pickup process, Carmen never once cracked a smile. She kept a serious face through all the paperwork. Through the introductions. Through the awkward session in the driveway when everybody hugged and waved goodbye.

She didn't have a whole lot to say, either. On the long drive through traffic to Costa Mesa she kept her mouth shut and lips sealed. Hands gripped the steering wheel at ten and two. She turned on the radio, tuned in a Spanish station and tuned this new foster kid out.

Sticky sat Indian style in the empty back of the car, leaned against his bag. Around corners he'd put a hand out to keep from falling over. To pass the time he stared out the back window and kept a running head count of all the cars they passed.

When Carmen pulled up to a run-down apartment complex under the freeway overpass, security bars on every window, a good-looking light-skinned Hispanic dude came rushing out of the corner apartment with an electric guitar around his neck. He swung open the back door and helped Sticky get out. *Hey, bro, I'm Ruben,* he said. *I'm gonna be your new dad.* He smiled so big you could see all his teeth.

Ruben picked up Sticky's bag and carried it around to his wife. He kissed her on the cheek and said: *Thanks for going for me, baby. We couldn't quit until we worked out that chorus.*

Ruben carried Sticky's bag inside and slid it next to a buzzing amp, which he flipped off. He stuck his guitar on an empty guitar stand and turned his attention to Sticky. *Bro, you don't even know. I'm totally stoked to have a kid.* He pulled a couple picks out of his pocket and set them on the amp. *We found out six months ago that my old lady can't have no babies. She can get pregnant and all that, but somethin always happens before it gets born.*

Carmen overheard Ruben and stormed out of the room. She slammed their bedroom door.

Ruben looked at Sticky, said: *That's why you here, bro.*

Before Sticky could even hit the bathroom, Ruben lobbed him a baseball glove and pulled him into the street to toss a ball around. He squatted like a catcher and told Sticky to fire it in there. *I'll let you know if it's a ball or a strike,* he said. *I played ball in high school.*

The shadow from a tall tree hung over Ruben like a giant tarp. Sticky stood in the sun. There was a line between them on the pavement where shade was creeping in on sunlight. Sticky stared at that line, tossing the baseball into the heel of his glove, trying to make the perfect popping sound. He tossed the ball into his glove, again and again, and thought about how much different it was with Francine on the first day. Tossed the ball into his glove. Pulled it out and tossed the ball into his glove. How Francine smiled so much on their drive to her house, stopped off at a mall and let him pick stuff out for his bedroom.

Tossed the ball into his glove. Pulled it out and tossed the ball into his glove.

Finally Ruben called out: *Come on, bro! Just peep the target and let it go!*

The street smelled like *carne asada* grilling on a barbecue. Like refried beans. Like fresh-rolled tortillas bubbling up with steam on some old Mexican lady's griddle.

Ruben smacked his glove, waiting.

When the popping sound sounded right Sticky wound

up and threw a wild ball that Ruben had to pick up on the short hop.

Sticky threw pitch after pitch that first afternoon. He threw a few strikes, but they were mostly balls. A couple bounced off the pavement and dug into Ruben's shins. One sailed wide right and smacked somebody's truck. Ruben grabbed the spinning baseball after that wild pitch and scoped the neighborhood for witnesses. He fingered the fresh dent on the side of the pickup and said, *It ain't nothing, bro. Just a little scratch. No worries.* He walked back toward the makeshift home plate and tossed the ball to Sticky.

At one point, when Sticky struck out an invisible batter on three straight pitches down the middle, Ruben went crazy and made crowd sounds with his mouth.

You lucky, bro, he told Sticky after he walked out to the mound and wrapped an arm around him. The tree shadow was now only inches from Sticky's feet. *My pops didn't never wanna play catch with me when I was a kid.*

After catch it was a couple horror flicks and microwave popcorn. Carmen went to snuggle in close to Ruben, but he thought Sticky should sit in the middle. Said it would make him feel more like a part of the family. Ruben turned off all the lights and turned up the volume.

After every scary scene Ruben would turn to Sticky and whisper: *That's some scary stuff, right, bro?*

When the credits rolled on the second flick, Ruben ran through a few songs on his acoustic guitar and sang. He sat on a stool in front of the TV, strummed and picked soft at the shiny bronze strings. He closed his eyes and tilted his head back when he was really into it. Sticky and Carmen sat on opposite ends of the couch, watching.

When Ruben's voice got tired he put away his guitar and set up a bed for Sticky on the couch. *Good to have you, bro,* he said, and gave Sticky an awkward little hug. Then he pulled his wife into the bedroom, and she shut and locked the door behind her.

Through the door Sticky heard Carmen yelling about how having some random kid in the house wasn't the same as having a kid of their own. How he was a complete stranger and it creeped her out. He heard Ruben telling her over and over to calm down and give the situation a chance.

Sticky fell asleep that first night to a chorus of sirens outside the front room window and the Hispanic couple arguing in the bedroom.

The next day they worked off the same script: burritos, catch, a couple scary flicks and then some singing and fighting. The next week was like that too, in fact, except Carmen was gone during the day, Monday through Friday. It turned out Ruben played bass in a couple salsa bands but was taking time off to write new songs. Carmen worked part-time at a flower shop. Made lunchtime deliveries to all the businesses around South Coast Plaza. When she went to work, Ruben stayed home with Sticky.

On the one-week anniversary of Sticky's stay, Carmen came out for breakfast with a big smile. It was the first time Sticky had ever seen her smile, and he decided she looked prettier that way. Happy. Ruben followed her out and went right up to the couch where Sticky was lying under a blanket watching cartoons. He stuck his hands in his pockets. *We're goin on a trip today, bro.* He paused a second and then added: *To celebrate.*

Carmen laughed when he said that.

They had Sticky pack his bag back up and set it out by the car.

Where we goin? Sticky said between bites of cereal.

It's a secret, Carmen said, and she gave him a wink.

Just hold on, bro, Ruben said, and he shook his head at Carmen. *And remember, bro, it wasn't me who thought this whole thing up.*

On the road Ruben talked about his own dad. How he worked all day in a factory and then went straight to the bar. *We barely ever saw my old man,* he said. *When we did he was always wasted and yelling for us to do something.*

Sticky sat in the back again, leaning against his bag. He stared out the window and wondered where these people were taking him.

Ruben moved in and out across the four freeway lanes as he talked. Carmen sat in the passenger seat with her arms folded. She didn't say a word.

So, one day my old man comes in and moves all his things out, Ruben went on. *Just like that, bro. Right there in front of me and my two brothers. My mom.* He turned almost all the way around so he could see Sticky's face. When he swerved a little, started riding braille, he spun his face back to the road and straightened up. *But you know what?* he said, looking at Sticky in the rearview this time. *Everything was better when he was gone. It took me a while to realize it, but I didn't need him.*

Ruben directed his attention to the road again. He didn't say anything for a few minutes. Carmen was now filing her nails, sitting with one foot up on the dash.

I still don't need him, Ruben said. He raced by a station

112

wagon and looked in at the woman driver. He looked at Carmen to see if he'd been caught, but she was busy pulling nail polish out of her purse. *I'm just sayin, bro, people can turn out cool, you know? Without no dad.* He coasted down a familiar off ramp and stopped at a familiar red light. He turned around and looked Sticky in the eyes, told him: *I mean, just look at me.*

The long drive led them right back to the foster care pad, where the old Mexican director was waiting outside with his arms folded.

Ruben pulled the parking brake and hopped out of the car. Carmen stayed inside.

Ruben unloaded Sticky's bag and ran him through the whole hand-shaking thing. *Sorry about this, bro,* he said. *It just didn't work out.*

Before Sticky had time to say anything back, the old Mexican director was pulling him away.

Things Are Heating

up at Lincoln Rec. Sticky cuts through the lane and Rob busts an elbow in his ribs. Knocks him to the ground and scowls.

Sticky springs back up and continues through the lane.

Dallas swings the rock over to New York on the right wing. New York holds it against his hip, surveys the situation, then chucks it over to Sticky at the head of the key.

Sticky sizes Rob up with a couple jab steps and spies the lane. He makes a quick hesitation and slashes past. Rob reaches out to hold on, but Sticky's too slippery. As he scoots into the lane, Trey steps over to cut Sticky off, but this leaves Dante all alone up top. Wrong answer. Sticky instinctively whips the ball over his head and hits Dante in perfect rhythm for the jumper.

Ball rips through the net.

Dante points at Sticky as he backpedals down the court.

Sticky points back.

Tied up, Dallas says.

Next bucket wins, Trey says.

Now y'all playin some ball, Old-man Perkins yells from the side. He reaches down and starts lacing up his old-school Nike Airs.

It don't matter which one of y'all wins, though, Johnson says. *Cause we on next, and we ain't losin.* He nods his head at Perkins. Reaches out a fist for some daps.

It's one-thirty in the afternoon and Lincoln Rec is bursting at the seams with guys waiting to play. Everybody dribbling around on the sidelines to get warmed up. Throwing bounce passes to each other and sneaking up jumpers when the action's at the other end of the court.

Next team that scores sits the other five down. Sends them to the back of the line. A five- or six-game wait means a good two hours sitting up in the bleachers, watching.

Watching instead of playing.

Only guys with heart look for the rock when it's game point. When everything's on the line. Guys confident enough to put a team on their shoulders and good enough to bring it home. This is where you find out who came to win and who's happy just playing. Who's willing to rip somebody's head off when the pressure's on, and who's likely to cower in the corner like a puppy.

Bring it down to me, Rob says in the post, digging an elbow into Sticky's middle. Holding and grabbing. Pushing. *Come on, Slim, bring it down.*

Slim dumps it in, clears out to the top of the key.

Rob backs Sticky in, frees up enough space to work his unpolished post moves.

Trey comes over to set a screen but Rob waves him off.

He spins into the lane and makes his move to the cup, muscles toward the basket like a linebacker. Lowers a shoulder and blasts Sticky in the face as he powers the ball up to the rim. The skin under Sticky's right eye splits from the blow and blood starts zigging and zagging down his face. He goes down on one knee and watches Rob's shot toilet-bowl around the rim and fall through.

Game over! Trey yells, and fires wild fists through the air.

Get off my court! Big Mac says.

Rob stands over Sticky and flexes his biceps. *Too strong, white boy!*

Sticky runs his fingers across his cut and stares at the blood.

The next five are already making their way out onto the court, stretching arms and legs, jogging in place. Shooting warm-up jump shots and talking matchups.

Dante scoops the ball up and fires it against the backboard. When it ricochets back at him he punches it with a closed fist. The ball caroms past Dallas, who's squatting next to the door, covering his face with his hands. *I can't believe we lost to them fools,* he says to no one in particular.

Trey and Slim give each other daps and head for the drinking fountain.

Sticky presses his shirt against his cut and studies the red blotch of blood. He gets up and walks toward the wall behind the basket, leans against it. Dabs his shirt against his cut again and studies the red blotch of blood.

Fat Chuck takes earthquake steps up to Sticky and touches a fat hand to the back of his head. He pulls Sticky's shirt away from the cut and investigates. *Damn, Stick. Looks kinda deep*. He turns Sticky's face into the light, investigates some more.

Sticky shakes out of Chuck's grasp and presses his shirt against his cut, studies the red blotch of blood. *It ain't that bad*, he says, talking more to himself than Chuck. And what flashes through his mind at that point is Anh-thu. He was planning on hooking up her birthday perfect. Walking up to her at nine tonight with a big shiner wasn't exactly what he had in mind.

Check it out, Fat Chuck says. *I got some Neosporin in the car*. He holds his hands up in the air. *At least you gotta let me help you clean up in the bathroom, Stick. It ain't like you gonna be playin anytime soon anyway*. He points to all the guys on the sideline, waiting to play.

Sticky looks at all the guys, does some quick math in his head and figures he won't be playing again for another hour and a half, minimum. For a second he considers taking off. Handling the stuff he's gotta handle for Anh-thu's birthday early and worrying about ball tomorrow.

Rob struts by with a devil-like smile on his face. He ducks into the drinking fountain for a few seconds and comes up gargling. He spits.

On the strut back he leans in near Sticky's ear, tells him in a quiet voice: *You know you can't handle all this muscle in the post, white boy*. He flexes his guns and laughs when Sticky shoves him out of his face. Then he pimps back out on the court for the next game.

Chuck wraps a meat hook around Sticky's neck. *Don't worry about him, Stick,* he says. *Rob ain't nothing but a fool. You can trust me on that one.*

Sticky presses his shirt against his cut, studies the red blotch of blood. He looks up just as Old-man Perkins checks the ball into play and another game starts rolling.

It digs in Sticky's stomach when he thinks about Rob hitting the game winner on him. How he let Dante down. Dallas. How because he didn't play good enough defense they're all sitting on the sideline now. Waiting. Watching. Not a worse feeling in the world, he thinks. And then Anh-thu's face flashes through his head again and it makes him feel better. Maybe his day of hoops is off to a bad start and he has a cut on his face, but at least he gets to see his girl later on. At least he gets to chill with her. And the fact that these thoughts make him feel better surprises him. He wonders if it's a good thing or a bad thing in terms of his dedication to hoops. In terms of the fact that hoops has to be number one in his life. Always. The truth is, maybe he shouldn't be so excited. Maybe this feeling is wrong. Especially considering he just lost the game for his team.

Stick? Fat Chuck says. *You comin or what?*

Sticky looks up at Chuck. He presses his shirt against his cut again, studies the red blotch of blood. Then he pushes off the wall and follows Chuck out the gym door and across the parking lot, toward the run-down public restrooms.

Fat Chuck Is

dabbing at Sticky's face with a wadded-up rag.
One he pulled out of the bag he wears around his waist. (Big
red blotches framed by white cloth.) *Hold still, boy,* he says,
and moves Sticky's head to the side.

Wet concrete is cracked under their feet. Jagged fault
lines running into cement walls full of graffiti: thick black
ink, spray-painted vato letters, blood. The kind of thing you
might find in any kept-up-by-the-city restroom. Saturated
toilet paper clogs both floor drains, forming ankle-high
puddles you have to step over to get where you're going. And
there's no getting around the sour smell.

Chuck's breath is tequila. Fingers salt. He puts pressure
on the cut and Sticky flinches. *Yeah,* he says. *Just like I sus-
pected. Looks like you gonna need a couple stitches, Stick.*

Sticky pulls away to check himself in the eroding mirror. Moves his face right up to the glass for a closer look: A thin uneven cut jetting across the skin under his right eye. He takes the rag from Chuck and wipes away the blood. Watches it quickly pool back up.

Chuck takes Sticky's head, tilts it to the side again and squints: *Maybe a butterfly, though.* He moves him into better yellow light. *But I'm thinking . . . Yeah, I'd say most likely some stitches.*

Sticky leans against the sink and flips through daydream channels: clipboard forms, explanations, rides to and from, insurance numbers, fancy doctors, rubber-gloved fingers, long needles in his cheek, a sun-bright dentist light. He puts his fingers to the cut and cringes when the salty sweat stings. *Nah, man,* he says. *I ain't got no time for no stitches.*

Chuck stares at Sticky's reflection and shakes his head, puts a fist to his mouth to catch a cough.

Chuck is: fat boy licking double-scoop all grown up. Gray sweatpants, gray sweatshirt, grass-stained high-top Converse. Celtic colors. Chuck is: Lincoln Rec's team mom or resident die-hard fan. Never even tossed up one jumper in all the months he's been showing up. Old-man Perkins warns everybody: *Don't let the man plop down in front of you up in them bleachers. That cat's so fat he'll cause a total eclipse of the court.*

Chuck catches another cough and spits in the sink. *All right, Stick,* he says, wiping his mouth. *It's your call. I'm just sayin, you could use about three or four.* He folds up his fat arms and leans against the wall.

I was takin Rob, too, Sticky says.

I saw the game, Chuck says.

120

Sticky pushes away from the mirror and goes for one of the stalls. The first three are occupied by homeless. Green trash bags next to callused streetfeet. None of the stalls have doors. Homeless dudes pick heads up slow as Sticky passes, show empty eyes. The fourth is wide open and Sticky quickly slips down his hoop shorts and reads the walls.

Chuck steps up to the mirror, plays with the ends of his chewed-up mustache. Twirls uneven hairs together and then smooths them out. He tries on six or seven different facial expressions and then laughs at himself. *Where you from anyway, Stick? I mean, where was you born?*

Sticky is: hands on knees, back straight. Defensive stance so that none of him is touching the metal bowl. He says through the wall: *I was born in Virginia, I think. That's what my papers say. But I don't remember it none.*

Chuck runs nubby fingers across the gray stubble of his cheeks and neck. *Well, you gotten pretty good at ball,* he says. *I been watchin, and you gotten pretty damn good.*

Sticky pulls up his hoop shorts and flushes.

A guy with flies comes staggering up to Sticky's stall and knocks on the wall twice. Politely. Sticky whips around wide-eyed.

This cat's a rotting burrito. Greasy gray hair and beard sticking out of a tightly wrapped Mexican blanket. Half-dead eyes. Callused clay feet under nappy frill. *Excuse me, sir,* he says, drawing out each word. *You sharing this room with anyone?*

Sticky smooths out his shirt and shorts on the scoot-by, tells him: *Go ahead, man, take it. I'm done.* He walks the six or seven steps back to the sink and thuds the faucet with the heel of his hand. Water shoots out strong and he washes up. He turns and watches the blanket dude slowly stagger into the stall until it's just his clay feet under the stall wall.

The water shuts off and Sticky dries wet hands on hoop shorts.

Gotta watch them vagrants, Chuck says. *They'll creep up on you sometimes.* He moves closer and puts a hand on the back of Sticky's head. Positions salt fingers next to the cut and pulls it open a little.

Like I said, Chuck says. *It's up to you. It's my cut, I have em stitch me up so it don't leave no scar. Don't mess me up down the road with the ladies.* He elbows Sticky in the ribs and laughs.

I already got a girl, Sticky says, checking himself in the mirror again. The blood is coming back molasses-slow now. It's caking up everywhere except in one little spot. *Matter of fact, I gotta go get some stuff for her birthday tonight. That's why I gotta hurry.*

Chuck shows the whites of his eyes. He finds Sticky's eyes in the mirror and says: *So you already gots you a little honey then?*

Sticky nods.

And you tryin to get her a little somethin? Chuck reaches both hands behind the back of his head and links his fingers. He looks up at the ceiling. *I see,* he says.

Sticky's mind is hoop channels again: three-game wait, max. Dante and Dallas probably got picked up already, but he could hook up his own squad. Get one more shot at Rob. Redeem himself. Anh-thu's birthday stuff can wait. He's still got business to attend to. His heart picks up its pace and he holds the rag out to Chuck (white framed by red at this point). *What should I do with this?*

Chuck looks at the rag. *Don't give it to me, Stick. Go on and throw it away.*

Sticky dabs one more dab. Nothing. He throws the rag on top of the overflowing trash. As he turns to leave the bathroom, Chuck wraps a meat hook around his thin elbow. *Hold up, Stick,* he says. *I know you all anxious to get back and ball, but let's first figure out this birthday thing.*

Chuck releases Sticky's elbow and folds up his arms. He glances at the door, looks over at the stalls. *How much money you got?*

Twelve bucks.

Twelve bucks?

Sticky nods his head.

Shit, Stick, Chuck says. *You can't do nothing with no twelve bucks.* Chucks looks at the floor, takes his right mitt and adjusts himself a little. *Well, hell, you ever snatch some lady's purse?*

Sticky leans back against the sink and starts messing with the empty soap dispenser. *I ain't gonna take no lady's purse,* he says. *I'll swipe somethin from a store, you know, but I can't be rippin off no lady's purse.*

Oh, I see, you some sorta moral thief, right? Chuck throws his hands in the air. He reaches up to scratch the top of his head and looks Sticky right in the eyes. *Stealin is stealin, Stick. Don't matter if it's from a store or some little old lady, it's the exact same state of condition.*

Sticky hops up on the sink and stares at the floor. He gets his legs swinging like a little kid might.

Chuck walks over in front of the door, puts his hands on the overhang and looks out. Fat-man sweat stains under both arms. Shirt raised where you can see his stretch-mark stomach climbing up over his sweatpants drawstring. *You need money, Stick. I'm gonna tell you that right now.*

Sticky gently touches his cut with his fingers.

Chuck lets his eyes wander outside again, looks both ways. Brings a hand down to adjust his sweatpants a little. He turns and lumbers back into the bathroom. *That's your only option, the way I see it.* He puts a round hand on Sticky's shoulder.

Sticky slides off the sink. Feels warm Fat Chuck energy pass through his shirt and skin.

First-stall resident pipes up. At first he's whining and coughing. Both Chuck and Sticky turn to the sound. Chuck drops his hand. Then the homeless guy starts slurring out some crazy political statement. *Down with the white man,* he says. *It's the white devil that done it to us,* he says.

Shut up, old man! Chuck yells.

It's the white devil, the guy says again.

Shut up!

Sticky gets the water shooting out again, splashes it on his face. This type of talk never gets to Sticky simply because he's never seen himself as white. He hears it all the time. The antiwhite stuff. It's up in the bleachers. It's out by the hot dog stand. It's in Jimmy's office. Guys always talk a little lower when they spot him coming. Or they say things like *We don't mean you, Stick.* Or *You're different, Stick.* But the truth is, it never would have crossed his mind. That they might group him with the whites. It's something that has never even occurred to him.

Sticky cranks out a few paper towels and rubs his face dry.

Anyways, Chuck says. *What you gotta do is find some old rich-looking broad walking an empty street. Come up from behind her and snatch her purse. Simple as that. If she tries to scream, smack her over the head.*

I hear what you sayin, Sticky says, hoping the lecture is over. He nods a couple times and tosses the damp paper towel on top of the rag. But as he starts toward the door, Fat Chuck picks him off again.

Only one other idea I could come up with, Chuck says, running a fat left hand up Sticky's inner thigh.

Sticky fights to get away, but Chuck has too much bulk. Too much power. Like being posted up by Rob on game point. *Do me this one favor,* Chucks says, struggling to keep Sticky still. *Do this one thing for me and I'll personally drive you there. Buy whatever she wants.*

Sticky jerks his arm back, yells: *Come on, man! Lemme go!* But before he can gain any leverage, Chuck shoves Sticky's hand into his lap.

Sticky fights even harder. He pushes and pulls, kicks, scratches, bites. But Chuck won't let go.

That's it, white boy, he says. *I'll buy your little girlfriend whatever she wants.* He grabs Sticky's head with one hand, pulls down the front of his sweatpants with the other.

The homeless guy starts whining again. Sticky's Nikes squeak against the concrete. Something pops when Chuck leans all his weight against the sink.

Sticky finally spins out and pulls away. He boots Chuck in his sloppy stomach two times quick and darts into the parking lot.

125

Chuck doubles forward and holds himself. He goes down on one knee and then hurriedly grabs the sink and pulls himself back up. Before both feet are even on the ground he is sprinting out into the parking lot toward his car. Duck-footed. Stomach bouncing.

Sticky rushes into the gym and goes straight up to Dallas, who's sitting in the bleachers. *That faggot Chuck,* he says, sucking in breaths. *He tried to . . .*

Dallas straightens up, says: *What, boy?*

Chuck tried to make me . . . Sticky shoots a look out the gym door and tries to wipe Fat Chuck off his hand.

New York and Dreadlock Man stop shooting. Dollar Bill looks up from tightening his laces.

Dallas stands up.

Sticky tries to catch his breath. Tries to wipe Fat Chuck off his hand. Onto his shorts. He points out the door, toward the parking lot. *Chuck tried to make me suck him off.*

Dallas looks down the barrel of Sticky's finger. Outside the gym. He spots Chuck lumbering through the parking lot and takes off sprinting. New York takes off too. Dollar Bill. The game stops and Trey and Slim ask what's going on.

A group of Lincoln Rec regulars drop everything and take off after Dallas and Dollar Bill.

Jimmy hears the rumbling outside his office window and rushes out. *Wh-wh-wh-what is it?* He brings up the rear of the pack, yelling the whole time for someone to tell him what's going on.

Sticky races after the pack.

When they reach the parking lot, New York spots Chuck squeezing into his old, paint-chipped Buick. Everybody charges after him.

126

The suits on the sidewalk stop walking to watch this pack sprinting through the lot, cutting and leaping over cars.

Chuck slams his heavy door shut and fumbles through his bag for his keys. When he finally gets ahold of them he frantically shoves the car key into the ignition and cranks it. As the big boat coughs and turns over a few times, he looks over his shoulder. It finally starts and he pulls it into reverse, tires squealing as he hastily backs out of the parking spot.

New York is the first to arrive just as Chuck is slamming it into drive. He pounds on Chuck's hood and kicks the door in. He reaches for the handle but misses, yells: *Faggot!*

Chuck floors it. Tires spinning to grip pavement. Smoke lifting into the air.

Dollar Bill and Dallas catch up to New York. Dreadlock Man picks up an empty forty bottle and heaves it at Chuck's car. It shatters against the back door. Old-man Perkins and Johnson catch up. They both pick up rocks and fire them at the Buick as it speeds through the lot. One of the rocks crashes through the driver's side window. Chuck ducks, puts a meaty hand up to save his head.

They all stop running when Chuck rounds the last island in the parking lot and peels onto the street.

Sticky watches as Chuck's Buick blazes down the road and out of sight.

Heads shake. Language flies. Old-man Perkins says he knew there was something not right about that cat. They all underline fierce words with forceful hand motions. Declare what they would have done if they were just a couple seconds quicker.

Sticky kicks the tire of somebody's Pathfinder. He lowers

his head and wishes he was invisible. The Fat Chuck thing was bad, yeah, hell yeah, but this is even worse. All the guys asking him to explain, asking him to review the situation. In detail. The sun pounding off the pavement. His knees all weak like a sissy. This is the worst part of it. He messed up the games by running in there like a little bitch and now everybody's looking at him, waiting for him to speak, telling him it's OK. But it's not OK. It's all messed up.

Everything's messed up.

The suits that were walking the sidewalk are now in one big group, speculating. There are curious faces pressed against most of the business windows. Sticky reaches up to his cut and discovers that it's bleeding again. It's dripping blood onto his shirt, his shorts, the pavement. He starts back toward the gym, tries to wipe Fat Chuck off his hand.

Everybody asks him question after question, about what happened, where it happened, why it happened, and Sticky keeps his cool. He answers clinically. Detached. But the minute Dante comes up, something changes. Sticky's face looks like a little kid's and he stares at the ground. He doesn't want Dante to see him like this. Like a victim. Like he can't take care of himself.

What happened? Dante says.

It was Chuck, Sticky says. And then he kicks another SUV tire as hard as he can. He clenches his fists and slams the hood of an SUV. His face turns into a vicious frown and he quickens the pace of his walking.

New York and Dallas come jogging up. New York tells Dante: *Chuck tried to fuck with Sticky.*

Dallas says: *We gonna find that fat-ass, though. Trust me.*

128

New York says: *Might not be today, tomorrow, but we'll get him.*

Dante looks at the blood streaming down Sticky's face. Nods his head.

Dollar Bill adds: *We'll get em soon enough. Don't you worry.*

Big Mac comes jogging out of the gym all sweaty and asks what happened. Carlos comes out. Even Rob peeks his head through the doors.

Jimmy marches past the others and goes right up to Sticky. He takes him by the arm and marches with him toward the gym. *L-l-l-l-let's g-g-g-g-go*, Sticky! *We g-g-g-gotta c-c-c-call the p-p-p-p-p-po-po-po-po—armed forces!*

Mrs. Smith Brought

her whole family to Sticky's foster care pad for
the pickup: Mr. Smith with his Coke-bottle glasses; Tammie
and Jamie, their two well-developed and wide-eyed daugh-
ters (seventeen and fifteen); and Johnny, their seven-year-
old son with the two missing front teeth. Sticky was fourteen
when they pulled along the curb in a sparkling white minivan. When they filed out wearing big smiles and hustled up
the driveway together.

This was Sticky's third try at finding a family that fit.

Mr. and Mrs. Smith shook hands with all the counselors. Mrs. Smith placed her hand on the old Mexican
director's shoulder like they were old friends and told
him: *We both have degrees in social work*. She turned and

smiled at her husband. *So don't worry, we know what we're getting into.*

All the counselors nodded their heads. They smiled, too.

When Sticky came walking into the office with his bag, Mrs. Smith gave him a long tight hug. She pressed his cheek against hers and told him: *Welcome to our family.* Then she tousled his hair with her hand.

Sticky bristled under all that touch.

Mr. Smith walked up when it was his turn, wrapped hairy arms around Sticky's stiff frame and squeezed. *We know about the troubles you've had finding the right home,* he said, pulling his face away and fishing for Sticky's eye. *Well, that search is over now.* He placed a soft hand on the back of Sticky's head and took a deep breath. *Young man,* he said, *I'm going to let you know this right up front, the only way you're going to see this place again is if you want to visit a friend. Either that or I drop dead of a heart attack.*

Honey! Mrs. Smith said, poking her husband in the arm. *That's a terrible thing to say.*

Well, that's how strongly I feel about this, sweetheart.

Mrs. Smith blushed and looked at the old Mexican director. *Hopefully it's just to see a friend, right?* she said. *I mean, my God.*

The director nodded.

Let's hope, Mr. Smith said, and he laughed.

Tammie walked up and gave Sticky a hug, told him: *We're really happy to have you.*

Jamie giggled a little and hugged him next. *Nice to meet you,* she said.

Mrs. Smith shot a look at little Johnny, and he timidly

131

stepped up for the hug too. *Do you like the Dodgers?* he asked as they separated, and everybody laughed. Sticky nodded.

Then the Smiths loaded all their own kids, plus Sticky, into the van and drove off toward their home in Oxnard.

The only problem was, by the time the Smiths got their hands on Sticky he'd already started to figure out who he was supposed to be. How he was supposed to fit in. And for the first time in his life he was determined to play the role.

The Smiths tried their hardest to treat Sticky like one of their own. Bought him new shirts, new jeans, shoes and socks. Mrs. Smith cooked dinner every night. But Sticky was trying even harder to be a thug. On the way to those dinners he would cruise past a crowded park and ride home on somebody's unlocked ten-speed.

The Smiths set up "family hour." Every night they'd all sit around the living room with the TV off and talk about their days. Something good that happened and something not so good. But the first week Sticky missed a meeting. He was hanging out in a baseball dugout on the other side of town with some kids from school. A pack of black dudes who stayed in a local group home. Two crazy Mexican cats who somehow managed to smuggle beers from their dads' stashes.

The second week Sticky missed two meetings. One of the black dudes showed up with a stack of old *Playboy*s. One of the Mexican dudes brought smokes. They started setting up meetings of their own after school. Told people they were forming a new gang. Every night, as the sun set over the right-field fence, they'd file into the dugout with new recruits and try to one-up each other. The shadier the show-and-tell, the bigger the impression.

After a month Sticky stopped showing up to "family hour" completely.

He started skipping certain classes to smoke out behind the track-and-field shed. A couple hits off a buddy's blunt and he'd be flying above the goalposts. Or he'd bail out on school altogether and cruise down to the arcade with his boys. Street Fighter and Mortal Kombat, old-school Mr. Do! and Police Trainer.

Foosball.

One night when Sticky walked into the house, Mr. and Mrs. Smith were sitting at the kitchen table waiting for him. *Sticky,* Mrs. Smith said, *could we talk to you for a minute?*

Grab a chair, son, Mr. Smith said.

Sticky took a seat and Mrs. Smith held up his report card: five Fs and a C in PE.

Now, this is just a progress report, son, Mr. Smith said. *You have a chance to turn this around if you put forth the effort.*

But it's unacceptable, Mrs. Smith said. *We called the school and your attendance is horrific. Why aren't you going to class?*

Mr. Smith took his wife's hand and told her: *All right now, sweetheart, this is about turning things around from here. We have to remember to look forward.*

I know it, honey. OK.

I think the boy needs to know that we believe in him. That we love him.

And that we're here no matter what.

Exactly.

They both turned to Sticky.

You do know that, don't you, son? Mr. Smith said. *That we love and support you one hundred percent?*

The following Saturday Sticky was brought home by the cops. He got caught swiping a pair of binoculars from Kmart by undercover security. (This was back when he was still refining his skills.)

Mrs. Smith was stunned when she opened the front door and found her foster boy in handcuffs. *Oh, my God,* she said, and yelled for her own kids to hurry upstairs.

Mr. Smith tried tough love after that situation. Restriction. Extra chores. An early curfew on Friday and Saturday nights.

Son, Mr. Smith said a couple nights later, as he moved Sticky's bed, piece by piece, out of little Johnny's room and into the sewing room. *I want you to know that I understand what you're feeling inside.* He lifted one side of the single mattress and Sticky picked up the other. They moved awkwardly through the door frame and into the hall. *I've seen it all before, you have to realize.* They leaned the mattress against the sewing room wall and walked back into Johnny's room, picked up the headboard. *I know how awful you must have felt after what happened with your mother.*

Sticky dropped his side of the headboard after that comment. Just dropped it on the rug and walked out of little Johnny's room without a word. One mention of Baby and he was gone. He cruised straight down the stairs and out the front door.

At around four in the morning, Sticky staggered back into the house through the side door. He was so high he passed out in the middle of the kitchen floor with an open half-gallon of orange juice in his hand.

Jamie found him like that when she walked into the kitchen for a drink.

Sticky? she said. *Oh, my God. Sticky!*

Sticky lifted his head to look at her. There was blood all over his face and hands, and he was smiling.

Jamie dragged him into the upstairs bathroom and gently cleaned his face with a warm washcloth. *What happened to you?* she said.

Sticky shrugged his shoulders.

You're, like, on drugs, aren't you?

He reached up and touched her face. *You look good,* he said, and ran a finger through her long blond hair.

Well, you better go back to your room and act like you're asleep, she said. *I'll tell them you're home. They've been, like, freaking out all night.* She wrapped Sticky's arm around her neck and helped him walk to his room. She put him on his bed, pulled off his shoes and socks and covered him with a blanket.

Sticky was asleep before Jamie even left the room.

This prompted a big family meeting the following night before dinner. There were discussions about hard-core counseling and antidepressants. Mentor programs and out-patient drug rehab centers.

But Sticky talked his way out of everything when Mr. and Mrs. Smith brought it up again over dessert. *I'll change,* he said. *I swear I'll change.* He put down his fork and gave them both his most honest expression. *I wanna be better now.*

Mr. Smith turned to Mrs. Smith, told her: *You know, honey, I think he means it.*

I do too, Mrs. Smith said.

I think it's about trust right now.

It's a trust issue.

135

I wanna be better, Sticky said.

Mrs. Smith turned her attention back to Sticky and reached over the table for his hand. *All right, son, we're going to trust you on this one.*

Mr. Smith nodded his head and smiled at them both.

But two weeks later, Sticky took things to another level.

It was a Sunday afternoon and Mr. Smith was putting in extra hours at work. Mrs. Smith was out running errands. Sticky flipped off the TV and headed upstairs. Knocked on Jamie's door. *Hey, Jamie,* he said, and knocked again. *You in there?*

Jamie pulled the door open and waved him in. *Of course I am,* she said. She was listening to Incubus and filing her nails. There were posters all over her walls: Bob Marley, Blink-182, Pearl Jam. Sticky was standing at the door, looking around the room, when Jamie told him: *Um, you can, like, come in, you know. I'm only doing my nails.* She stood up and pulled him by his arm, closed the door behind them. She sat Indian style at the edge of her bed, and Sticky lounged into the big purple beanbag on the floor.

Jamie handed Sticky a photo album of all her friends, told him he could look through it if he felt like it. While Sticky turned the pages, she excitedly played parts of all her favorite songs. *I love Rage,* she said, pointing to a series of posters on her wall. *But I love Radiohead and Coldplay, too. I think there are, like, times you wanna hear slow songs and times you wanna hear fast songs. I like any type of music that inspires me.*

Sticky laughed at her energy.

They were both quiet for a while, listening to the first

few tracks off the Toadies album. Jamie pulled a glittery pink nail polish from inside a drawer and started applying careful strokes. When Sticky was done looking at all the pages of pictures in her photo album, he started at the front again.

So, you got a boyfriend? Sticky said, studying a picture of Jamie posed with some guy at a dance.

Not really, she said. *That guy, like, thinks we're together, I guess. His name's Ricky. But I'm over it.* She blew on her wet nails and said: *What about you? You have a girlfriend?*

Nah, Sticky said.

Jamie screwed the nail polish cap back on and tossed the bottle behind her on the bed. She stretched out on her stomach and faced Sticky. *Have you ever, like, been with somebody, though?*

Huh? Sticky said. He set the photo album on the floor and sat up in the beanbag.

You know, have you ever . . .

Yeah, I been with somebody.

Who?

This girl Maria.

Was it before or after you started living at our house? Jamie leaned her chin in the palms of her hands and stared at Sticky, fascinated.

She used to stay at the same place I stayed, Sticky said.

Did you like her?

I mean, we was friends and all that.

Jamie covered her face with her hands and giggled. She looked at Sticky and told him: *God, that's so weird if you think about it.*

Sticky stood up from the beanbag and sat next to Jamie on the bed. *What about you?* he said.

No. Never.

You'd probably like it.

I've never even been to second base. Jamie rolled her eyes and laughed at herself.

Sticky reached over to the stereo. He turned off her Nirvana and tuned in his favorite hip-hop station.

Jay-Z filled the room with rhyme.

Mrs. Smith arrived home in good spirits.

She walked into the house leafing through a stack of junk mail and humming under her breath. She tossed the mail on the end table by the couch and headed upstairs. When she opened the bedroom door, singing out Jamie's name, she found Sticky and Jamie half naked on the bed. Sticky's hands all over her daughter. Shorts and skirt thrown recklessly on the floor.

Mrs. Smith freaked out.

She slapped her daughter across the face and called her a whore. She reached over the bed and punched Sticky in the back, in the neck, on the shoulder. When he ducked out of the way she got him in the leg.

She swung a few more wild fists at Sticky and then ran out of the room holding her hands over her face. She rumbled down the stairs, picked up the phone and called Mr. Smith at work. Through hysterical tears, she told him to come home right away. Then she hung up the phone and rumbled back up the stairs to slap her daughter again and try and hit Sticky some more.

Jamie was crying too. She screamed at the top of her lungs when she caught another one of her mom's hands across the face.

Sticky managed to dodge most of Mrs. Smith's flailing while at the same time pulling on his shirt and shorts.

An hour later, Mr. Smith came rushing through the front door and immediately locked Sticky out in the garage with the dog. Sticky spent that night sleeping on a cold cot next to a rusty tool bench.

The next morning Mr. Smith packed up Sticky's bag and stuck it in the back of the van. He opened the passenger door and let Sticky in. Then he took his seat at the wheel. He stared out the window for a few minutes before starting the motor. For this leg of the trip it was just him and Sticky. There would be no more big family affairs. No more upbeat conversations. No more hugging and talk of trust.

Sticky sank into the passenger seat and hung his head. He had succeeded in playing a role.

Mrs. Smith stayed inside with her kids. She watched her husband through the living room window as he turned the key, flipped the car into reverse and rolled down the driveway.

Tammie and Johnny sat at the kitchen table eating oatmeal with their heads down. Neither said a word.

Jamie watched from her bedroom window with glassy eyes as the white van made its way down their street, stopped at the stop sign and then turned out of sight.

When Mr. Smith pulled up outside the foster care pad again, not even a year after he'd come to pick Sticky up, the old Mexican director was once again standing out on the curb, waiting.

We've got young children, Mr. Smith said after he shut off the engine and hopped out of the van.

I understand, the old Mexican director said, and he crossed his arms.

You know how it is, Mr. Smith said, and he stood there a second, slipped his hands in his pockets. *They're impressionable.* He watched Sticky walk around the van, then pulled open the sliding side door and reached in for Sticky's bag. Set it down on the sidewalk and shook his head.

The director picked up the bag.

I have to think about my own kids right now, Mr. Smith said, and then he climbed back into the van and drove away.

Dave Was Snapping

his fingers to the rhythm of the reggae when Sin pulled his Impala along the curb and shut off the engine. They were about a block from Milo's Liquor in Venice, the place they always ended up on the nights they hung together. Where the forties were cheap and nobody asked for ID.

The buzz of the big play-off win was still spinning in their heads, and the fellas were set on prolonging their night.

Sin reached underneath his seat for his beanie, pulled it on over his shaved head and checked himself in the rearview. Sticky slipped out of the backseat. He leaned back in and slipped out again.

Leaned back in and slipped out.

Leaned back in and slipped out.

Leaned back in and slipped out.

When something in the process was precise, and just before Dave and Sin turned to look, he slammed the door shut cool and joined his boys.

In all the commotion, an old white man lifted trash-can eyes from his sleeping bag. He was lying between rusted fence posts near an old abandoned shed. All the windows were busted out and the rotting plywood served as a practice canvas for up-and-coming taggers.

It was a cool spring night. The streetlamps looked like little yellow suns hanging from concrete posts.

Dave pushed Sticky in front of the homeless dude. *Hey, old-timer,* he said. *See this kid right here? Yo, he just single-handedly beat Dominguez Hills, man. Goddamn single-handedly.*

And dude's girl was right there to see it all, Sin said.

And Annie's fine, too, Dave said. *Especially for an Oriental.*

Sin and Sticky laughed when Dave started popping without music. The homeless dude shifted around his sweatshirt-pillow, dropped his head and closed his eyes.

They walked along the vacant sidewalk three deep, pulled open Milo's security-barred door and headed straight for the beer section. Sticky swung open the spidered glass door and reached in for three cold forties.

I got the beer, Sin said, pulling out his Velcro wallet on the way up to the counter.

When Milo handed Sin his change, Dave hopped up on the counter and pumped his fist into the security camera. *Venice High, yo! Venice fucking High!* He twisted the cap with his shirt, put the bottle up to the camera and let the cold beer run down his throat.

Sin and Sticky watched Dave dance to the strange music coming out of Milo's old transistor radio. All 6' 6" of him grooving on the counter, ducking his head slightly to avoid the ceiling.

Yo, this is a jam, Dave said, and he turned to Sticky and Sin. *You all don't know about this.* He got his arms into it, snapped in rhythm with his empty left hand. *I could make love to this beat.*

Milo tugged at the bottom of Dave's pants. *Must come down,* he said in his jacked-up English. He grinned at Sticky and Sin, pulled on Dave's pants again and repeated himself: *Must come down.*

Dave put his forty up to the camera again and then went to get down. *My bad, Milo. We just beat Dominguez Hills tonight and I'm super up.* He hopped down to the floor with the grace of a power forward and wiped off the counter with a bare hand.

Milo smiled.

The fellas loved Milo. Not just because he sold to them, but because he was always smiling. The liquor store was all he had. No wife. No kids. No car. Whenever Sticky used the bathroom in back, he'd spy the unmade futon-bed where Milo slept. But still, he always had a smile. Even for three punks that came into his little store looking like trouble.

Dave grabbed a roll of paper towels from behind the register. He wadded up three and wiped away the giant footprints his Nikes had left.

Let's roll, Sin said, and he took a long swig.

Milo pulled out an open box of Tootsie Pops and pointed for the guys to take some.

Dave shook his head.

Sin politely told him: *No thanks.*

But Sticky's eyes lit up. *Man, I dig these,* he said, unwrapping one and popping it in his mouth. *We used to get em as a reward back at the place I used to stay.*

Sticky took a couple little hits off his lollipop and then a big hit off his forty. The candy made him remember that he was a year older today. Seventeen instead of sixteen. Almost a man. He wondered if maybe he was too old to eat candy now. Maybe it wasn't cool anymore. He considered this for a quick sec and then reached his hand in the box for a couple backups. A blue one and an orange one. Stuck them both in his pocket, waved to Milo and followed his boys out of the store.

The fellas rolled down Broadway, buzzing, recapping the big game. Dave said his favorite play was when Sticky took two guys baseline and spun in a reverse. He made Sticky and Sin stop so he could show how the move looked from his seat.

Say this beam was the hoop, he said, pointing to the makeshift sidewalk that had been put in front of a construction site. *Sticky came in from the side like this.* Dave ducked his shoulder and pretended to dribble low to the ground. *He barely got by em and I was like, oh, man, big guy might swat this. But thing is, Sticky used the rim to protect the ball.* Dave took the ball up on one side of the beam, ducked and came up on the other side. *That was a smooth-ass layin right there,* he said. *Most guys don't know how to do it, protect the ball with the rim.*

A block later, Sin came up with his. *I know what the play of the day was, though. Besides the game winner.* Sin set his forty down so he could involve his hands in his story. *You know that little guard they got? Number twenty-three or whatever? The play of the day was when he came flyin through the lane and Fat Jay straight put em to the ground.*

Oh, damn, that was a nasty foul, Dave said, holding a fist to his mouth.

Jay had to slap em down, though, Sticky said. *He had to let em know whose lane it was.*

Fat Jay did just like this, Sin said, and he put his arm out clothesline style and swung it through the air. *That's the kinda foul that could set the tone. Like Sticky said. After Fat Jay did that, wasn't no little number twenty-three flyin through the lane no more, right?*

Sin yelled out at a car speeding by: *Ain't no free shit in our house, boy!*

They all laughed and kept walking.

The wind increased slightly, picked up loose grocery bags, scraps of paper, then set them back down. Background sound. Broadway is a sad gray face after the sun goes down, with Santa Monica Boulevard and Wilshire shining bright only a couple blocks north. Dull light from fading street-lamps, peeling billboards, tired and stained sidewalks that crumble in places under the weight of heavy feet. Lifeless homeless bodies curled up sleeping under old-school CLOSED signs. As they walked, a range of different cars sprayed music out from open windows as they zipped past. Sticky booted a rock ahead of them. It rebounded off a cement wall and Sin kicked it.

Dave stopped in front of Corona Imports and pointed

inside the window. *Yo, I wish I could just roll a Ferrari around one time,* he said. He put his hands and face up to the glass. *Look at that car, man.*

Sin stepped up to the glass too. *For real, that's a smooth ride right there,* he said. *I'd just wanna sit in it one time.* A black convertible Ferrari sat inside the glass sparkling like jewelry under a security light.

Yo, just one time, Dave said.

Sticky listened to Dave and Sin go on and on about the car, how fast it goes from zero to sixty, how much rich cats are willing to pay to drive right off the showroom floor. He looked at the way his boys stood there, hands against the glass, on the outside looking in. Drooling over something completely out of their reach. He set down his forty, picked up a chunk of concrete from the broken sidewalk, shooed Sin and Dave out of the way: *Look out, look out.*

What? Dave said.

What the hell you doin? Sin said.

Sticky took a couple running steps and heaved the concrete through the glass. Just like that. Without thinking. Chucked it right through the window so shards of thick glass spilled onto the showroom floor on volume ten.

Go ahead! Sticky yelled over the screaming alarm. *Go on and sit in it!*

Sin's and Dave's eyes bugged out of their heads. Their mouths hung open like old socks.

People in passing cars slowed and stuck heads out of rolled-down windows.

Holy shit! Dave said.

Damn! Sin said. *Let's get the hell outta here!* And they took off running through an alley behind Lincoln.

It wasn't four blocks before the first cop car spotted them running.

Dave and Sin followed Sticky as he made a sharp right behind Denny's and Ralphs. They shoved their way through a group of hipsters smoking outside and ducked behind a boarded-up flower stand. The cop screeched around the corner and turned his lights and siren on.

The fellas raced back up to Lincoln, past the art supply shop, the Italian deli, the long string of antique shops. There was nothing but the sound of heavy air whipping past their ears, the loud siren gaining on them by the second.

Sticky led them west down Santa Monica Boulevard and then north along Seventh. He sprinted with his hands fixed sharp like Carl Lewis. Whizzed past Al's Guitar Shop, Primavera Pizza, the building where a Nike Outlet once stood. At the 7-Eleven on the corner of Wilshire and Seventh, he shot west past Wahoos and Chevron and Houstons. The avant-garde bagel shop. Then to throw the cops completely off their trail he led them through the crowded promenade. Weaved in and out of thick packs of people.

Dave and Sin followed their point guard wherever he went. Sin directly behind. Dave a couple steps off the pace.

Sticky swung into an alley between Third and Fourth and ducked behind some trash bins. The cop car screamed by. They all huddled there for a while, laughing nervously and sucking in quick, choppy breaths.

What the hell? Sin said, grabbing for air.

Jesus Christ, Dave said. *You outta your mind?*

Sticky shrugged, hands on knees. He brought a devil grin up to both of them.

147

They started sneaking back through the Promenade in silence, but just as they rounded the corner onto Third, another black-and-white spotted them.

As they took off running again, the car screeched to a stop and two cops hopped out to pursue on foot. The cops ran back the other way, down the same streets, past the same businesses. Keys rattling, clubs swinging, leather boots clopping against the pavement.

Sticky, Dave and Sin tried jumping the fence to the Boys and Girls Club back up on Lincoln, to hide behind the skateboard ramps, but one of the officers grabbed Dave by an ankle and pulled him back down.

Sticky and Sin made their way back over too, and all three put their hands up on the fence like they were told.

Both cops were sucking hard for breath as they patted the fellas down: slapped hard on the chest, hard on the hips, hard on the back of the legs, grabbed hard around the ankle. They got names and ages and one of the cops talked into his radio.

Dumb decision you gentlemen just made, the other cop said.

Which one of you threw the rock? the radio cop said.

Nobody moved.

Simple question, guys. Which one of you threw the rock?

Sticky put his eyes on the pavement. Drips of sweat ran down the back of his neck. Sin and Dave picked up their heads and snuck glances at him.

Another car rolled onto the scene, lights flashing without sound. It slowed to a stop and a woman cop stepped out. She stayed back and talked into her radio.

So, what's it gonna be? one of the cops said. *We gonna have to do this the hard way?*

Just as the cop finished his sentence, Sticky raised his hand off the fence. He turned around and looked at the cop.

That's more like it. A little cooperation would be a good thing right about now. The cop moved over to Sticky and pulled his arms down one at a time, slapped on the cuffs. *Some pretty dumb shit you just pulled, kid.*

The cop with the radio came walking over with a grin on his face. *You're not gonna believe this,* he said, tapping his partner on the shoulder with the radio antenna. *The kid who threw it, it's his goddamn birthday.*

Say what?

This kid here. He pointed at Sticky with his radio. *Travis Reichard. It's his birthday today.*

Well, what a way to bring in a new year.

They both laughed a little and then one of them asked: *So, why'd you do it, Travis?*

Sticky cringed at the sound of his real name. He didn't look up.

The other cop put his right thumb through his belt loop and stared down at Sticky. *I don't get it, ace. Why not just get a piñata like normal kids.*

Both cops thought that was pretty funny, too.

The woman cop walked over and they gave her the scoop.

It's your birthday? Dave said while the cops were huddled together, talking.

The lights spun around the cop car without sound. A flash of bright blue light spinning around methodically. Cars slowed as they passed, stared out at the fellas as they were led from the fence toward one of the cop cars, guided into the backseat. A motorcycle cop rolled onto the scene. He shut off his engine and flipped out his kickstand. Took off his helmet and started walking toward the other cops.

An old homeless black woman rolled her cart by without looking. She had a black bandana covering her hair, a soiled USC sweatshirt and boots without laces. She kept her head down and hummed to herself as she passed.

There were muffled voices coming over the cop's radio. The tinny echo of the rattling cart. The soothing sound of the woman humming as she slowed by. Never once did she look up to see what it was all about.

Check This Move,

Sticky said, and Anh-thu turned around to watch.
This is for when some dude gets all up on me. Sticky jab-stepped with his right foot, hesitated, and took off baseline. Cupped the ball between his right hand and forearm and spun it in cool off the glass. *Just like that, Annie. These fools can't hold me.*

Too bad nobody's really guarding you, Anh-thu said, and she went back to reading her book.

It was Saturday night back in mid-April, and the park Sticky'd pulled Anh-thu into was dark. She had to put her book right up to a yellow floodlight to make out the words.

But if there was, Sticky said. *That's how I'd do em.*

On their way to some high school party on Second

Street, at some guy named Cyrus's house, Sticky spotted the baskets and veered Anh-thu onto the empty blacktop with pleading eyes. He just couldn't resist it. Needed to fix. It was his last Saturday of community service, the court-ordered 100 hours he'd been given for the window-breaking incident, and he was hyped. No more ten-hour weekend days cleaning up graffiti. No more orange vest.

He pulled his beat-up ball out of his backpack and ran his fingers along the grooves. *Just a couple quick jumpers,* he'd said. But Anh-thu knew better and rolled her eyes. Sticky ripped off his sweatshirt and dribbled over to the nearest hoop. Anh-thu sat with their stuff and pulled out the novel she was reading for English class.

Over an hour spiraled by and here they were, still holding down the same spots.

I'll post this dude up, Sticky said, crab-dribbling with his back to the basket, digging a couple elbows into an imaginary defender's chest. He spun quick and rose up off two feet. Dunked the ball with two hands and hung on the rim. *Too strong,* he said, and let himself drop. *These fools gotta get in the weight room.*

He picked up his ball and dribbled out to the wing. *This ain't no fair, Annie. These dudes ain't got no defense. I need someone out here who could at least put on a little defense.*

Anh-thu, without looking up from her book, told him: *What happened to you taking me to that big party?*

I am, Sticky said. *I just gotta finish off these fools.*

The park had four hoops, all without nets. One of the rims was bent so far it pointed right back down at the blacktop. The old-school wooden backboards were all tagged up with different-style gang markings. Sticky knew how to take care of stuff like that, though. He'd even kept some of the community service solvent thinking he might one day clean up the outside of Lincoln Rec. Figured there shouldn't be any taggings on a dude's home away from home.

Anh-thu looked up at Sticky for a second. Watched him spin in a reverse layup and point at an invisible crowd. She shook her head and reached into her bag for a pack of Starburst. She unwrapped a red one and popped it in her mouth.

You better get up on me, Sticky said to a new defender. *I'll knock em down all day.* He was dribbling around at the top of the key, through his legs and close to the ground. Sizing up. Then he blasted to the basket and dunked the ball with two hands. *Too slow, man.*

Sticky kept on like that, talking trash and clowning, no matter who was guarding him. Most of the time he took the ball to the bucket, but sometimes he'd pull up for a deep jumper.

After a while, Anh-thu got tired of reading in such bad light. She closed her book and slipped it back into her bag. She watched Sticky for a bit and then lay down with her back against the blacktop, balling up Sticky's sweatshirt and using it as a pillow. There was a slight break in the night clouds and she could see the faint light of a couple stars peeking through.

It wasn't long before she closed her eyes and drifted into sleep.

Jumpers is all about rhythm, Sticky started chanting. *Point your feet at the bucket. Elbow at the bucket. Middle finger in the groove, thumb between the 7 and the F, bend knees, and put it up*. He spied the writing on his ball to check his fingering and lofted up a shot from the free-throw line.

Ball went straight through.

He retrieved his rock and marched back out to the free-throw line. *Middle finger in the groove, thumb between the 7 and the F, bend knees, and put it up.*

Ball went straight through.

Retrieved his rock and marched back out to the free-throw line. *Middle finger in the groove, thumb between the 7 and the F, bend knees, and put it up.*

Ball went straight through.

Once he started getting in a rhythm like this, he could go on for hours without missing. Like a robot.

Cabs started to fill up along Wilshire. They crept along the curb outside Renee's waiting to gobble up the first group of people who waved or gave a loud whistle.

Middle finger in the groove, thumb between the 7 and the F, bend knees, and put it up.

Ball went straight through.

Anh-thu looked like a little girl lying on the concrete. Her fingers linked on her stomach, feet crossed. Breaths long and deep. The dull yellow glow highlighting her pretty face.

Middle finger in the groove, thumb between the 7 and the F, bend knees, and put it up.

Ball went straight through.

Deep thumping from a nearby club filled the black night with bass. A black-and-white flipped on its siren, screamed past Fifth, Sixth and Seventh, and headed south down Lincoln. Another black-and-white flew after without a siren, for backup.

Eventually Sticky stopped chanting and shot with his mouth shut. The sprinklers came on in the grass field beside the courts, making the cool air smell like rain. In the distance he could hear two women yelling at each other outside a bar.

Sticky lofted another shot up and the ball went straight through.

There were the faint sounds of the faraway sirens, a few honking cabs and the hollow tap of rubber on blacktop as Sticky dribbled back out to the free-throw line for another shot.

Sticky and Anh-thu

made six months just before school let out for summer. Sticky was already seventeen, but Anh-thu was still two months away from her sixteenth birthday.

Sticky rolled into Midnight Liquor on Rose with his backpack strapped tight. Slipped two bottles of black-label champagne in beside his books and took a pack of Hostess Cup Cakes to the counter.

This it? the old man said, looking Sticky up and down.

This is it, Sticky said, looking right back at him.

The old man bagged the Cup Cakes and dumped the change in Sticky's palm.

Sticky took the back way to Paradise Park, the place he and Anh-thu had agreed to meet. He was a shade early, but he didn't mind. It was a Friday night and the school year was coming to a close. The air was warm. The sky was just starting to change colors. June bugs were starting to show up, flying around all loud and clinging to everybody's screen door.

Earlier in the day, Sticky had pulled a letter out of the mail that informed him he'd been invited to some prestigious summer basketball camp. "Only the top players in the country will attend," the letter read. Every college coach would be up in the stands, scribbling things down in notebooks. Kentucky. UCLA. Duke and Indiana. Sticky's heart picked up its pace every time he thought about it. This was his chance. This was his dream. Two more weeks yawning in the back of a classroom, scanning sports page box scores, and then he could spend all-day-every-day at Lincoln Rec working on his game.

Sticky unwrapped his cupcakes on the way, took giant bites. Left uneven tooth marks in chocolate icing. He kept a running head count of all the BMWs that cruised by. Tried to picture what model he'd hook up if he was getting paid. What color. How fast he'd drive late at night when the roads were empty. As he walked, he made sure to step over every line. Sometimes he had to take a triple jumper's stride, sometimes he had to shorten up. But never on lines, and the whole time in his head keeping a BMW count.

The closer Sticky got to the park, the bigger the houses got. Dark green lawns, baskets set up over garages, wind chimes. Shiny cars pulled into sloping driveways. There were kids out front chasing each other around with spurting hoses. Laughing. A dad holding his baby on his shoulders.

Somebody's mom snipping red and white roses out of a perfectly manicured flower bed, laying them side by side on a spread-out towel. Little kids racing around on tricycles and older kids playing Wiffle ball in the street. All of them watched Sticky out of the corner of their eyes as he took another bite of cupcake and stutter-stepped to avoid a line.

In the park, he watched couples stroll by holding hands as he tossed chocolate crumbs to the pigeons waddling around at his feet. He watched the birds dart in for the grab and then back off quick. Watched them set their little dinners on the cement path and then pick pick pick.

He had his best gear on, the blue collar shirt he swiped from the Foot Locker Outlet in Venice, a pair of ironed jeans. His newest hoop shoes. It was a weird deal to think about, having an anniversary with a girl. Six whole months. But Anh-thu made him feel happy.

When he made it to their spot he found Anh-thu already hanging out on a bench. Her long black hair falling down her back. White tank top. Short khaki skirt and flip-flops. Always flip-flops. She was reading a book.

He snuck up from behind and touched his hands lightly on her shoulders. Kissed her hair.

Anh-thu turned around, smiling. She closed her book and set it down. Grabbed Sticky's face and kissed him on the lips. *I can't believe you're on time,* she said.

The sun was drifting below the rooftops. Dark colors trapped in clouds. A slight breeze played tree leaves quiet. Anh-thu reached down and picked up her book. She stuck it in her bag and pulled out some nicely folded blue tissue paper, handed it over. *Happy anniversary, Sticks.*

Sticky ripped the paper apart and let it fall to the grass, held out a brown bead necklace. *I made it myself last week,* Anh-thu said.

Sticky held the necklace up to his eyes to check it good. He wrapped it around his neck and hooked the clasp. *This thing's smooth,* he said.

Six months, she said. *That's a big deal.*

Sticky pushed his backpack over to Anh-thu, told her: *Go ahead. See what's in there.*

She unzipped the pack and reached in her hand. She grinned as she pulled out one of the bottles. *Wow, Sticks, champagne. Two bottles.*

Sticky took the first bottle and tried to figure out how to open it. *A half year we been together,* he said. *We gotta celebrate.* He pushed hard on the cork and it shot off. A few of the suds ran down the neck of the bottle and onto his hand. *There's some glasses in there too.* He wiped his hand on his pants.

Anh-thu reached in and pulled out two cream-colored coffee mugs. *You just thought of everything, didn't you?* she said. *I bet you think you're being pretty romantic, don't you?*

I'm like that one cat. The one you're always talkin about you read in English class.

Romeo?

Yeah, I'm like him. Sticky poured the champagne slow, first in Anh-thu's mug and then in his own.

I guess you're some kind of modern-day version, Anh-thu said. *How'd you get this champagne anyway?*

Sticky smelled inside his mug. He pulled back and smelled again. Pulled back and smelled again. He shrugged his shoulders. Then he smelled the mug again.

You stole it, didn't you? Why do I even have to ask? Anh-thu took a sip, said: *Watch, someday you're gonna get caught and then what?*

Ain't nobody can catch me, girl.

Oh, yeah?

Trust me, Annie, Sticky said. *I know what I'm doing.*

I just don't want anything to happen to you, Sticky. That's all. They looked at each other and Sticky laughed. They both put their mugs to their lips.

As the sun slowly dipped below the neighborhood, the automatic park lights clicked on and started buzzing. They took a few minutes to come to life. At this exact moment, a strange thing happened—most of the nice middle-class couples instinctively headed back to their safe houses and cars, while packs of street zombies seemingly came out of the bushes to take their place. But that's the way it is in a place like Paradise Park. Sunlight fades and the whole face of the park changes. One well-off couple gets up to go, two shopping cart women come out from hiding and stretch out their stiff arms and legs.

It's like two completely different worlds exist in L.A.: one that operates under the sun and another that slinks out under the shadows of the moon.

Sticky tipped back and emptied his first mugful. When Anh-thu followed his lead, he picked up the bottle and poured them both full again. He shook out the last couple drops over her mug.

Let's play a game, Anh-thu said. She held her mug up to her face and looked closely at the chipped rim. Took a sip. *Let's play five questions. We each get to ask five questions*

160

about anything, and the other person has to tell the truth no matter what.

Sticky shrugged his shoulders.

You go first, Anh-thu said. *No, wait, I'll go first.* She took a sip and stared at the ground. *I know. What in the whole world makes you the most happy?*

What do you mean? Sticky said. *Like anything?*

Yeah, what makes you feel the most happy inside?

You do.

You can't say me, silly. Anh-thu reached out and pushed Sticky's shoulder. *Besides, that's something we already know.*

Sticky ran a finger along a skinny crack on the outside of his mug. He took a sip. *I know what it is,* he said.

What?

Sometimes I get on this streak playin ball. I make like five, six straight buckets and I get this feelin inside. I'm, like, locked in or something. I feel like I could make any shot I try. Falling away from twenty-three feet, driving in on a big man, off the glass, left-handed, whatever. It's crazy. It's like I'm doin magic or somethin. And everybody on the sideline gets all louder every time I hit another one. And I get this feeling all through my body. My skin gets hot. Yeah, it's like magic. Like I could just cast a spell and make anything happen. And I get all this energy in my chest when it's like that. Cause I feel so alive.

Sticky stopped talking and tossed a stick against a tree. He took a quick sip of his champagne. *I don't know. Sometimes I wish I could just keep on playin when I got it like that. I wish I didn't never have to stop.*

Anh-thu stared at Sticky but didn't say anything.

Sticky looked at her, then quickly put his eyes on the

grass. *Anyways,* he said, and he reached up to scratch his head.

She took his face and made him look her in the eyes, said: *I swear to God, Sticks, I know you're gonna make it to college playing ball. You can see it in your eyes when you talk.*

We gotta break out bottle number two, Sticky said, reaching into his pack. He pulled the bottle out and shot off the cork. He peeked into Anh-thu's mug and it was still half full. *You gotta finish this off, Annie. You drinkin like you ain't never drank before.*

She took the mug and gunned the rest in one motion, handed it back to Sticky with a sour face. *Better?*

Sticky poured both mugs full again.

OK, now you ask me one, Anh-thu said.

Sticky watched a homeless guy digging through the trash for cans. *What makes you the most sad?* he said, turning back to Anh-thu. *You know, when you think about it.*

Anh-thu took a long sip with both hands on her mug. *That's easy,* she said. She took one of her hands off the mug and started playing with the tips of her hair. *It's my mom. I think every time I think about her I get sort of sad. I mean, especially for my dad. He was always so nice to her and then she just leaves.* She pulled her hair behind her ear and stared into her drink. She took a sip.

Sticky picked up another stick and tossed it against a tree. He took a sip.

But it's weird, Anh-thu continued. *Why should I even worry about something that's completely out of my control? I mean, I was only six when she left. How could I have really even known her, right? But still, I have this picture of her in my* drawer. Under my pajamas. I mean, I could just throw the thing away and try harder to forget about her. But, you know, for whatever reason I know I won't do that.

That ain't right, Sticky said, touching his knee against hers.

Anh-thu smiled at Sticky. *I know one thing, though,* she said. *I'm gonna be such a better mom when I have kids.* She brought the mug to her lips, let the cool champagne run onto her tongue and then down her throat. *What about your real mom, Sticks? You still haven't told me about her.*

Sticky shifted his weight on the bench. He reached down and picked up another stick, twirled it around in his fingers.

That's my second question. And remember the rules, you have to answer.

Sticky twirled the stick faster and then switched hands. *I ain't playin this game no more,* he said.

Come on, Sticky. We've been together six months now, why won't you ever talk about your mom? I mean, I'm your girl-friend. I want to know everything—

I said I'm done playin! Sticky shot back. *All right? I don't have nothin to say about it!* Sticky fired his stick at the tree and scooped up another one.

Anh-thu smoothed her hair behind her ears and then looked up at him. *Don't yell at me, Sticky.*

Sticky dropped the new stick and picked up his champagne, took a sip. He didn't want to talk anymore. He didn't understand why everybody always wanted to talk. Why? What good did it do? He wished he could just live his life. Do his thing. And never have to talk. But he also felt bad for snapping at Anh-thu.

I didn't mean to get all loud, he said.

Anh-thu took a drink, said: *You have so much stuff bottled up inside, and, I don't know, sometimes I worry.*

Sticky looked at his girl. He felt the buzz of the champagne spreading into the tips of his fingers, all through his chest and back. She actually cared about him. How strange, he thought. To be around somebody who cares. Who worries. He wanted to tell her how much he liked her. Right then and there. But when he tried to think something up in his head, it didn't sound so good. Nothing cool was coming. Instead he set his mug on the grass and moved in on her, knocking over the empty bottle. He kissed her and said in her ear: *I hope we don't never get messed up.*

Anh-thu kissed him back. It was the first time she'd ever heard Sticky say something like that and it made her skin tingle. *I love you, Sticky,* she whispered in his ear. *I mean it.*

They both pulled away and looked at each other. Anh-thu giggled and a smile grew on her face. She touched her mouth and told Sticky: *I think my lips are numb.*

Sticky picked up his backpack and Anh-thu's bag and pulled her by the hand. He spied the public restrooms up ahead and hurried through the grass. Anh-thu giggled again as she allowed herself to be pulled. Everything blurred around her except the back of Sticky's favorite shirt.

Sticky set both packs down in the women's restroom and checked the stalls for homeless. Nobody. He moved back in on Anh-thu, put his hands on her face, ran his fingers through her hair. He kissed her and could smell the scent of fruit on her skin. She kissed him back. It was so dark in the bathroom it didn't matter if their eyes were open

164

or closed. But they'd been together six months now. They didn't need to see anymore. And as the rest of the park fell asleep outside the restroom, Sticky and Anh-thu were alive inside. Together.

Outside, they fell against the tree beside their bench and tried to find faces in the night clouds. Sticky leaned his head back against the tree. Anh-thu rested her head on Sticky's shoulder. They watched a woman walk by rolling a duct-taped suitcase and talking to herself in Spanish. Watched a cat slinking underneath a bench. Neither one of them said much, their heads still buzzing from the champagne and all, but they held hands.

Sticky let his eyes close up shop. He thought about how he was happy where he was. With Annie. He squeezed her hand.

Anh-thu kissed his cheek, then let her eyes slide shut too.

A few homeless bodies were curled up around them. Sleeping.

There was the sound of a long train grinding by slow in the distance. A Santa Fe train maybe. Its muted whistle blowing subtly under the purr of a thousand crickets.

When Anh-thu woke up it was already past midnight. She looked at her watch and shook Sticky's arm.

Sticky jumped out of sleep with his fists raised. *What are you doing?* he yelled. He sucked in quick breaths as his eyes darted around the park.

It's OK, Sticky, Anh-thu said, backing her face away. *It's only me.*

He dropped his fists and looked at her through blurry eyes.

I didn't mean to scare you. Anh-thu stood up next to him and put her hands on his cheeks.

You didn't scare me, Sticky said.

I just have to go, Anh-thu said.

They both reached down to pick up their bags. *You gonna get in trouble?* Sticky said, putting his backpack straps on his shoulders.

Anh-thu smoothed out the creases in her shirt. *No. I told my dad I was staying at Laura's house. And she said I could go over there at whatever time.*

Sticky walked with Anh-thu the twelve blocks to Laura's place. Down the middle of the quiet side streets lined by pale streetlamps. They didn't hold hands, but they kept their bodies close. Arms sometimes brushing. It was late and all the kids Sticky had watched on the way were tucked safely in their houses now. Manicured lawns were abandoned. Doors were shut and locked. Alarms were set.

That's the kinda house I'd want, Anh-thu said, pointing to a big cabin-style pad with a steep roof and huge windows. *I'd put in secret rooms and stuff. Secret passages.*

Sticky kicked a rock. Walked up to it and kicked it again. *I got some letter today,* he told her.

About what?

It said for me to come to some basketball camp this summer. It's for the best players in the country. You have to be invited. Sticky slipped his hands in his pockets. *It said there's gonna be all these college coaches watching us.*

Wow, sounds like a big deal, Anh-thu said.

You know, them colleges cut you checks every month to live on. And you fly big-ass jets to away games. Sticky took his hands out of his pockets, moved them all around with his story. *And I heard the pilot tells everybody that a college team is on the plane. They say it over the loudspeaker. And then all the passengers cheer and turn around to look at you.*

The letter said all that?

Nah, I heard it, though. From the guys at Lincoln Rec. And if you play good at a school like UCLA or Kentucky, you're almost guaranteed a shot at the NBA. That's what Dante says. Sticky reached down and picked up a rock, threw it up into a tree. It sliced through the dense leaves, cracked against branches and fell onto somebody's perfect lawn.

I wonder if we could go to the same college, Anh-thu said, slipping her arm through Sticky's. *I took my transcript to the counselor and he said I'll have an excellent chance to get in most schools. Even the UCs.*

That'd be cool, Sticky said. *Going to the same school. I'd ball and you could keep up with your studies. We could get an apartment with the money they give me.*

See, Sticky, I told you there's a reason why I study so much. Anh-thu gave a little I-told-you-so face. *I'm not just being some nerd like you always say.*

You still kinda nerdy, he said.

They crossed to the other side of Rose and left the nice neighborhood behind. Walked right into the shady side of town. It happens that fast in Venice: One street you're surrounded by nice big houses with driveways holding fancy cars, and a block away all the streetlights have been shot out. Houses shrink up and are bunched closer together.

Lawns shorten and turn brown. Cars lose their luster. Old Chevy Novas and pickup trucks. Impalas with crushed front fenders. Newspapers cover cracked windows. Mailboxes are tagged by gang signs and all the sidewalks are crumbling.

There's her apartment, Anh-thu said, pointing to a run-down complex with sagging wood steps.

Anh-thu and Sticky sat down on the curb in front of Laura's place. Sticky shot rocks across the street like marbles. Anh-thu crossed her legs and played with her sandal. *Hey, Sticks,* she said.

Yeah?

You're not gonna be at that basketball thing all summer, are you?

Nah, he said. *It only goes for like a week.*

Cause I was just thinking maybe we could hang out like this more when the summer starts.

Sticky put a hand on her leg, told her: *That's cool.*

They stayed sitting on the curb awhile longer in silence. Anh-thu leaned her head against Sticky's shoulder. Sticky carved his name into the concrete with a sharp rock. The street was quiet aside from the two crackheads standing on the corner talking.

Then Anh-thu stood up. She brushed off the back of her skirt and told Sticky: *I should probably go. I don't even know if she's still awake or what.*

I'll stay here till you get in, he said.

Bye, Sticky, Anh-thu said. She wrapped her arms around his neck and squeezed. She kissed him. *We had the best anniversary.*

Anh-thu walked up the wood steps and knocked on door #17. She stood there waiting and looked back.

You could hear locks being fumbled with, and then the heavy door creaked open. Laura popped her head out and hugged Anh-thu. She waved to Sticky.

Anh-thu blew Sticky a kiss, and then she and Laura both stepped into the apartment, pulling the door shut behind them.

Sticky Tapped Every

mailbox he passed twice on his long walk home from dropping off Anh-thu. One tap on the firm corner for a stale sound, the other in the hollow middle. Bass. When the sounds didn't sound right he'd slap twice more. Then he'd back up and do it all over. And he still stepped over lines.

As he walked he was surrounded by the nighttime rhythms of his world: old dirty women wrapped in plastic bags, pushing rattling shopping carts full of their lives down a side street; thick-bearded men curled up on bus stop benches, sleeping, faces like old leather shoes; a crackhead stumbling out of an abandoned building having just scored a fix, talking crazy: *A fine night, huh, boy? Marvelous night, boy. You wanna have this dance, boy?* Sticky shook his head and kept on walking.

An occasional car full of dudes coming back from a bar would slow up to flip Sticky off. Music thumping out of open windows. Drooping faces. They'd yell out: *Hey!* And then when Sticky turned around to look: *Fuck you!* Their laughter trailing off as they screeched away. Sticky always handled this by flipping them right back. There was the beat of an after-hours club, tucked nameless between an empty warehouse and a condemned apartment building. The sturdy black bouncer out front gave Sticky a what's up with his head and watched him walk by.

A slightly overweight white girl, tight spandex shorts cut so high you could see all of her legs, whistled for Sticky from across the street. *Hey, guy, you need a date tonight?* She swung her purse and smacked on gum.

Sticky started across the street toward her.

You need some company tonight? she said.

Sticky walked up to the girl and slipped his hands in his pockets. *You ain't cold?* he said.

The girl's face was a third-grade finger-paint project gone bad. Bright red lipstick, pink blush. Eyelashes clumped together with black gunk. Blue eye shadow and hair a bad-perm blond. When she looked at Sticky, something in her eyes made him think of Baby. *I'm a little cold,* she said. *Not that much.*

An old Honda Civic slowed. The driver leaned himself across the passenger's seat to get a good look. She motioned with a finger for the guy to come get her. He stopped, rolled his window down and stuck his head out. He looked her up and down and shook his head. Then he sped off down the road.

The girl made a face and turned back to Sticky. *You seem real young. How old are you?*

Sticky looked straight in her eyes. *I'm about to be twenty-one.*

You ain't look that old to me.

Well, I am.

The girl pulled out a cigarette and lighter. Cupped her hand over the cig and flicked the lighter on. She sucked in a long drag and said: *I'm twenty-two. By the way, you got any money?*

Sticky shook his head. *Nah.*

The girl stepped out of her heels, reached down and rubbed one foot, then slipped the shoe back on, rubbed the other and then slipped that shoe back on. *These shoes are killing me.*

Another car rolled by. There was a long silence and Sticky sat down on the curb. The night clouds had cleared and all the stars were naked. A McDonald's cup started rolling on its own down the road with a gust of wind. An old club flyer chased after.

One thing I learned out here, the girl said, breaking the silence. *Men don't know how to treat no woman.* She frowned as she spoke. Took a drag and let the smoke leak out her nostrils. *I'm talkin about the men I dated, too. Not only tricks. My baby's daddy didn't know the first thing about how to kiss no woman's hand.*

Sticky looked up at her.

She pulled him up by his arm, said: *I'll bet you don't know the right way to kiss a woman's hand neither.*

172

Sticky shrugged his shoulders.

Figures, she said. *Most men don't.* The girl took Sticky's right hand in hers. *By the way, you got a girlfriend?*

Nah, Sticky said.

Well, I'm gonna show you something for when you get one. She dropped her cig and ground it out with the toe of her shoe. Told Sticky: *First, here goes the wrong way.* She leaned her head down and kissed soft, her blond hair spilling across Sticky's wrist. *That's the wrong way. Ya got it?* She paused for a second so Sticky would have time to let it sink in. *OK, now here goes the right way.* Same thing except she kept her eyes on Sticky's eyes through the whole deal. *See the difference?* she said, and she held Sticky's hand and waited for his answer.

I don't know, maybe you was lookin at me.

That's exactly right. She let go of Sticky's hand and reached in her purse for another cig. She lit up and held it in her fingers. *So, now you know. Girls will be impressed if you know how to kiss they hands right.* She put the cigarette to her lips and sucked in.

Another car rolled up slow to check the girl. The window came down and an old gray-haired guy stuck his head out. The girl twirled around. She flicked her ashes all sexy.

The guy pulled it to the curb.

Sticky leaned back against a pole, put his free hand in his pocket and watched the deal go down. When the girl hopped in the guy's car Sticky continued down the road.

Three blocks later Sticky was at Lincoln Rec.

He cut through the grass and cruised into the dark parking lot. Thought he'd check it out before cruising back home. He went right up to the gym doors and shook the handles. Locked. He peeked through the crack between the doors and was able to make out all the lifeless bodies lying on the floor. He thought about how soon he'd be back to ball. Only five hours. He imagined sneaking in the gym somehow and curling up next to all of them, along the three-point line.

Sticky startled when he heard a rustling in the bushes. *Hey, yo, Stick,* somebody said. *Yo, Stick, that you, boy?*

Sticky turned around and found Dallas and Dreadlock Man sitting against the dark gym wall behind some bushes, holding paper-bagged bottles.

Dallas stumbled getting to his feet but caught himself on the wall. *Hey, yo, Stick, my brother.* He held out his fist and Sticky gave him daps. *What you doin out here, boy?*

Sticky glanced at Dreadlock Man. His eyes were half shut. *I was just walking around,* he said. *What are you guys doin?*

Dallas fell back a little but caught his balance by grabbing a handful of bush. He peeped down at Dreadlock Man and then looked at Sticky. *Yo, you ballin in the mornin?* He put a fist to his mouth and laughed. *What I'm talkin about, I know you ballin. Tomorrow's Saturday. You always ball on Saturday. Boy, you might as well stay here with us, man. We gots blankets and stuff up in the van.* He teetered when he put hands on his hips. *It's a nice night out.*

Nah, I gotta get back to the house, Sticky said.

Come on, Stick, Dallas said. *If you look at it a certain way, this sorta* is *the house.* He cleared his throat and spit into the bushes. He held out his bottle, said: *Plus you gotta try this juice we got for you. I know you be drinkin juice sometimes.*

Sticky stared at the bottle.

Dreadlock Man laughed through his teeth.

A siren wailed in the distance.

Sticky took the bottle and sniffed the mouth. Then he poured a healthy swig down his throat. He coughed and spit some of it out. *Damn!* He wiped his face on the bottom of his shirt. *That's strong as hell!*

Dallas and Dreadlock Man started howling with laughter and slapping fives. *Shit, boy*, Dallas said. *This juice right here could make you a man. Put some hair on your chest.*

Sticky cringed as he swallowed a smaller sip.

Dallas took the bottle and tilted back. He took a super long swig and shook his head: *Goddamn it, that's what I'm talkin about!* He passed the bottle to Dreadlock Man, who did the same.

I better take off, Sticky said.

Nah, Dallas said. *Hang with your peeps.*

Chill with your boys tonight, Dreadlock Man said.

We's hidin out from my old lady, Dallas said. *She after me again. Been up and down this parkin lot three, four times already lookin for me.* Dreadlock Man grinned and shut his eyes completely. He leaned his head against the wall. His green ten-speed was leaning against the wall behind him. He took the bottle from Dallas and tipped back, held it out for Sticky.

Dallas watched to see if Sticky would take it.

Sticky turned around and looked at the empty parking lot, the quiet road that would take him back to his couch in Georgia's living room. He looked at the bottle.

Nobody moved for those few seconds, when Sticky was thinking. Dreadlock Man held the bottle out. Sticky stared at it, looked back at the road again. Dallas watched Sticky.

Finally Sticky reached for the bottle.

Dallas started talking about his girl again. Dreadlock Man flipped three or four dreads out of his face and yawned. Sticky slid down the gym wall and put the bottle to his mouth.

It's All Set,

Counselor Julius said as he and current foster lady, Georgia, walked out from the office together.

Sticky took his hands off the foosball handles and reached down for his bag. By the fourth episode he had the whole checkout process down: prepacked, papers signed, ready to roll.

Looks like you're gonna be living out in Venice Beach, big guy, Julius said, and he shot a smile at Georgia. *You'll probably turn into a surfer or something.*

Georgia laughed and told Sticky: *Be sure to tell your friends goodbye. And take your time. I'll be waiting outside in the car.* She shook hands with Julius again and walked duck-footed out the front door.

Sticky strolled over to the TV room, stuck his head in.

The other residents were glued to the couch watching a video on MTV. After Sticky's checkout, Julius had to load everybody up in the foster pad van and make the long drive out to the Getty, their scheduled outing for the weekend.

I'm out, Sticky said, and gave the group a head nod.

All the residents got up and circled around him, took turns saying their goodbyes. Long-haired Tommy shook Sticky's hand. Angie and Lisa, fourteen-year-old twins from the valley, stuck out their bottom lips all sad-like and gave tight hugs. *We'll miss you, Sticky,* they both said at the exact same time.

Be cool, Jerome said in a Barry White voice. He slapped Sticky five and pulled him in for a quick dude-to-dude-style embrace.

Six-year-old Pedro, who was new to the house and spoke only Spanish, didn't say anything. He wrapped his skinny arms around Sticky's legs and clung tight. Wouldn't let go. Two tears fell down his brown cheeks as Sticky patted him on the top of the head. After a couple minutes, Counselor Julius had to peel Pedro away.

Everybody loved Sticky because he was OG. The seasoned veteran of the house. The resident who knew the system inside and out and could go into detail to some new kid with questions.

What was strange about the whole goodbye scene, though, was that it didn't include Maria. She was Sticky's closest companion. His first lady of the foster world. But when everybody else got up to see him off, she stayed with the video. And this was something Sticky didn't understand.

He leaned his head forward, tried to make eye contact and told her: *Hey, Maria, I'm takin off.*

Oh, bye, Maria said, pretending to be distracted by the video. She put her hand up no-look style and then let it fall back into her lap.

Sticky shrugged and turned to take off, but Maria spoke up: *They're just gonna bring you back here in a couple months, Sticky. You know that by now. They always bring us back.*

Sticky shook his head and walked away.

Julius was waiting in the hall with his arms folded. He pulled Sticky into the counselor's office. *I wanna give you something,* he said, and he walked around the desk and reached into the closet. Pulled out an Old Navy bag and set it up on the desk. *It's not that big of a deal, but I thought you might want it.*

Sticky pulled open the bag and found the old beat-up house basketball. The one he'd learned to play the game with.

Julius pulled the ball out and looked it over. *This thing's seen better days, man.* He spun the ball on his finger and looked at Sticky. *Listen, the supervisors are always trippin about house equipment, so don't go tellin everybody.*

You could really just give it to me? Sticky said.

I can't, Julius said. *But I just did.* He faked a pass and Sticky flinched.

That's real cool, Julius. Thanks.

Julius reached out and shook Sticky's hand. *I'm not gonna lie, dude, you turned out to be a pretty good baller. Now hurry up and get out of here. That fat broad is sittin out there waitin for you.*

Sticky cruised out of the house with the Old Navy bag over his shoulder and a small bag of clothes in his left hand. As he went to pull open the passenger door of Georgia's minivan, the old Mexican director came speeding around the corner in his little Honda Civic. He pulled up along the curb and cut off the engine. Jumped out. *I barely caught you,* he said, shutting his door. He walked over to Sticky's side of the van and waved through the window to Georgia. She waved back.

Julius did all the paperwork, Sticky said.

I'm not worried about the paperwork, the director said. He looked Sticky in the eye and gave him a firm handshake. *You and I have known each other a long time.*

Yeah, Sticky said.

I'd like to think we've become friends.

Yeah, Sticky said.

Well, I wanted to tell you this, Sticky, as a friend: Over the past eight years I've seen a few families pick you up only to turn around and bring you right back. And that's confusing. It's real confusing. But you need to realize that it's not your fault. That it has nothing to do with you. In fact I consider myself the lucky one. I've had the pleasure of watching Sticky-the-boy become Sticky-the-young-man. And what's special about you, son, is not the way you play foosball or basketball or any other game—it's who you are. He pointed to Sticky's chest. *You're a good person, Sticky. A good human being.*

Sticky didn't know what he was supposed to say to that so he didn't say anything. Instead he nodded his head and stared at the pavement.

The director smiled and drummed his fingers on the roof of the van, said: *I hope you never lose sight of that. You mean a lot to me.* As Sticky climbed into the passenger's seat, the director exchanged waves with Georgia again. Then he shut the door and motioned her back onto the road.

Georgia merged onto the 10 heading west. She pulled open a big bag of chips, set it in her lap and reached inside. *You're my fifth foster kid,* she said, shoving a couple chips into her mouth. *This makes two whites, a Oriental, a black and a little Mexican girl.* She reached back into the bag. *I tell friends: It's like the flippin United Nations at my house.*

Sticky pulled the house basketball out of the Old Navy bag and set it in his lap. He examined the tiny rips in the synthetic leather.

Now, I run a pretty laid-back house, Georgia went on. *You kids do your chores and don't give me any headaches, everything's fine. It really boils down to this: You make life easy for me, I make life easy for you. I like to think of it as a kind of business arrangement.*

Sticky ran his fingers along the grooves of the ball. He spun it around and stared at the thick black initials of his foster care pad: 7 FLOW. Stuck his fingers in the groove, thumb between the 7 and F, and imagined lofting up a soft twenty-footer over the outstretched hands of some over-matched defender.

My husband's gone all day. He works like sixty-hour weeks so you'll hardly see him. Of course, I work just as hard as he does. We got in a big fight about that just last night. He thinks all I do is sit around the house watching TV. I told him: Uh, no, honey, I don't think so. I told him: I got a full-time job just the same as you do—I take care of other people's kids.

Georgia kept on talking, but Sticky wasn't listening. He

181

had his daydream channel set on more important things. Like, where was he gonna play ball in Venice? He'd seen some famous court by the beach in a movie. And Julius told him about some gym called Lincoln Rec. He started thinking about other things too. Like, what was the old Mexican director trying to tell him when he was leaving? That he was a good person? And how strange was that? He'd never had anybody talk about him like that. It didn't make any sense. But maybe that was just part of his job. Something he was supposed to say.

Georgia's voice turned into background sound. Like the wind rushing in through the rolled-down windows. Like the sound of the traffic report coming in over the AM radio. Sticky traced the letters on the ball and did some other kinds of thinking too. He thought about what Maria said. How he'd probably get dropped back off in a couple months. How if that came true he just wished the director hadn't said what he said. It seemed like the kind of thing someone says to someone when they know they'll never see that person again. And he figured if it was true, that this chip-eating lady would one day bring him back too, like the rest of them, then he should at least know in advance. That way he could think up something good to say to the director. Something that might make him feel right about what he said. About Sticky being a good person. Something that might make him feel like it wasn't a mistake.

Sticky stared out the window and tried to remember all the billboards they passed: Chevron Gas, Gateway Computers, In-N-Out Burger, Staples, The Sports Club/LA. That way he could know what's up if they ever passed them again, going back the other way.

Pop Songs Echo

through the tiny staff bathroom in Millers. Britney Spears drops bubblegum beats that bounce off the stall walls and into Anh-thu's throbbing head. When her tune fades, Justin Timberlake takes over. OutKast. Matchbox Twenty. Jennifer Lopez. Their melodies filling the blue-tiled box of a bathroom with cotton candy.

Anh-thu leans on her elbows over the toilet bowl. One hand gripping white porcelain, the other holding back her long black hair. She spits and stares into the water: a rippling reflection of her puffy brown face. She heaves again and coughs. Flushes. Everything is pushing at the back of her watery eyes.

She spits again and stares.

The summer music mix bumps into an old-school Rob

Base jam: "It Takes Two." It's the third time Anh-thu's heard this song today and her ears anticipate every shift in melody. She pictures the way customers always react, busting a couple quick dance steps near a mirror or keeping time with a subtle head bop.

She wipes away forehead sweat with the back of her hand.

Shift leader Dori creeps up to the locked bathroom door and leans in with an ear, taps her knuckles. *Everything OK, Annie?* She fingers the end of her long blond ponytail.

Anh-thu spins around, says through the door in her best smiling voice: *Everything's fine.*

All right, Dori says. *Just checking.* She listens at the door a few seconds longer and then heads back out onto the floor.

Anh-thu turns back to the bowl. She digs her fingers into her stomach again and starts to cry. She's picturing Sticky's face if she really is pregnant. She's so nervous her stomach feels nauseous again. She heaves and coughs. She spits. Flushes.

Ten minutes ago Anh-thu was folding clothes with the rest of the girls. Folding and talking about some guy that gave Laura his cell number. They were gathered around the fifty-percent-off table, listening to Laura and cleaning up the two-story mess left by thoughtless customers—people who pull every item off a sale stack, unfold and throw back. Laura was dropping serious insight about UCLA dudes, what a girl has to do to catch their eye. She was doing heavy analysis, but Anh-thu had stopped listening.

Anh-thu was thinking about Sticky again. How her situation might mess everything up. It was her birthday, she was sixteen today, and Sticky would show up with a gift. He'd want to touch her and kiss her. But what if everything was different now?

She tossed an unfolded shirt on a stack of sweaters and hustled for the staff bathroom holding her stomach.

Somethin up with Annie, Laura said, watching Anh-thu hurry off.

She's not being normal, a girl named Julie said.

Shift leader Dori finished folding a sweater and watched Anh-thu turn the corner into the break room. She figured she'd give her a couple minutes before she went over to investigate.

Anh-thu picks herself up from the toilet and moves to the sink. She turns the water on full blast, cups her hands and splashes her face. She rinses out her mouth. She shuts the water off and pulls down a clean towel from the cupboard. As she dries her face, she stares at herself in the mirror. Her hair matted to her forehead. Her swollen eyes and puffy cheeks. This is the way her face looks after a long night of crying.

But when she locks in on her own eyes for too long, starts thinking about her situation, her and Sticky's situation, that nervous sick feeling comes spinning back into her stomach. She plants a hand against the sink and looks away.

Eminem starts flowing through the speakers: "Lose Yourself." The song Sticky made Anh-thu listen to over and over a few days back, on the tape deck of a borrowed car.

He drove them up to a small empty lot between two

giant houses with tall fences. Somewhere in the Pacific Palisades. There were dense trees and bushes so nobody could look in. Signs that warned in big black writing: KEEP OUT. There were construction postings and idle tractors, a streetlight dug out of the ground and lying on its side. Sticky maneuvered the car past all that stuff and up to the edge of the cliff, where he cranked the parking brake. He and Anh-thu looked out at the stars hovering above the big black ocean. There wasn't a single cloud in the sky. Sticky bopped his head with the beat and pulled Anh-thu in close. They held hands and kissed.

At one point, he motioned to the tape deck and told her: *This dude got skills, Annie.*

Anh-thu agreed.

He said: *You know what? I wanna be the Eminem of hoops.*

Anh-thu laughed.

When Eminem spilled his last line of lyrics and the beat trailed off, Sticky hit rewind and started the song all over again.

Anh-thu feels like crying again but instead she stomps her foot to stop herself. *Quit acting like a little girl,* she says to her image in the mirror, and she grits her teeth. *Just stop it already.*

She takes a few deep breaths and tries to pull herself together. She tosses the towel in a bin, runs a finger under each eye and straightens her clothes. She takes another deep breath and unwraps a stick of gum. As she pops the gum in her mouth she devises a plan. What's done is done, she thinks. All she can do is deal. She'll tell Sticky the situation tonight, and then go from there based on how he reacts. It might not go perfect at first, but they'll figure out what to do.

A Jewel song comes on, one she doesn't really dig, but Anh-thu feels okay about her plan. She takes another deep breath and unlocks the door. Then she heads back out onto the floor.

Two Old Cops

climb into the bleachers next to Sticky and pull out notepads.

The white cop has a salt-and-pepper crop of hair starting halfway up his head. A beer gut that lips over the buckle of his belt. He plops down on one side of Sticky and strains for breath.

The black cop is a tall lanky dude, 6' 5" at least. He has juicy Jheri Curls spiraling down the back of his neck. He sits on the other side and pulls a pen from behind his ear, says: *Now the suspect, you say he's a light-skinned brother?*

Sticky nods, eyes glued to the court. Sticky's been a prisoner since the Fat Chuck thing happened a couple hours earlier. Sure, the games are rolling again, Dallas and Dante are back on against Rob's squad, but right now Sticky is Stuck in the bleachers.

Out on the court, Old-man Perkins sets a hard screen for Johnson, who dribbles toward the wing and dishes to Dreadlock Man in the corner. Dreadlock Man lofts up a prayer that somehow hits nothing but net. He yells out *Peanut Butter!* three times as he runs back on defense. And then, in case someone still isn't sure who scored, he yells it out again: *Peanut Butter!* His raspy voice cutting through an otherwise silent game. The whole gym quiet and cuss-free due to the two busters with badges sitting up in the bleachers with Sticky.

Off the court, every couple minutes a different guy will cruise by the bleachers and pat Sticky on the back. Tell him in his ear: *We gonna find him, Stick. Don't even trip about that.* Then walk away.

And he's been in here before? the white cop says.

Sticky nods.

What about his clothing? the black cop says. *What's this brother wearin?*

Sticky shrugs his shoulders. He kicks at the bleacher in front of him and leans back. Kicks again, only softer this time, and puts on a mad-dog glare. He can't believe this has happened. Can't believe he's stuck up here going over the play-by-play again with a couple of cops.

Now don't get all sassy, kid, the white cop says. *That certainly won't get us anywhere.*

Just play it cool and answer the questions, the black cop says. *We'll take care of the rest.*

Sticky leans forward with his elbows on his knees, rests his head in his hands.

I can't say I understand the attitude, the white cop says. He fingers the sweat off his forehead and wipes it on his cop pants. *We're here to help you. We're on your side.*

Know what, Tom? the black cop says to his partner. *This kid looks kinda familiar.* He turns to Sticky, says: *Why do I get the feelin I've slapped some cuffs on you before?*

Sticky stays with the game, but his mind floats back in time. He pictures leaning against the chain-link fence next to the Boys and Girls Club in Santa Monica, the black cop patting him down and calling him an asshole. He remembers the sound the metal cuffs made behind his back when they clinked together. The feel of the cold metal digging into his wrists as the cop pulled him to the car, shoved him in the backseat and slammed the door.

I'll be damned if he don't look familiar, the black cop says.

He who is the victim one minute, is the perpetrator the next, the white cops says to his partner. He laughs a little, says: *You know how this city works, Sam.*

That's poetic, man, the black cop says.

The white cop turns back to Sticky, says: *Now let's try this again, kid. What type of clothing was the suspect wearing?*

Sweatpants, Sticky says, still staring at the game. *Gray, I think.*

After Chuck sped out of the parking lot, Sticky had begged Jimmy to keep the cops out of it. He walked through the office door and explained that it wasn't that big of a deal. Bringing cops in would be an overreaction. He claimed he and the guys in the gym could handle business on their own. It's called street justice, he said. But Jimmy told Sticky he had to make the call, that it was part of his job. Something goes down on his watch and he makes the call. That's the way he was trained to do it. Somebody finds out he didn't follow protocol and then it would be *his* job on the line. After he said that, he nudged Sticky out of the way and pulled the office door closed. Picked up the phone.

Through the window, Sticky watched Jimmy put the receiver to his ear and punch in the numbers. Watched his mouth lock and twist and twitch as he tried to form the words that would explain what Fat Chuck had tried to do to him in the public restroom.

The two cops fire question after question at Sticky, they want to know everything: what did the suspect say? when did he try to touch? was there actual sexual contact? was there a scuffle? They take turns, one after the other like they're singing a duet. And they barely allow time for an answer. When Sticky speaks up they scribble his words down on notepads. Sticky thinks back to his court appearance for throwing the concrete through the glass at that car dealership. He had to answer the same questions posed the same way. He wonders how this, being the innocent person, is any different from being guilty: where do you live? how long have you lived there? who needs to be contacted? how will you get home?

At one point, the white cop leans in close and tells Sticky: *You really think this is the type of place you should be hanging around, kid?*

Sticky turns and looks him in the face for the first time, says: *I always play ball in here.*

Oh yeah? the cop says.

Yeah, Sticky says. *And I always will.*

The cop scans the gym, laughs a little under his breath and says: *All right, kid. All right. But look around a little bit. Open your eyes. I mean, I'm just saying.*

Jimmy walks up and hands the two cops ice-cold Cokes, says: *Such a h-h-h-hot d-d-day.* Both cops crack open their cans.

The black cop puts the can up to his forehead, says: *Ah, man. It's a hot one, all right.*

Sticky watches their necks vibrate as they suck down soda. Checks out the dark blue of their uniforms. The club and gun on either hip. The radio. The shiny leather shoes and cuffed pants. And right then he realizes something: cops are just normal people dressed up. They get hot and drink soda and clear their throats just like everybody else. They used to be seventeen, same as he is. And this is a strange idea for Sticky. Strange because cops have always just been blue robots to him. Nothing more, nothing less. Blue uniforms he had to avoid on the streets. Like a video game.

Jimmy folds his arms and leans against the side of the bleachers. Checks out the action on the court. *N-n-not m-m-much t-t-t-t-trouble in here m-most d-d-d-days,* he says.

No, you do a hell of a job, Jimmy, the white cop says, and he sets his empty can on the bleacher in front of him. *Hardly ever get calls about this place.*

You run a tight ship with these characters, the black cop says. *Don't you, Jimmy?*

Jimmy cracks a baby smile and buries his hands in his pockets. He stands there awhile longer, watches Dante pick off a pass at half-court and streak down the right sideline all

192

by himself. Watches Dante take off just outside the key, lean through the air and flush in a one-hand jam.

The sideline erupts.

Oh, man! the white cop says.

D-d-d-d-damn, D-D-Dante, Jimmy says.

The black cop sets his Coke can down and stands up, yells through megaphoned hands: *Somebody tell that brother it ain't right to get up that high! It just ain't right!*

Sticky feels a surge of energy rush through his skinny frame. All that action on the floor and he's stuck in the bleachers, yapping. All the highlights are going down without him. Everybody's running up and down the court making music with their squeaking sneaks, and he's no more than a spectator. No more a part of the show than the business guys watching in ties. He squeezes his fists together and sits up straight. Watches Rob inbound to Trey and everybody rumble back down the other way. He punches at his own legs a couple times. Feels the burn in his muscles and then sits on his hands.

Jimmy picks up the empty cans and adjusts his glasses. *Well,* he says, *I g-g-g-g-got s-s-some p-p-p-paperw-w-work in the off-ff-ff-ff-ffice.* He reaches out a hand and both cops shake it.

All right then, Jimmy, the black cop says.

Be good, the white cop says.

Jimmy nods his head, his magnified eyes gleaming with pride, and walks back toward his office.

The cops put away their notepads and pens, their questions. They chill in the bleachers like everybody else for a while, watching the game.

Sticky's eyes follow the ball. Trey's handling it at the top

193

of the key. He swings it over to Slim and cuts through the lane. Slim holds the ball above his head while he surveys the scene. Sticky's eyes are on the action, but his mind is somewhere else. It's almost three in the afternoon according to the clock above the door. Not much time before he's gotta break for the house, drop his bag off and grab a shower. Then he's gotta pick out some smooth gear to wear and review the different ways he might swipe the bracelet.

He spies the cops out of the corner of his eye.

And then there's the stuffed bear he's gotta buy. Eleven bucks and some change at the old lady's card shop. He peeks through the bleachers for his bag. Still there. That's a lot of stuff to do before nine tonight. He touches the back of his fingers against his cut and checks them for blood. Nothing.

The white cop nudges the black cop with an elbow, tells him: *Used to be pretty good back in my day, Sam. Second leading scorer on the team in high school.*

The black cop shoots out a deep belly laugh and slaps a hand on his partner's shoulder. *About thirty years and fifty pounds ago, right?*

Both cops laugh.

Sticky spies the clock again and does some minor math in his head. He should probably leave the gym by five-thirty. That would give him enough time to walk home, shower and figure out some gear. Then he'd bus it out to the promenade and size up the bracelet. According to his calculations that leaves him barely enough time for two more games. And he's gotta get on it right now if he wants to make even that happen.

We done? he asks the cops politely, standing up.

194

I think we got the information we need, the black cop says.

Don't worry, kid, the white cop says. *We'll get right on this one.*

We'll do everything we can, the black cop says.

In fact, the white cop says, nudging his partner, *it's about time we start heading out.*

Let's do it, the black cops says.

Sticky nods and hops down from the bleachers. He walks over to a pack of guys waiting against the wall, asks them who has next. Does the guy have five? Who's got the game after that? Does he need one? Yes? Cool.

When his slot is secure he glances back up at the bleachers and discovers that neither cop has moved.

My Name's Sticky,

Sticky said, first time a group of Lincoln Rec regulars got him in a corner and came with their questions.

Nah, man, what's your real name? Johnson said.

Sticky is *my real name.*

What kinda name is Sticky? Dallas said. He turned and laughed with his boys, told them: *Y'all ever heard some crazy stuff like that?*

Sticky? Old-man Perkins said, trying hard to put his finger on it. *Like, I spilled beer on my dashboard and now the shit's all sticky, Sticky?* Dallas nodded his head at the question. Johnson stopped laughing and waited for an answer, his mouth hanging open in a little *o*.

But Sticky had nothing more to say. He was new at the

gym and didn't know these guys. He leaned his weight against the wall by the door. Pushed off with his fingertips and let his weight fall back to the wall again. Pushed off and fell back.

Pushed off and fell back.

I ain't know no dude named Sticky before, Dreadlock Man mumbled. He was sitting on the seat of his beat-up green ten-speed, rolling a little forward and then stopping himself with the hand brake. Rolling back and then the hand brake.

It was the sixth straight day Sticky had shown up at Lincoln Rec, and these guys had a right to their interview. They stood around him in a horseshoe. Old-man Perkins with his arms crossed; Dallas with a bag slung over his right shoulder and a little white stuff in the corners of his mouth; Johnson's feet shoulder width apart, Raiders cap backwards; Dreadlock Man rolling back and forth on his bike. Slim hung behind a few feet. He sat with his back turned, stretching out his long legs—whenever somebody said something clever, you could hear his deep Carolina laugh. They were all digging for some background info on this new white kid coming in every day. Where'd he come from? What's he thinking, trying to ball with a bunch of black folks? They asked all kinds of different questions that day, one after another, when the games had died down and Jimmy started going up and down the floor with a wet mop, but they couldn't seem to get past the whole name thing.

That the name that's on your papers? Johnson asked.

Sticky nodded. He stared down at their high-tops, said: *It's been the same thing since I was born.*

Know what, kid? Old-man Perkins took a couple steps

forward, got right in Sticky's face this time with his dead-serious look. *Know what I got to say about that?*

There were a few seconds of heavy silence in the gym. Sticky snuck a quick look up at Perkins's scowl and quickly went back to his shoes, Dreadlock Man stopped his bike cold, Slim turned his body all the way around.

Dallas peeked around the gym to see who was watching.

Perkins pulled a knife from his pocket and flipped the blade out, puffed up over Sticky and swung a violent knife hand through the air. The blade wooshed by Sticky's chin and Perkins yelled: *That's a stupid-ass name!* leaning in extra hard on the word *stupid*.

Everybody laughed.

Dallas put a fist to his mouth, stomped the floor with his heel. Dreadlock Man made a whistling sound through his gold teeth. Perkins folded the knife up and stuck it back in his pocket. He pointed a finger at the side of Sticky's head, told him: *Your momma must of been all up in the pipe when you was born.*

Johnson pumped his fist at that line. His laugh was high and loud.

Old-man Perkins reached out a fist and gave Dallas daps.

But Sticky was telling lies.

He started out Travis Reichard back in Virginia. Travis after Randy Travis, Baby's favorite singer. But when they moved all the way out to Los Angeles, the name Travis quickly disappeared. Their apartment was above a Hostess wholesale shop. In the beginning, Baby would go downstairs and buy Cup Cakes every Sunday evening when they were half price. It was a once-a-week treat, and Sticky looked forward to their dessert. He had a system for eating the Cup Cakes: cakes first, the creamy filling, and then the sweet frosting. Baby would look at her boy after he'd polished off a pack, the chocolate all over his face, and she'd shake her head. *You're my little sticky boy,* she'd say.

But eventually Baby started making more frequent runs downstairs. Whenever she wasn't in the mood to cook she'd go get a bunch of cupcakes and serve them on paper plates. And before long, she was always calling him Sticky Boy.

For real, though, kid, Old-man Perkins said. *Anybody can't come in here tellin people what to call em. Look at this Dreadlock Man fool, he been tryin to get people to call em Peanut Butter since he first showed up two years ago. Peanut Butter, like the goddamn sandwich. You heard em yellin that out every time he shoot that broke-ass jumper he got.*

Come on, man, Dreadlock Man said. He laughed a little and shook his head. *It ain't like all that. I could shoot sweet when I gets my rhythm. For real. It's just y'all ain't never gonna pass me the ball enough.* He looked at Sticky and pulled a thick dread out of his face. *I ain't never said to call me it. They just ain't figure out when I gets my rhythm, that ball come bustin through that net like—*

D-man, Dallas interrupted. *You sittin here lyin to that white boy. You know you came up to me and Dante way back and said you go by Peanut Butter. I remember like it was yesterday, right over there* (he pointed and everybody looked) *by the soda machine. You straight-up lyin to the kid.*

Nah, Dallas, nah. I ain't never said to call me it, nah, it's just when I gets my rhythm, that ball look like peanut butter goin through the net. The creamy kind with no nuts.

Dreadlock Man held his hands up in the air. It all seemed pretty obvious to him. *That's what I said back when you talkin about, Dallas. I swear on my moms on that one.*

Dallas raised his eyebrows at him and shook his head. *All right, if that's how you wanna say it then.*

What I'm sayin, Old-man Perkins said, looking at Sticky, *is you can't be comin in here tellin people what to call you by. They may call you Sticky where you from, but that don't apply here. This is a whole nother world.*

Sticky shrugged his shoulders and avoided Perkins's eyes.

Two, three weeks down the road and we'll have somethin for you, Dallas said. *Maybe sooner.*

I don't care what you all call me, Sticky said. *Cause I know my name's still Sticky.* He broke through their horseshoe and made a beeline for the bleachers where he had his bag tied up.

The guys all looked at each other as he walked away. Dallas and Dreadlock Man laughed.

You ain't gotta go runnin off when grown people tryin to talk, Johnson said.

Old-man Perkins fingered his stubble. He looked perplexed. *I don't think this dude understand who he talkin to.*

He think this place like Disneyland or some shit, Johnson said all excited, proud of his analogy. *He think anybody can just come in here whenever they want and ride the rides and watch the shows and then just go home.*

All the guys nodded in agreement.

And it sure ain't no Disneyland, Dallas said.

No Mickey Mouse, Dreadlock Man mumbled.

Ain't no line for no Space Mountain, Johnson added.

Sticky reached under the bleachers for his bag. He unzipped the zipper and pulled out his headphones, carefully slipped them over his ears, making sure the duct tape was still holding strong. He pulled them off and put them back on.

Pulled off and put back on.

Pulled off and put back on.

These dudes were coming at him and he wasn't quite sure how to handle it. He didn't wanna go home, but he wasn't gonna let anybody call him something other than Sticky.

Pulled off and put back on.

Pulled off and put back on.

Pulled off and put back on.

When the worn-out pads on both phones were up against his ears just right, he pressed a thumb against the Play button and Tupac came to life.

Slim stood up and slung his bag over his shoulder. *Why don't you all just leave the kid alone. I mean damn, he's just here cause he wants to play ball. He didn't show up lookin for no lecture about nicknames.*

There's more to playin ball than just playin ball, Dallas said. *You know that just as much as I do, Slim.*

Old-man Perkins walked over to the bleachers and swiped the headphones off Sticky's ears. *Hey, white boy,* he said. *We about to get this straightened out right now.*

Sticky stood up and yanked his phones out of Perkins's hands, shot his eyes toward the open door. His escape. He glanced back at Perkins, who now held his hands up in the air, like he was trying to show some invisible referee it wasn't him that fouled anybody. *Easy, kid,* he said.

Don't get stupid, Johnson said.

Sticky eyed the door again, then Perkins.

Easy.

Slim walked over with his bag and climbed into the bleachers, sat a couple feet to Sticky's left. He folded his arms and stared at Perkins.

Sticky, trusting Slim for some reason, slowly sat back down and left the phones off his ears.

I ain't tryin to mess with you, kid, Perkins said. *I'm just lettin you know.*

We tryin to teach you somethin, Johnson said.

This the way things been, Old-man Perkins said, *since long before you stumbled in here from wherever you stumbled in here from.*

Know why we call Slim, Slim? Dallas said, walking closer to Sticky. He looked at Slim and started laughing. *We call this cat Slim cause even if he stood right between you and the clock, you could still tell what time it was.*

Everybody laughed. Slim laughed.

Johnson sat up in the bleachers, too. Dreadlock Man coasted over on his ten-speed, one foot on a pedal, the other pushing off the wood floor. Jimmy leaned the mop against the wall near the homeless court and started going around the gym tearing off old outdated announcements.

Slim stood up in the bleachers and pointed at Dallas. *See this dude right here?* he said, his eyes stuck on Sticky. *You probably thinkin he must be from Dallas or somethin, with a name like Dallas. But he ain't. New York was in here earlier, now we call him New York cause he legit. Born and raised in Brooklyn. My man Dallas, though, he's from right down the road. Right over there on Washington next to the ninety-nine-cent store. Pure L.A., this dude. We call him Dallas cause he used to come in here talkin about that stupid-ass TV show called* Dallas. Slim winked at Sticky, and that wink eased Sticky's mind.

Ain't that right, big D? Old-man Perkins said, laughing. *You black as night and watchin some show with a bunch of white folks sippin on champagne.*

Don't make no kind of sense, Johnson said.

One time I mention that show in here. Dallas crinkled his face and rolled his head around. *One time and all these dudes jump on it.*

Slim pounded the bleachers, laughing, and sat back down. Dallas waved him off.

Same thing happened to me, though, Johnson said. *My real name ain't no Johnson. I came walkin in here three years ago as Dimarcus Jackson, same name as my granddaddy. A distinguished name. Jackson, not Johnson. And then cause I occasionally wore this one specific T-shirt I got for Christmas—*

Lemme stop you right there, Old-man Perkins interrupted, putting his hand on Johnson's shoulder. *Yeah, you came in Dimarias Jackson or some shit like that—*

Dimarcus!

But for the first three months I seen you, no lie, you wore the same Big Johnson T-shirt every damn day. Never washed it, neither. That's how we started callin em Big Johnson. Like the T-shirt. Old-man Perkins wrapped Johnson up in a bear hug and they stumbled out of the bleachers. *Tell em bout that Big Johnson shirt. All them rips under the arms. Like you was some kinda homeless cat.* They both laughed and wrestled around a little. *And you supposed to be some big man workin for the city.*

Always talkin about his damn benefits, too, Dallas said. *We was like, yo, forget Blue Shield, what they need to do is buy your ass a new shirt.*

Slim stepped off the bleachers and acted like he was gonna drop a WWF elbow on Johnson. Old-man Perkins let go when Johnson's Raiders cap fell off his head. Johnson reached down and picked it up, pulled it on his head and adjusted the bill.

And what about Jimmy over there, Dallas said. He pointed toward the homeless court where Jimmy was kneeling down next to an old Indian-looking woman. *His real name wasn't even Jimmy, right?* He looked over at Old-man Perkins for him to pick the story up from there.

That's right, Perkins said, and he paused a sec to catch his breath.

Sticky unzipped his bag and threw his Walkman inside, zipped it back up. He set the bag on the bleacher next to his feet.

Dreadlock Man started rolling back and forth on his ten-speed again.

Johnson took off his cap and checked out the bill. He brushed off some dust from the floor and pulled it back tight on his head.

His real name is Sam, Old-man Perkins said. *Me, Johnson and this guy Shotgun was all sittin right here in these bleachers talkin about that movie* Hoosiers. *Jimmy was walkin by and heard what we was talkin about. He says to us, Oh, I l-l-l-l-love that m-m-movie, man.* Everybody laughed at Old-man Perkins's version of Jimmy stuttering. *Then Shotgun says, You like that movie, Sam? What you like about that movie, Sam?*

I remember that Shotgun cat, Dallas said. *He was always startin up fights on the court.*

Yeah, Shotgun was a real mean cat, Old-man Perkins said. *Cops came in one day and slapped the cuffs on em, too. Grabbed him right in the middle of a fast break and pulled him out by his elbows. Ain't nobody seen em since.*

Damn, Slim said.

Guess you could figure out why they call him Shotgun, Johnson said.

So anyways, Perkins said. *He starts tellin Shotgun what he liked about the movie. He says, Ah man, I th-th-th-think that Jimmy ch-character c-c-could sure sh-sh-sh-sh-shoot the ball. Then he sits up in the bleachers with us cause he all happy we ain't talkin about nothin illegal. You remember all this, Johnson?*

Johnson nodded his head and laughed.

Perkins continued: *Sam says, M-makes em all d-day on that d-dirt c-court, that Jimmy. So Shotgun says, You kinda shoot like Jimmy yourself, Sam. I seen you out there knockin down jumpers between games when nobody be payin atten-tion. And Shotgun's one hell of a lie about all that, cause you all know that dude Jimmy couldn't throw a rock in the ocean if he was standin on a pier.* He pointed over at Jimmy, who was kneeling next to some homeless man now. *But it pumps him all up inside, see. He says back, F-f-for r-real, y-you s-s-s-s-s-s-*

seen me? Shotgun nods his head up and down like that's the straight truth what he said.

Old-man Perkins stared at the floor for a few seconds and shook his head. *From that point on everybody called Sam Jimmy. He liked it so much he crossed out his own name* Sam *on his office door with a black felt pen and wrote in* Jimmy *right above it.*

He was so hyped about his new name, Johnson said. He pulled his cap off again, scratched the top of his head, put the cap back on. *Next few days he was comin up to everybody, telling em to call him Jimmy.*

Still does, Slim said.

Ain't no Sam no more, Dreadlock Man said.

Plus he don't stutter none when he says Jimmy, Dallas said, his eyes all big like he'd stumbled onto something important. *I ain't never even heard him slip up on it once.*

That's gotta tell you somethin, Johnson said.

Hell yeah it does! Old-man Perkins said, looking right in Sticky's eyes. *Tells me something, all right. Tells me we gave that cat a whole new life when we changed his name.*

When Baby yelled out from the tub—her voice piercing like boiling water from a teapot, the late-night sound of two cats screeching outside the bedroom window—Sticky was standing next to the one window of their sixth-story apartment, holding a chunk of government cheese and trying to spit into the bed of a dirty red pickup parked below.

STICKKKYYYYYY! she screamed, over and over. *STICKKKYYYYY!*

It was the first time she'd said his name like that, just Sticky, without the *Boy* coming after, but it wasn't the first time she'd screamed out for him. Baby was always getting loud about some crazy thing: She screamed if there was a trail of roaches running around the fridge, or when the fat rat that lived in their bedroom peeked its ugly head out; she screamed at the TV if she was unhappy with something going down in her soap opera, or if a bill came that she couldn't possibly pay; and she always screamed when she needed a fix. *Oh, my God! Baby needs her medicine! Baby needs her medicine!*

The screaming was nothing new, and Sticky spit a few more globs of orange saliva down at the red pickup before he even thought about moving.

Even back then, at age seven, Sticky knew how he was about things. How if he spit once he might be stuck there all day. He'd definitely been down that road before, spitting at some target outside his window. An empty Burger King bag or some stray cat. There were days he'd be in the window spitting for hours, until there was no more spit in his mouth and his throat went sore. He'd slap at himself to stop, pull at his own hair, but nothing could slow his momentum. He had to keep on going until something clicked. Baby would eventually give up and close the curtain around him, saying: *I don't understand. What's wrong with you? Acting all weird all the time. Normal boys don't do things like this.*

And this time was no different. Sticky spit again and missed wide right.

STICKKKYYYY! Baby yelled.

He spit again and grazed the bumper. He knew he should at least check on Baby, but the pull to get one perfectly in the truck's bed was too strong.

He knew the next one would hit perfect, and when that missed, the next one.

STICKKKYYYY!

He knew one of the next five at least, cause he had a knack for stuff like that. He gathered saliva up and spit again: windshield. He glanced back at the half-closed bathroom door. Listened for his mom. Baby. She was screaming. He was trapped again, and he had no idea how to break free. He felt like crying, but he wouldn't let himself do that, either.

STICKKKYYYY!

Just *Sticky* she's yelling out. He leaned out the window this time for a better angle, felt the cool breeze against his face, held on to the wall for support and spit again: wide left. Just *Sticky*. Why just *Sticky*?

Spit again: left door handle. His mom. Baby.

Spit again: missed everything.

Just *Sticky*.

Spit again: missed.

Spit again: missed.

Spit again: missed.

When the screaming stopped, the apartment went silent. His mind went silent. His life went silent. There was only the sound of what was outside: the wind in his ears, a distant siren, the honk of an impatient car, the guy walking by holding his daughter's hand and whistling. His life went silent. Everything that was inside him went silent.

There was nothing left inside.

And outside, it was just the sound he made as he spit again.

We gotta think up somethin else for this kid to go by, Oldman Perkins said. He stared at Sticky and thought hard.

What about Little Bird? Dallas said. *He got that nice little jumper from the outside.*

Pistol Pete, Slim said, jumping off the bleachers, pointing at Sticky's socks. *Look at them limp-ass socks. Same as Pistol Pete use to wear.*

How about Eminem? Old-man Perkins said, and all the guys laughed.

Yeah, Johnson said. *Or maybe Little Norm. For Norm Nixon.* He laughed hard at his idea. Old-man Perkins, Dreadlock Man, Slim and Dallas looked at Johnson with straight faces, trying to make out the connection.

What's that mean? Slim finally said.

You know: Norm Nixon.

We know who goddamn Norm Nixon is, J, Old-man Perkins said. *But why you wanna call a white boy Little Norm?*

It just sound right, man. Plus Nixon was a light-skinned brother.

That's just plain stupid, J, Perkins said. *It don't make no kinda sense.*

Sticky grabbed his bag in his hand again. The frustration bubbling in his stomach was becoming too much. He clenched the straps as hard as he could and shouted: *I don't need some stupid name! I already got a name! My name's Sticky!*

Dallas shook his head. *Nah, kid, that ain't no kinda name.*

That just ain't natural, Perkins said.

I can't be callin nobody Sticky, Johnson said. *I could tell you that right now.*

Sticky sound like Dicky, make em sound like some little homo from West Hollywood, Dreadlock Man mumbled. He lifted his front tire and smiled gold teeth. Sometimes the guys couldn't quite make out what Dreadlock Man was trying to say, but half the time they laughed anyway.

Sticky stood up to leave. He started stomping down the bleachers, but Old-man Perkins reached out and snatched his forearm. *Where you goin, kid? I ain't done talkin to you.*

Sticky dropped his bag.

He been disrespectin all day, Johnson said.

Old-man Perkins glared right in Sticky's face. Dreadlock Man got off his bike, set it on the floor. The back wheel was still spinning.

Let em go, Slim said.

Nobody moved.

Let the kid go!

Jimmy's head whipped around from the homeless court. *H-h-hey!* he yelled out. He dropped the blanket he was holding and stood up.

Sticky ripped his arm from Old-man Perkins's grasp and jumped down from the bleachers. When he reached back to grab his bag, Johnson moved behind him so he couldn't go anywhere.

You gonna keep playin ball here, Old-man Perkins said, *then you gotta start showin some respect.*

Jimmy started walking over. *Wh-wh-what's the p-p-p-problem?*

Sticky slipped by Johnson and made his move for the door.

Johnson and Old-man Perkins threw their hands up at the same time and said, *Ain't no problem, Jimmy. There ain't no problem here.*

It's all good, Dallas said.

Sticky turned around and looked all the guys in their eyes, each one of them, first time he'd done that, and shouted: *I already got a name! My name's Sticky!*

Come on, kid, Dallas said. *It ain't gotta be like all that.* He walked toward Sticky, said: *Lemme buy you a hot dog or somethin. From the food cart.*

Let us buy you lunch, Perkins said, eyeing Jimmy.

There's a food cart right out front, Johnson said.

But Sticky shook them all off. His name was Sticky and nobody was going to call him anything different. Nobody. He turned away from them and walked out the gym door.

Whenever Sticky pictures himself walking into the bathroom that night, to check on Baby, his memory locks up. It stops him cold and spins him back around the other way. He remembers her yelling, *Sticky!* He remembers spitting over and over out the window at a truck. He remembers feeling something strange in his chest when her voice dropped off. The sudden quiet of the apartment making him nervous. But when he finally pulls himself away from the window and walks through the bathroom door, that's the part he can't get to. Everything crumbles in his head. It slips away. The images disappear. But he remembers her calling him Sticky. That's the last thing she said. *Sticky.* So that's who he is now, Sticky. That's what his mom called him. And he's never gonna answer to anything else.

It's Just Hoops

now. Ten guys, two buckets and a basketball.
Everything else shut off like the beats on Sticky's duct-taped
Walkman. No more Fat Chuck. No more two old cops in the
bleachers posing questions. No more sunlight-glare sneaking through the open doors. No more waiting on a sorry
sideline, watching. No more cleaning out a cut or coming up
with a birthday game plan.

No more thinking.

It's just Sticky and a game now. His game. Hoops. Ball.
Pickup. Fives. It's Sticky in his secret world, His haven. And
he's making plays that look like magic tricks. He's clowning
whoever's guarding him so bad the guys on the sideline are
on their knees, laughing. Whistling. Hooting and hollering.

What does it matter how the rest of the day goes? Getting home on time, swiping a bracelet, buying a bear? Sure, there's a time and a place for all that. Of course there is. Real life always comes whipping back around at you like a boomerang. But right now there's one last game to play. And Sticky's right here. In the zone. Flowing. Every shot ripping through a nylon net and playing the same song. And it's almost mean the way he does it, making people look so bad. So sad. So human. But this game is Sticky's drug. It's his stage. This court is Sticky's home. It's his hiding place. It's his church. And he's the one who gets to talk to God.

It took two games and forty-five minutes for Sticky to get back on the court, and even then he had to get a lucky break. TJ and Daway from the winner's squad had to hustle off to their jobs at Chevron, leaving two open slots. Dreadlock Man picked up Dante first and then yelled out: *Hey, yo, Stick! You wanna run with us? We need a point guard!*

Sticky hopped down from the bleachers, pulled off his Walkman and stuck it deep inside his bag. Then he ran out onto the court and the game began.

At first Boo was checking him, a long-limbed, light-skinned brother who plays for Santa Monica College. But that was no match. Boo face-guarded Sticky all around the court, nose to nose. He was oblivious to everything else. His breath like the bottom of a soup can. Eyes bugged like he just got tapped on the shoulder by the devil. Boo played defense so tight that if Sticky had run out of the gym midgame, to score a quick dog and Coke at the snack cart, Boo would have run right out of the gym with him.

Sticky handled Boo like a puppet. The game wasn't ten

minutes old and he had all four of his squad's points. That's when Rob called for the switch. *I got white boy,* he yelled out, and he shoved Boo out of the way.

Boo backed off and sought out Rob's man with his head down and his tail between his legs.

Rob checked ball and stuck a forearm in Sticky's chest, told him: *Forget all that, white boy.* Said: *You ain't scorin not one more bucket.*

But Sticky played deaf to all that. He dropped in two quick jumpers and asked Rob how bad it hurt to have a skinny white boy school him like that. Asked could he at least get a hand up in his face. Call for a double team. Anything so it wasn't so damn easy.

Rob kept his mouth shut and ran back the other way. But a man's shifty eyes are like a window to his busted-up ego.

The only thing that stopped Sticky's barrage on Rob was when Crazy Ray came stumbling out onto the court for a second time. He lifted himself off his piece of cardboard on court two, started launching into his typical tirade, pointing his finger at the guys in the game and walked right into a fast break. Three players trampled over him on their way to the basket.

New York, tripped up on the play, let the ball sail out of bounds and got up pissed. *Now that's some dangerous shit right there,* he yelled. He stood over Ray. *I ain't tryin to get hurt out here, now. I got my kids to feed.*

Ray lay flat on his back, holding his head.

Dallas had to come to his rescue again. He helped Ray up, wrapped an arm around his shoulder and pretty much dragged his ass back to the homeless court.

That's when Sticky first looked up and saw it on Rob's

214

face. The confusion. The helplessness. The look of a trapped animal. And he knew it might turn bad.

Sticky gets the pass out on the wing and sizes up. He swoops by on the drive, but Rob reaches out two tree-trunk arms and wraps up. Holds on tight so Sticky can't go anywhere.

Check ball, Sticky says.

Dante checks the rock up top. He flips it back in to Sticky and tells him: *Go to work, boy.*

Sticky stutter-steps and spins into the lane, but just as he's about to let it go, Rob swings his arm out and cracks Sticky in the face.

Sticky springs off the ground and throws an unpolished right hook that thuds against the side of Rob's neck.

Rob stumbles back, puts a hand to his neck. He looks back at Sticky, stunned.

The gym goes silent.

I'm sick a them fouls! Sticky yells, and he steps up and wings another wild right. Rob ducks it and wraps Sticky in a headlock. Slams him to the ground and pounces. He throws muted blows at the top of Sticky's head. He knees him in the ribs. Sticky reaches back and claws for Rob's face.

Dante and Trey move quick to pull Rob off.

We don't need no fightin in here, Old-man Perkins says as he steps in on the action too.

Dante gets Rob's arms locked up behind him and pulls him backward. He doesn't say a word.

Rob tries to yank free but can't. *I'm gonna kill you, white boy!* he yells.

215

Dallas pulls Sticky away and holds him by his elbows, tells him: *Be cool, kid. Be cool.*

Sticky rubs the back of his head. Touches the cut from earlier and checks his fingers. Blood.

Rob breaks away from Dante and charges. Pushes Dallas and Perkins out of the way and cracks Sticky in the ear with a solid right. He wrestles him to the ground again, holds Sticky's head still and fires quick jabs to the mouth and chin.

Sticky puts his hands up to try and muffle some of the blows.

Dante strides up from behind and pulls Rob off by his face. When Rob stands up, Dante busts him in the mouth twice with a quick left-right combination. He doesn't say a word. Rob's knees buckle and he spills back to the hardwood. Blood trickles out of a tear in his bottom lip.

Jimmy comes hustling out of the office. *W-wh-wh-what the h-h-hell's g-g-g-going on?* he yells. A couple guys turn and watch him marching toward the scuffle.

Rob touches at his lip gently and eyeballs the red on his fingertips. *This wasn't none a your business, D,* he says, and looks up at him. *Wasn't nothin to do with you.* He clenches his fists and goes to get up again, but Dante blasts him twice more, above the right eye and on the chin.

Rob crumbles to the hardwood again. Blood is oozing from above his eye now and branching down his face.

Just stay down, Trey says.

Rob turns and looks at Trey. He frowns and goes to get up again, but when he's on his feet Dante cracks him in the ribs with an uppercut and smacks him on the chin again. Rob spills back to the ground and with a dazed expression on his face looks up at Dante.

I said to stay down! Trey yells.

Don't get up no more, New York says.

Dante stands over Rob and doesn't say a word.

Dreadlock Man steps up and puts a hand on each of Rob's shoulders. *You done fightin, dawg,* he says. *You done.*

Jimmy walks right between Rob and Dante and yells at everybody: *G-g-g-get outta here!* He's so mad, spit flies from his mouth.

Nobody moves at first. They all stare as Jimmy looks down at a trail of blood splotches that dot-to-dot through the free-throw lane. He yells again: *G-g-get outta here, all y-y-y-y-y'all! G-g-g-g-get out!*

Everybody scatters.

Sticky goes over to the bleachers holding the bottom of his shirt against his cut. He unties his bag and checks inside for his twelve bucks: still there. Then Dallas and Dante lead him out of the gym. New York and Slim head over to the bleachers and grab their bags. Old-man Perkins tosses the ball toward the homeless court and heads for the door. Big Mac rumbles out shaking his head. Three newcomers who were waiting for next cruise out of the gym together.

Trey and Dreadlock Man help Rob to his feet. Johnson tosses him an old gray towel. Rob presses the towel against his lip, his eye. When he sees the towel is full of blood he punches the wall.

Trey leads Rob through the doors, out of the gym.

Outside, Trey digs the keys out of Rob's bag and unlocks the passenger side door. He pulls the door open and helps Rob in. As Trey walks around to the driver's side, Rob pulls down the sun visor and checks the damage in the mirror.

There is blood all over his face and running down the front of his sweaty shirt. He slams the heel of his hand against the dash.

Trey gets in and pushes the key in the ignition, starts the car up. He looks over his shoulder and backs up, flips it into drive and moves slowly through the parking lot.

The rest of the guys aren't so quick to leave. They huddle around Big Mac's Caddy under the blazing sun and replay the highlights of the fight.

You see the quick combo D laid on em? New York says. *He said bam bam and put Rob's ass right back on the ground.* New York whips his fists through the air to show what it looked like from his angle.

Used to box Golden Gloves, Old-man Perkins says. *I been telling people all along, that's the wrong brother to mess with.*

I heard that, Johnson says, and wipes the sweat off his forehead. *But, damn, you see how quick he threw them punches?*

Rob went down hard, too, New York says. *He said just like this. . . .* New York falls to the hot pavement cross-eyed, arms and legs spread, tongue hanging out of his mouth.

The guys all laugh.

Boo laughs hard and hits his palm against Big Mac's hood.

Big Mac's face goes serious and he stares Boo down. *I don't know about all that, dawg,* he says.

What? Boo says.

That's my car you just slapped, boy.

Oh, man, Boo says. *My bad.* And he takes a couple steps back from the Caddy.

What about Sticky, though? Old-man Perkins says. *White boy gots some heart, don't he?*

I knew it was comin, Johnson says. *You could see it brewin all day.*

Socked em right in the neck, too, Dreadlock Man says.

New York nods his head, says: *Socked em right in his neck.*

Bound to happen, Big Mac says, and pulls a sixty-four-ounce Gatorade from a cooler full of ice. *Rob always be tryin to mess with that white boy.*

He makes Rob look silly, New York says.

Ain't Stick's fault he can play, Perkins says. *Hell, I can't guard em either, but it don't mean I'm gonna foul em every time he touches the ball.*

Everybody nods their head in agreement.

Big Mac unscrews the cap to the Gatorade and tilts back for a long swig. When he's done he passes the bottle to Johnson and wipes his mouth on his shoulder. Johnson holds the bottle inches above his mouth and lets the cool green liquid spill down his dry throat. They all lean against different parked cars and talk some more about the fight. The air is warm and thick, humid. The afternoon sun is like fire against their shiny black skin.

Lincoln Rec Shuts

down at eight on most nights. That's what the
sign on the door says: HOURS OF OPERATION—10 AM TO 8
PM. But when closing time rolls around and the games are
still solid, Jimmy's pretty flexible. He'll handle other business first: tally up the books or post new gym announcements. Help pass out bused-in meals to the homeless. Some
nights he doesn't start kicking guys out until well after ten.

But today's a different situation.

It's a quarter past five and Jimmy's taping a cardboard
sign on the door that says in thick black marker: GYM
CLOSED UNTIL FURTHER NOTICE. When he gets the sign up
sturdy, he turns around and scans the parking lot. He spies
all the guys jiving around Big Mac's Caddy and shakes

his head, says under his breath: *B-b-bunch a .kn-kn-kn-knuckleheads.*

Then he slips back into the gym, shuts and locks the door behind him.

Dallas steps up to the snack cart and tells the Mexican vendor he wants three waters. When the vendor says how much, he pulls a soggy five out of his sock and hands it over. He takes the waters and his change and tells Sticky and Dante he has some chairs stashed behind the gym. Then he hands them both a bottle and leads them around the corner.

There are four plastic chairs stacked between some overgrown bushes and the back wall of the gym. Dallas pulls out three and brushes off the leaves and spiderwebs. Sets them up as far away from the big trash receptacles as he can get.

Sticky sits down and tosses his bag on the ice plant, listens to the buzzing Rob's fist has left in his ear. Runs a couple fingers over the three or four lumps on the back of his head.

Dante swallows some of his water and sets the bottle down next to his chair. He checks his right hand, shakes it out and checks again: there are a couple small nicks on his knuckles from Rob's teeth.

Sticky sets his water down and looks at Dante's hand too. *Your hand messed up?* he says.

Nah, Dante says, and he stretches out his fingers. *This is what you gonna deal with when you dot a man in his mouth.* He picks up his bag and pulls open the zipper. *I just hope that dude don't got AIDS.*

The tall gym has the sun blocked out, but the air is still warm and thick. It brings out the sour smell of the overflowing trash bins, where buzzing flies dip in and out in clusters. Dallas wipes beaded sweat off his forehead with the back of his hand. Dante pulls a towel from his bag and wipes down his face and arms. Through a seam in the buildings, Sticky watches all the businesspeople filing out of their big glass building. Loosening their ties and marching toward their shiny cars. Women fan themselves with magazines and everybody chirps their alarm before reaching for a door handle.

You did good today, young Stick, Dante says. *You stood up for yourself, and I'm proud of you.* He throws a playful little jab that glances off Sticky's chin. Sticky smiles and looks at the ground. He takes a sip of water and screws the cap back on.

Hit em right in his neck, Dallas says. *Last place somebody wants to get hit.*

That's right, Dante says.

An old homeless white woman staggers past pushing a cart. Her eyes half-closed and empty. Mouth moving without sound. She holds a hand out as she passes. When nobody makes the move to give up any change, she continues by, parks her cart near the trash receptacles and reaches two hands into the mess. As she digs around, her soiled jeans slip down her backside.

Ah, man, Sticky says, pointing at the spectacle.

Come on, lady, Dante says, and he puts a hand up to shield his eyes. *Get em up!*

The woman reaches back with one hand and pulls her jeans up. But when she goes back to the trash, they immediately start the slow slide back down.

Go on, old lady, Dante says, laughing. *Ain't nobody tryin to look at that old flea-bitten ass.*

She pulls two cans from the trash and sets them in her cart. Continues forward. Holds her jeans up with one hand and steers with the other. The sound of her rattling cart becomes more and more faint after she rounds the corner of the gym, out of sight.

She don't know no better, Dallas says. *That's all.* He reaches into his bag and pulls out some foil and a pack of Zigs. Opens the foil and drops a clump of brown weed into his palm. He rolls it, lines it and licks it. *She just tryin to get herself some cans,* he says.

Dante throws his towel back in his bag. He takes out a baseball cap and pulls it low over his forehead. *You can get a couple cans without showin everybody the goods, right?*

It ain't easy livin on the street, Dallas says.

No, I ain't arguin that, Dante says.

People get all weird, Sticky says. *Look at Crazy Ray.* He takes in another sip of water and swooshes it around in his mouth, spits it out. *Why you always helpin that old dude out, Dallas?*

Dallas shrugs his shoulders and pulls out a yellow lighter. He flicks the fire on, cups his free hand to block the wind and lights the joint. He sucks in deep and passes to Dante.

Dante pulls in a drag, holds the smoke in long and then lets it slip out over his lips.

Sticky stares at all the years of graffiti spray-painted up and down the back wall of the gym. Ten years of gang names, he thinks. Fifteen. All the different colors on top of each other turning the white wall brown. Anything over six months old has been crossed out or covered up by something new. And then Rob's face flashes though his mind. The glimpse he got of Rob's expression through the flurry of punches coming at the back of his head, his face. And to get Rob out of his mind he thinks back on all those hours he spent painting over graffiti walls just like this one when he did his community service. The burn in his shoulders, the ache in his feet. It didn't sound so bad when the judge gave his ruling: 100 hours of community service instead of jail time. But those ten-hour Saturdays were no joke. Painting up and down, side to side, standing on ladders all day, the brush turning so heavy in his hand he could hardly keep it above his head.

He reaches down to untie his laces. When loose laces don't feel quite right he ties up and unties again. Turns a little to the side so Dante and Dallas won't recognize his process. Ties up and unties.

Ties up and unties.

Ties up and unties.

Ties up and unties.

Dante passes back to Dallas and pulls a clean shirt out of his bag. He peels off his sweaty shirt and says: *It's survival of the fittest out here, man. Too many people.* He slips the clean shirt over his muscled-up black shoulders. Takes his shoes and socks off and slides his feet into Nike sandals.

You say you wanna make it playin ball, right? Dante says. *And you good, Stick. I ain't gonna take nothin away, your game is real tight. But it's more than that. Every one a these guys wanted to make it playin ball. What makes you any different? What separates you?*

Sticky nods his head.

Look at Dallas here, Dante says. *How much you wanna bet he thought he was gonna make it too. And you seen his broke game.*

Now wait a minute, D, Dallas says, waving his hand in the air and laughing. *I didn't play no overseas like you, but I gets mine out there. You know that.*

I'm playin, money. You all right. Dante takes the joint, lights and sucks in. He holds the hit in his lungs and passes to Dallas. Blows out. *I'm just lettin you know, Stick, you can't back down from nobody on the court. I used to fight three or four times a week when I was comin up. And I was skinny, too. Like you. Sometimes cats would beat my ass, man. I'm not gonna lie. But them same cats found out quick, if anybody ever came at me, there was definitely gonna be some fightin.*

Sticky nods his head.

That fight with Rob, Dante says. *I'm gonna tell you right now, there's gonna be more where that came from.*

Especially cause you white, Dallas says. *Brothers don't like no white boy makin em look bad playin ball.*

That's right, Dante says.

Damn, Dallas says, fumbling what's left of his joint. *That's the only stuff I got.* He gets on his hands and knees and digs through the ice plant looking for it.

Look at you, man, Dante says. *Like a damn crackhead.* He and Sticky both laugh.

Dallas finds the joint and sits back in his chair. He flicks off a little mud hanging from the tip and pulls a roach clip from his bag. *What?* he says, looking up at Sticky and Dante. *I don't even care.* He lights up and pulls in as much smoke as he can get.

225

Dante reaches into his bag and pulls out his watch. When Sticky sees the watch a wave of panic rushes over him and he straightens up quick in his chair. *D, what time you got?*

Almost six, Dante says. *And, that's right, Stick, you still ain't done nothin about no birthday gift.*

Whose birthday? Dallas says.

His old lady's, Dante says.

Stick, you messin up, man. Dallas laughs and tosses the lighter back in his bag.

Sticky stands up, pulls his Walkman out of his bag and puts the phones around his neck. *I gotta go,* he says. *I gotta jog home right now.*

Don't sweat it, Dante says. *I'll give you a ride.* He leans back in his chair. *But chill a minute. Sit down. Let's discuss what options you got.*

How much time's left? Dallas says.

Until she gets off work at nine, Sticky says.

How long you been together? Dante says.

Over six months. I got it handled, though.

What you got handled, boy? Dante says.

I'm swipin this bracelet from Macy's.

Macy's? Dallas says. *You know department stores got all kinda security, right?*

Sticky nods.

I'm just sayin, Dallas says, *my dawg just got busted at a department store. He was tryin to make off with a toaster oven and security tackled him just as he was steppin into the parking lot.*

I hear you, Sticky says. *But I got a plan.*

Dallas rolls his eyes and laughs. *Oh, I see, Stick, you got a plan.*

While Sticky and Dallas go back and forth a little, Dante leans forward in his chair straight-faced and kicks Sticky in his leg, tells him: *Yo, it's me, I might mess around and rob somebody.*

What? Sticky says.

Back in my day I'd have probably hunted down some rich cat, stuck a knife to his throat and told him to give me his wallet.

You crazy, Dallas says. *Sticky don't know nothin about muggin nobody. He ain't got no experience.*

I ain't sayin for him to do it, Dante says. *I'm just sayin what I'd do. If I had some cash I'd figure I could buy the bracelet and take my girl out to a nice little dinner somewhere. Italian. And some cats, man, they got enough extra cash that they could fund a little somethin like that.*

Nah, Sticky says. *I wouldn't wanna rob somebody. That ain't right. Stores, man, they don't even know the difference, but robbin a person ain't right.*

What's the difference between stealin from a store and stealin from some rich cat? Dante says. *Huh, Stick? Explain your logic behind that last statement.*

Sticky looks up at Dante and thinks hard about it for a minute. He says: *Cause stealin from a store isn't as bad.*

But why? Dante says. *I want to hear your reasoning.*

I don't know, Sticky says. *It just isn't.*

Damn, boy, Dante says, shoving his shoes and socks in his bag. *You ain't listened to a word I said since I met you.*

Yeah, I have, Sticky says.

You heard me talkin, but was you listenin to my words?

Sticky looks at Dante, but he keeps his mouth closed this time. He can tell Dante's getting frustrated, and that's the last thing he wants. He thinks about the question again: What's the difference between stealing from a store and stealing from some rich guy? Dante must think it's the same thing, but why? It doesn't make any sense.

Dallas sips his water quietly, glances back and forth between Sticky and Dante.

Dante picks up a stick and lobs it against the back of the gym, says: *I'm not sayin for you to do the shit. In fact, I'll tell you this right now, Stick: Don't do it. For real. It ain't in your nature. But just hear me out for a minute. No matter how you look at it, this ain't no righteous world. It just ain't. I mean, there's no debatin about that. The laws we operate under are set up by those who have everything, in order to protect themselves from those who have nothing. That makes sense, right? Now, let's take me for example. When I was comin up on these same Westside streets, I was one of the ones who had nothing. Just the same as you. So it was up to me to find ways to acquire the basic things that other people already had. That was my reality, and I understood the situation. Now, when you don't got enough to live an adequate life you can do one of two things: either you can sit there and accept your fate, or you can do somethin about it.* He shakes his head and leans back in his chair. *I chose to do somethin about it.*

I know what you sayin, D, Sticky says.

No, Stick, you don't know nothin about what I'm sayin. That's the problem. You ignorant to your own circumstances.

Dante reaches down and grabs a couple stones off the

ground. *See that wall in front a you?* he says. *In America, life's like a race to that wall. That's the way I see it.* He sets the first stone less than a foot from the wall, points and says: *If you born white and got money then you start the race way up here. Ahead of everybody. These cats got nice clothes and eat at nice restaurants. Their parents send em to private high schools and expensive colleges so they can one day be in a position to get the best jobs. And when they make it they'll do for their kids just like their parents did for them. It's a cycle.*

Dante stares at Sticky. He waits for it to sink in for a bit and then sets the second stone a couple feet behind the first. *But say you ain't white and you ain't rich. Say you poor and black. Or you Mexican. Puerto Rican. Well, guess what? You don't get to go to that nice private high school, that expensive college. In fact, you may not even have enough food to eat a balanced meal every night. You suffer from a lack of nutrition and that ain't no good for a young mind. In this case you startin the race of life way back here.* He points to the second stone. *Only a fool would think someone who starts here has the same opportunities as cats startin at the first stone.*

Sticky feels Dante's eyes burning through the side of his face, but he doesn't look up. He just stays staring at the two stones and their different distances from the wall.

Now I didn't make all this stuff up, Dante says. *This life-being-a-race thing. America did. But I sure as hell gotta deal with it, don't I?*

God knows it, Dallas says, nodding his head. *We all gotta deal with it.*

And let me tell you something. If you some scrubby white boy who's been moved in and out of different foster homes since you was little, then you off the charts, boy. Dante physically lifts Sticky's face up to his so he can look in his eyes. *How many foster homes you been in?*

Sticky looks Dante in the eyes but doesn't say anything.

Answer me, boy. How many houses?

Four.

That means three of em, plus your real momma, didn't want your ass no more. They straight up gave you away like you wasn't nothin. I gotta be real with you, brother. I gotta tell it like it is cause that's my *nature. All these people, Stick, they decided you wasn't worth a damn thing. They decided you was a nothing. A zero. Add to the fact you got that mental thing, where you gotta do stupid stuff over and over and over. . . .* (Dante snatches up another stone and puts it even further back. Points at it. Moves Sticky's face so he has to look at it) *. . . and fuck it, boy, you startin out way back here. You three stones back.*

Sticky stares down at that third stone. He refuses to look up. He's hearing what Dante's saying, about people giving him back, about the stuff he does over and over, but he doesn't want to think about it. That's the last thing he wants to think about. The only thing he wants to think about right now is hurrying home and getting ready. Picking out some gear to wear and catching the bus. Getting the bracelet and the bear and meeting up with Anh-thu. He only wants to think about the next thing he has to do. The next hour. The next day maybe. But all this other stuff, what Dante is talking about, this is exactly the kind of thing he's tried to put out of his mind all his life.

Dallas nods his head, staring at the three stones. He

230

looks up at Dante, glances at Sticky and then looks down at the stones again.

Dante turns Sticky's face back to his, digs into his chest with crazy eyes and tells him: *You the nigger, too, boy*.

Sticky jerks his chin out of Dante's grasp and goes back to the third stone. He concentrates on the way it looks. How it's small and chipped on the side facing him. How it's caked with dirt and a couple blades of dead grass. He realizes that his phones are unplugged from his tape deck and he reaches down to connect them back up. When they don't snap back in with the perfect pop, he goes to do it over again but stops himself short. He goes back to that third stone, stares at it. The chip on the side. The brown blades of grass. He battles the urge to pull the plug back out and snap it in right. He fights with everything he has to leave it alone. To leave it the way it is.

And we supposed to worry about rules? Dante says. *What rules? The ones set up to keep us way back here?*

Sticky shifts in his chair and looks up at Dante, he opens his mouth to say something but decides to keep it put away. He shifts in his chair again and then finally breaks down: he unplugs the phones and plugs them back in. He unplugs and plugs back in.

Unplugs and plugs back in.

Unplugs and plugs back in.

Unplugs and plugs back in.

Dallas sits back in his chair, watching Sticky. He folds his arms up and shakes his head.

Sticky unplugs and plugs back in.

Unplugs and plugs back in.

Unplugs and plugs back in.

Dante picks up all three stones and tosses them against the gym wall. He picks up his bag, zips it closed and fingers the edge of the zipper. *I ain't gotta do that stuff now,* he says. *I played ball overseas and made some money. I invested. I'm successful now. But when I was comin up, man, I'm gonna tell you right now: I did what I had to do.*

When the popping sound finally sounds perfect, Sticky stops unplugging and hangs his head.

All three of them remain quiet for the next few minutes. There's only the hum of the hundreds of cars starting and stopping on the nearby highway. Dante stares at Sticky, pulls in a few deep breaths to slow himself down. He shakes his head at all this stuff he's just said. Maybe he shouldn't have done it. Maybe he shouldn't have launched into all that. It wasn't the time or place. And he doesn't want Sticky to rob anybody. Definitely doesn't want that. He just wants him to see the world for what it is. For how it works. Because even though Sticky's white and he's black, there are obvious similarities: the passion for playing ball, the grace with the rock, the way every move on the court comes from some inherent instinct. He looks at Sticky and he knows basketball is all he has. A game. A sport. He knows there's nobody looking out for him. Nobody talking to him about life or waiting for him to come home at night. Sticky's completely alone. Just like he was when he was a kid. Sometimes just looking at Sticky brings back painful things about his own past. Things he thought he'd long since put away.

The stones are gone, but Sticky's still staring at the ground where they were. Where Dante had put them. Everything he has just heard, all the words and phrases out of Dante's mouth, all the important things he was meant to learn, rattle around in his head. But all of it messes up when he tries to come up with meaning. He knows he can't rob anybody. He knows that's something he wouldn't be able to do. But he wishes he could. He wishes he could bum rush some business dude and bring the wallet back to Dante for proof. Because even though what Dante has said is not the kind of stuff he wants to think about, he knows Dante said it because he cares. And the fact that Dante cares about him is incredibly important. There may not be anything more important. There's a low whistle in Sticky's ear now. And it's sore. Really sore. He can't stop touching his fingers against the part that hurts worst. The cartilage just above the ear-lobe. He flips daydream channels to the way it would go down if he could do it: putting a knife to some rich dude's neck, snatching his wallet, shoving him down to the pavement and taking off running.

It's the truth, Dallas says, staring at the ground. He nods his head and wipes a hand down his face, *It's the truth what he's sayin.*

Dante and Sticky look at Dallas.

Dallas brings his eyes up and stares at Sticky. He scratches his head and chuckles a little to himself, says: *That's my pops, man.*

Who? Sticky says.

Crazy Ray, Dallas says. *From the gym. That's my daddy.*

Sticky returns Dallas's stare but doesn't say anything more.

Dante nods his head and looks at the side of Dallas's face. *I know it is,* he says.

Wong and Rolando,

two of Sticky's foster bros, are at the TV playing Madden. Wong is fifteen and Korean; he walks around the neighborhood all day in thick army fatigues, clutching a water gun and pretending it's the real thing. Rolando is fourteen and black, but he looks like he's twenty and Samoan. One of his eyes is set a little lower than the other, and there's a two-nickel gap between his front two teeth, but nobody ever mentions these things. Both stop arguing when Sticky walks through the door.

Hey, Stick, Wong says.

Sticky gives him a what's up with his head.

Yo, you been ballin? Rolando says.

Yup.

Wong pauses the game and walks over to the kitchen counter, grabs a letter and hands it over. *This came for you today,* he says. *I think it's for college.*

Sticky peeps the return address: UNIVERSITY OF SOUTHERN CALIFORNIA TROJANS. He rips it open and reads the words: it says one of their scouts saw him play against Dominguez Hills. Says they liked his skills. Says they wanted to contact him early to let him know they're extremely interested in recruiting him. Says if he fills out the enclosed questionnaire and sends it back, that they'll be in touch real soon about having him as a guest at one of their home games next season. It's signed by the head coach.

Sticky folds the letter up and shoves it back in the envelope. Coach Reynolds told him the letters might start rolling in soon. Do work in the play-offs and college coaches will track you down. He said by the time Sticky's a senior it will be like a circus. Calls at all hours of the night. Coaches knocking on his door. Letters from prestigious alumni and offers to host him on recruiting trips. But all that was just talk. It was nothing like this. Nothing like having that first letter from a college right there in your hands.

What they said? Rolando says. *They gonna give you a scholarship or what?*

That's what they want, Sticky says, and he tosses the letter in his bag like it's no big deal. *But I'm waitin to see what UCLA says. And all them Big Ten schools. The ACC.*

I'd go to Duke, Rolando says. *All the best basketball players go to Duke.*

Yeah, Duke's all right, Sticky says.

Hey, what happened to your face? Wong says.

235

Nothin, Sticky says. *Just playin ball.*

Rolando starts the game back up while Wong is still standing by Sticky. He maneuvers his linebacker through Wong's offensive line and crushes his quarterback. *That's right, boy!* he yells. *Fifteen-yard loss.*

Wong sprints back around the table and grabs his joystick, finds his quarterback lying motionless on the turf. *What the hell you doin?* he yells. *I wasn't ready.*

You the one ain't been playin by the rules, Rolando says, laughing.

I am playing by the rules, Wong says. *You just mad cause I'm beating your ass three games in a row.*

Rolando throws his joystick to the side and tackles Wong. They wrestle around on the dirty rug, laughing and talking trash. Knocking things over with erratic arms and legs.

Sticky cruises into the bathroom and shuts the door. When he flips the light on, roaches scurry back into corners of the room. Underneath the cracked linoleum or behind somebody's tossed-to-the-side towel. He turns the shower on and rips off his gear. Sets everything on top of the cracked toilet seat. He steps in with a foot and when it doesn't feel right, steps back out. He thinks about what Dante just said. Reaches in to touch the cool water with his hand and wonders if everybody knows. If everybody sees it. And if so, do they look at him like he's some kind of freak?

I ain't doin that no more, he says under his breath, and he steps back in the shower. And even though it feels all messed up the way he went in, he stays put. Even though just standing there feels completely wrong, totally unbalanced, he won't let himself move. He clenches up his fists and fights the urge to do it over. Grabs for the soap and forces his head under the water. But it's only a couple seconds before he gives in and backs everything up. He puts the soap down and steps a drenched foot back out of the shower. He drops his head as he steps in and out again, tells himself he's gonna fix this about himself. Starting tomorrow he's gonna practice at doing things regular. Doing things like a normal person. But for now he lets himself do what he's gotta do. He steps a foot in the shower and then steps back out. Tomorrow he's gonna start fresh. Change his ways. Be more normal.

He steps a foot in the shower and steps back out.

Steps in, steps out.

Steps in, steps out.

Steps in, steps out.

It's a shade past seven when Sticky finally finishes his shower. He hops out and stands in front of the mirror toweling off. Moves his face in close to get a good look at his cut. It's still open a little, but it's not that bad. Definitely doesn't need stitches like Fat Chuck said. He fingers the lumps on the back of his head. Listens to the hollow fuzz filling his sore and bright red ear.

While brushing his teeth, Sticky stares at his face as a whole. His eyes, ears, lips, cheeks, chin. His color. He looks at the way everything comes together. Anh-thu says he has a beautiful face. She says a lot of the girls think that about him. But why? he wonders. He imagines Dante looking at this face when he was talking about the stones. Telling him how nobody wants him. This face. Telling him how everybody keeps giving him back. Dropping him back off cause he's nothing. This face. These dark eyes. These cheekbones. These lips. At some point in their life, he thinks, maybe everybody looks at their face like this. Wishes they could change one or two things. But has anybody ever experienced this situation? Feeling that none of it makes sense? Cause he's looking closely at his face, closer than he ever has before, and he doesn't recognize himself. He doesn't see himself in himself. This isn't the Sticky he's always imagined in his head. It's a picture of somebody else. A mask. Something off a TV show. He doesn't know this face. It's a complete stranger. And the whole thing freaks him out to the point that he has to look away.

He finishes brushing his teeth by staring at a big hole in the wall. Thinking of nothing. He stares at the hole he always stares at instead of looking in the mirror. An ex–foster brother made it a while back. He locked himself in the bathroom one night for almost two hours and clawed at his own skin. Ripped down the moldy shower curtain. Put a fist through the wall. The cops had to break the door down to finally get him out. It was Sticky's first week in the house, and he didn't ask any questions. Nobody offered up any info on their own, either. Not even a few days later, after the kid was shipped back to wherever he came from and a new kid was brought in to take his place.

Sticky walks into the hall and pulls out his bag full of gear from the closet. He always keeps his clothes stuffed in a bag now. Georgia offered him a couple shelves in one of the bedrooms, but Sticky told her he wanted to stick with the bag. Call it superstition or reverse psychology or whatever you want, but he's always ready for the next time somebody tells him it's time to move again.

He pulls out some boxers and socks, the fresh retro Nike Airs he swiped last week from a shoe shop in Culver City. He pulls out some baggy jeans and a wife-beater and then puts everything on in a particular order: first the drawers and the jeans, second the wife-beater, third the socks. He goes to one knee and pulls on the left Nike first, makes loose laces look perfect, and then does the same deal with the right. He grabs his bag and rolls into his brothers' bedroom, pulls open a drawer and snatches Rolando's favorite shirt. Light blue button-up with a collar. He sticks the shirt in his bag on top of his ball and his letter and then zips up.

Out in the living room, Wong and Rolando are still battling on the video-game football field. And little Julia has come back from class. She's sitting on the far end of the couch reading the funny pages. Julia started out as a temporary in the house. Way back before Sticky arrived. A temporary is a kid who's scheduled to stay in the system only a couple months or so on paper, until a mom or dad can get a handle on things financially or a group of counselors working the case give the go-ahead. But like so many other temporaries, Julia's two months has turned into two years and now nobody mentions her real parents anymore. Including Julia. But Sticky has spotted her a couple times, writing long letters in the middle of the night on the back of old homework assignments.

Julia spends her summer days in a science class for eighth graders, even though she's only eleven.

What up, Jules? Sticky says, and pats the top of her shiny black hair.

When she turns around her face lights up. *Sticky,* she says, all long and drawn out, and slugs him in the arm.

You have fun in class today? Sticky says.

Yeah, she says. *I learned how astronauts use this stuff called polymers in space that they grow food in,* Julia says. *It absorbs four hundred and eight times more water than dirt.*

Say what? Sticky says as he cruises into the kitchen. *They can grow stuff up in space?*

Wong stands up and leans into his long pass downfield. Rolando speed-taps his Run button to catch up. When the receiver drops the pass, they both yell out at the same time: *Ahhhhh!*

Rolando shoves Wong. *You can't mess with my DB's, man.*

You just lucky, Wong says.

Julia follows Sticky into the kitchen and leans against the overflowing trash. *They can grow all kinds of food up there,* she says. *They gotta eat somethin, you know.*

Sticky opens the cupboard and reaches in for the big bag of granola. He digs his hand in and grabs a fistful. *You just like Annie,* he says, chomping through a mouthful and swallowing, reaching into the bag for more. *She's always learnin about stuff like that.* He opens the drawer next to him and sifts through the silverware. Grabs hold of an old steak knife and flips it around in his fingers. He gives a quick peek over his shoulder and when he sees Julia's not paying attention, he slips it into his pocket on the sly.

Julia reaches her hand in the granola and takes out a handful of her own. She crunches through a mouthful and swallows, looks up at Sticky and smiles little kid teeth.

I don't know why, Sticky says, *but I just can't listen that good when I'm sittin in a classroom.* He palms his hand on Julia's head and shakes it around. *But you and Annie got it totally different. You all actually like learnin that stuff.*

When we gonna go shoot baskets? Julia says as she digs her hand in for more granola.

I can't tonight, Jules, Sticky says. *It's Annie's birthday.*

It's Annie's birthday?

Yeah. I'm about to go meet her right now. Sticky puts the granola away and scoops up his bag.

I wish I could tell her happy birthday, Julia says.

Maybe she'll swing by this weekend, Sticky says. *And then you could tell her.*

Yeah, yeah. Tell her, please? I'll get her a present and everything. Please? Please?

OK, I'll tell her. I promise. Sticky picks up his bag. *I gotta break, Jules. We'll shoot some hoops tomorrow, all right?*

Julia leans forward and hugs Sticky. She wraps her skinny arms around him and squeezes tight. *Bye, Sticky,* she says.

Sticky goes stiff in her arms. He's never been good at hugs. Even with Anh-thu. The feel of somebody's body next to his is always awkward. When she lets go he pats her on the head a couple times.

Outside, the sun is finally losing its grip on the day. It sits low in the sky like a giant orange ball, resting just above some stores on a patch of clouds. As Sticky walks down his street he stares at it, amazed at how big it seems. It's as if you could just reach out and snatch it in your hand, start dribbling it around the block or spin it on your finger. The air's cooled down a bit, too. The pleasant breeze smells like salt and seaweed and the exhaust of cars all mixed up.

Sticky cruises a couple blocks and sits down on his busstop bench next to a black lady dressed in a Ralphs uniform. He sets his bag down. She looks over at him and shakes her head, glances down at her watch and tells him: *Number three bus was supposed to be here ten minutes ago.*

Yeah? Sticky says.

Yeah, the lady says. *This damn bus driver is ten minutes late every single day. Like clockwork. But don't go tryin to work your schedule around him bein ten minutes late, now. Nah, you try to coordinate your schedule and that's the one day he comes on time. Trust me.*

Sticky laughs with her a little and fumbles with the zipper on his bag. He reaches past Rolando's shirt and his ball and pulls out the letter from USC. The lady says something else, about how hot it was today or how her air-conditioning unit doesn't pump out any cool air anymore, and Sticky nods his head at her. Two cars almost smack into each other in the nearby intersection during a yellow light. They both slam their horns and flip each other off. They drive around each other, cursing out of rolled-down windows, and then continue on their way. A group of Mexicans walks by with shovels on their shoulders, shirts soaked with sweat. Dirt-covered work boots. They laugh and say things back and forth in Spanish.

Sticky holds the envelope in his hands and stares at the

return address: UNIVERSITY OF SOUTHERN CALIFORNIA TRO-JANS. It's so official with the school name on the envelope like that. It makes it seem totally legit. Important.

He smiles at the lady, who is pointing at her watch again and shaking her head. Then he pulls the letter out of the envelope and unfolds it in his lap. He reads it again.

In the Heart

of Santa Monica, the beautiful people come out at night. They step out of fancy rides in hip gear, stroll into trendy clubs with no name above the door. You see dudes in black leather jackets, black leather pants, black leather boots. Surfers in sandals wearing a curvy blond girlfriend around their waist. Spiky-haired hipsters wearing cool throwback shirts plucked off a retro rack in some pseudo-thrift shop on Melrose. You see ladies in short skirts and backless tops. Tight jeans. Pointy high heels. Cowboy hats. You see some forty-year-old dude escorting a twenty-year-old model-type into some bar off Second Street. See a little white honey holding a big black cat's hand, checking out of one club and rolling into another two doors down. See two six-foot

French-looking ladies stepping out of a stretch limo and walking hand in hand into some crowded café. Smoking long fancy cigarettes and giggling at a crowd of gawking guys.

It's a little before eight and a bright moon has nudged the sun completely offstage. The air is warm and full of salt. Sticky watches all the different people from a patch of grass outside Sanwa Bank on Colorado. He takes big bites of the Hostess Cup Cake he swiped when he got off the bus and chews with his mouth slightly open.

Some suit guy walks past him to the ATM, slips his card in the mouth of the machine. Sticky wads up his wrapper and holds it in his hand, watches the guy from behind: punching in numbers and waiting, pulling out seven or eight twenties and shoving them deep in his wallet. The guy snatches his receipt and heads off toward a nearby bar.

Sticky reaches in his bag and pulls out his own stash of cash. Counts out the bills in his hand over and over. Slowly. Straightens out each buck and sets it on the grass in front of him. Licks a finger and peels off the next bill.

He does this repeatedly, but each time the total remains the same: twelve bucks.

Anh-thu stands next to Sergio as he totals up the sales from her drawer. He does the numbers, but she's staring across the store at a family. A young black man holding a baby on his shoulders, his wife's arm wrapped snugly around his back. They stop at the T-shirt rack and while the dude sifts through the extra-large section, his wife makes faces at their baby and pulls at its toes. The baby laughs.

Anh-thu feels her stomach tighten up as she stares. She feels the anxiety of her and Sticky's meeting climbing into her lungs, making it tough to get a deep breath. She turns her eyes away from the family and goes back to Sergio's counting.

When everything comes up even, Sergio points over to the broom. *Just the dressing rooms and the back, Annie,* he says. *Don't worry about the store floor, I wanna get you out of here a little early for your birthday.*

Anh-thu forces a smile and grabs the broom. As she walks over to the dressing rooms, she scans the store. Her tired legs carry her across the floor while her green eyes sweep over every detail in the store. The place is almost empty now—aside from the black family, a couple kids from the valley rifling through what's left of the half-off table, a guy with a bad flattop holding up a pair of baggy jeans and sizing himself up in the mirror—but the store looks like a tornado has just rumbled through. Shirts are scattered everywhere, pants are hanging from the jacket rack, sweatshirts are turned inside out and lying on top of the hat table. For the girls on the floor the real work starts not when Sergio flips the OPEN sign on in the morning, but when he cuts it off at the end of the day.

Julie is in the middle of the store sorting out a pile of swim trunks that somehow ended up on the floor by the jackets. She's folding and stacking according to size. Laura is at the far register ringing up an elderly guy. She smiles at the old-timer as she takes his credit card. She swipes it through and they both stand there waiting.

Anh-thu pushes open the door to the first dressing room

and thinks about Sticky again. How he'll act if she tells him how late she is. She runs through the different scenarios as she sweeps pins, tiny threads, ripped-off tags and dust into a little pile. As she reaches down and pushes the pile over the plastic lip of the dustpan.

Sticky watches a couple ladies stick their cards into the ATM one at a time. The first has long pasty legs shooting out of short khaki shorts. The second is shorter and heavier and is wearing a tacky pink skirt. They both have fake blond hair with awful dark roots. They stand next to each other and talk in voices so loud that everyone on the block knows their business.

Sticky's watching these ladies, but he's brainstorming about hoops. He figures if Lincoln Rec is shut down tomorrow, because of the fight, he might have to suck it up and ball with those scrubs on Twentieth and Pico. On that beat-up outdoor court with chain nets. Or maybe he could track down his school custodian, Manuel. Ask him to leave the back door of the gym open a crack. If he had the gym to himself all night he'd flip on the court spotlights and make like the dark bleachers were filled with screaming fans. Or maybe he'd smuggle in the new OutKast CD and slip it into the gym's beat-up old boom box. He'd shoot five hundred jumpers while jamming to his beats. A thousand jumpers. And after that he'd get in a little ball handling work. Do some passing drills off the wall. It's time to buckle down, he thinks. Time to get his game right, with that camp only a couple weeks away. And the mere idea of the camp hypes him up even more. Matter of fact, he'll shoot *more* than a thousand jumpers. He'll keep on shooting and shooting until his arms feel like they're gonna fall off. Dribble so many dribbles the ball will turn into an extension of his hand. Run home so hard from the gym that the muscles in his legs will feel like they're catching fire. He's gotta go into that camp with every part of his game clicking. Everything perfect. Dante says the most important hours of hoops you'll ever spend are the hours you spend alone.

Sticky decides only a few things really matter to him right now: his rhythm on the court, his performance at the camp, the college coaches who will be watching, the letter from USC in his bag, and Annie's birthday. Everything else is secondary, he thinks. Everything else is a million miles away.

As Anh-thu is diligently sweeping through the back of the store, Laura comes walking up to her with a brown paper bag. She hands it over and winks.

What's this? Anh-thu says, leaning the broom against the wall.

Just somethin I thought you might need, Laura says. *Don't open it here, though. Serious. Wait until you get off.*

OK, Anh-thu says, confused.

Trust me, girl. I been there.

OK.

And no matter what, Laura says, *know that I'm totally here for you.* Anh-thu nods her head. Laura gives her a long hug and tells her in her ear: *Later on tonight, it doesn't matter what time, call me. OK?*

I will, Anh-thu says back.

After Laura takes off, Anh-thu stares at the brown paper

bag in her hands, folded over at the top. She presses through the outside and determines it's a box of some kind. But a box of what? And is it for her birthday? Because Laura's already given her the picture frame. *Strange,* she thinks, setting the bag on top of a shirt bin and grabbing for the broom.

She begins sweeping again, though she can't help continually glancing over at the bag. What could be inside? What did Laura mean when she said she's been there? Been where? She rolls a rack of returned jeans to the side so she can sweep underneath, and a tiny spider scurries across the floor. Anhthu lunges back and smacks at it with the broom. She picks it up with a paper towel, throws it in the trash and continues with her sweeping.

A pack of tourists walks up to the ATM, talking all loud in a foreign language. Sticky can't figure out what language it is, but he knows it's not English. One guy goes to the machine at a time while the group hangs back. Each guy pulls out a wad of twenties from the slot and shoves it deep in his pocket. When all of them have had a turn at the ATM, and they're armed with enough money for their big night out in Santa Monica, they move quickly down the street as a group, like a pack of excited dogs. They hook around the big parking structure and head toward the Third Street Promenade. Even when they're completely out of his sight, little pieces of their loud language still funnel back to Sticky's ears.

A cab rolls to a stop in front of Sticky and a light-skinned black dude hops out of the back. He hands over some money to the driver and slams the door shut. The cab rolls off, and the guy heads for the ATM.

Sticky watches this guy and for some reason he thinks back on the incident with Fat Chuck. The way Chuck seemed cool at first, like he was trying to help, and then all of a sudden tried some crazy shit. Sticky feels himself getting pissed all over again. He should have kicked Chuck in his teeth, man. Blasted him with a heel to the back of the head. Booted him in the ribs over and over until he couldn't breathe. And Sticky wonders why he ran off to tell all the guys. Why didn't he just handle business on his own? Like Dante told him to. Like he did with Rob. And Dante's right about what he said. About him taking care of himself. Dante's right about a lot of things.

He leans his head back on his bag and stares up into the sky. He stares at the bright moon and watches his fight with Rob play out in his head. The way he leaped up off the hardwood and clocked Rob in the neck. The way Rob tackled him to the ground. Everything happening so fast, like when you're on some pitch-black roller coaster at Disneyland. Space Mountain. Everything flashing by before you even know what's happening. All you have time to feel is the exhilaration, the twists and turns, your heart climbing into your throat. And then suddenly it's over.

Sticky's eyes slide shut.

An old woman screaming at no one pulls Sticky out of his dreams. He wakes up as Dante's laying out that last stone. The third one. Look how far away he is from the wall. Look. He's the bottom of the barrel, man. The last rung on the ladder. He wakes up and acknowledges what Dante is explaining to him. That people keep giving him away. That they keep sending him back. But then Sticky sees himself playing

250

ball. Dominating guys twice his age, twice his size. He sees his grace on the court. His beauty. His secret refuge. Those foster parents never saw him play ball, he thinks. They never saw him on the wing with the rock in his hands. Something incredible happens out there, man. Something he can't even explain. If only they'd come to watch. Like Anh-thu did. Then they'd see it for themselves. That he's not retarded. That he's actually really good at something. Great, even. That he's been blessed.

Maybe then they would have wanted to keep him.

When Anh-thu is finished sweeping she puts the broom and dustpan back into the storage closet, picks up the brown paper bag and carries it with her into the employee bathroom. She takes off her work clothes, a brown Millers T-shirt and jean skirt, and pulls her summer dress out of her bag. She lifts it above her head and slips it on. She changes her shoes, too, all the while staring at the brown paper bag in front of her.

Anh-thu finally takes the bag in her hands, unfolds the top and slides the box into her palm. Her stomach drops. It's a home pregnancy test. How could Laura have known? Does everybody know? Does she even want to know what it will tell her? She's too young. Sticky's too young. He has his basketball, and there's college. Her dad and brothers would kill her. But then to have the chance to do right what her own mom did so wrong. Even if it started today, on her sixteenth birthday.

Anh-thu tries to push all of these thoughts out of her head as she follows the directions. Then she waits.

• • •

A chorus of honking pulls Sticky out of his head.

He looks over at the road and spies three cars stopped at a green light while an old man is trying to pull off a tight U-turn. The people in the waiting cars have no patience; they throw their hands in the air all dramatic and shout out their windows.

When Sticky snaps his attention back to the ATM, he finds a skinny-looking white dude in a suit standing alone. A briefcase at his side. He watches the guy pull out a chunk of money and take his card from the machine, then slip another card out of his wallet. He shoves the new card in, punches in a series of numbers and pulls out another stack of cash. He peeks quickly over both shoulders, as if aware that someone's watching him, and then reaches for the second receipt. He stands there organizing himself, slipping a thick stack of twenties into a gold money clip, then slipping the money clip into his back pocket.

Sticky sits up, leans his weight on his hands behind him and checks the big clock above the parking structure: 8:15. He's gotta go get that bracelet now. Before the store closes. The bear. He's only got forty-five minutes before he's supposed to meet Anh-thu, and a feeling of failure spreads through his stomach.

The guy walks away from the machine and cuts through the alley between Third and Fourth. Sticky gets up and grabs his bag. He follows the guy.

The alley behind Third Street is dark and grimy. The asphalt slick from all the years of trash bags being left outside the back doors of fast-food joints to rot. There are small cars parked against the wall, wet mops leaning against giant trash receptacles and mysterious warm smells drifting out of exotic restaurants. Sticky follows behind the guy like a private detective. He keeps him in his vision but stays far enough back that nobody would ever know. He wants to see where the guy's going, and then he'll go get the bracelet and the bear and meet Anh-thu.

Sticky slides his right hand into his pocket, fingers the twelve bucks, fingers the steak knife. He looks up as the guy walks out across Broadway and into the alley on the other side. *The thing about Annie,* Sticky thinks as he crosses the street, *is she wouldn't care if all she got for her birthday was a stuffed bear. She'd love it. That's just the way Annie is.* And maybe he doesn't need to be out stealing stuff so close to his basketball camp. What if he got nabbed? The judge warned him last time to straighten up. He brought up juvenile hall and military-style work camps. And how could he show those coaches what's up if he was standing behind bars? Annie just wants them to spend time together. That's what she's always telling him. She's doesn't trip on all that other stuff. Material things. That's not the kind of stuff she thinks is important.

And that settles it, Sticky thinks. He's not stealing anything today. He's gonna go get the bear and maybe take Anh-thu down to the Santa Monica Pier. They can watch all the different people circling around on the Ferris wheel and talk. The most important thing is to be with her on her birthday.

And without even thinking about it, Sticky starts kind of jogging through the alley. He's excited now because he's settled on a plan. The weight of decision has lifted from his shoulders. He's kind of jogging behind the suit guy, slowly cutting into his lead, while at the same time thinking about Anh-thu's face when she sees the bear. When he sings her "Happy Birthday" in her ear and kisses her sixteen kisses on the lips. And without even thinking about it, Sticky reaches into his pocket and pulls out the steak knife. He pulls the knife out and jogs through the dark alley with it clutched at his side.

The suit guy whips his head around when he hears Sticky's footsteps, but it's too late. Sticky slams into him like a free safety. He lowers his shoulder, lunges at the guy and sends him flying into some plastic trash cans. He thrusts the jagged blade against the guy's neck and grabs a fistful of his hair.

The guy's eyes are wide. His teeth are long and yellow, lips thin and white. His jacket is ripped at both elbows and tiny drops of dark red blood are starting to soak through. The tip of a dark green tattoo juts out above his collar.

Sticky spies the briefcase, which has sprung open in the fall. It's full of little white baggies of powder. Drugs. The guy's a drug dealer. He's tackled a drug dealer. Sticky goes back to his man, opens his mouth to talk but nothing comes out. Instead of talking he yanks at the guy's hair and watches his face cringe.

What the hell you want? the guy says, his voice altered by the pressure of the knife against his throat.

Gimme the money! Sticky says, pressing the knife harder against the guy's throat. *The money in your back pocket!*

OK, OK, OK, the guy says, and he holds his hands out to

his sides. *All right. Just hold on.* He reaches behind his back slowly, the whole time staring into Sticky's darting eyes, and into his back pocket. He pulls out the wad of cash and sets it gently on the pavement. Then he holds his hands out to his sides again. *All right, buddy,* he says, almost in a calm voice now, *there it is. There's the money. But you don't know who I am, buddy. You have the money, but I'm just telling you, you don't know me.*

Sticky releases the guy's hair long enough to pick up the money clip and push it into his own back pocket. He has no idea what to do next and this makes him panic. He cracks the guy in the back of the head with the butt of the steak knife and takes off running. He races down the alley as fast as he can. Fists pumping, mouth sucking in air. Chest pounding, burning. He sprints away from what he's just done as fast as he can, still clutching the steak knife in his hand.

Sticky flies out into Santa Monica Boulevard. He dodges a couple slow-moving cars and ducks into the alley on the other side. He whips his arms at his side, barreling through the length of the alley, and then pops out onto Arizona. A woman in a minivan has to slam on her brakes to avoid hitting him. Her eyes grow huge and she covers her chest with her hand. Sticky slips into the alley on the other side and hurdles a homeless man, an empty crate. On the run, he anxiously looks back over his shoulder but nobody's there. He pops out onto Wilshire and barely slips past a bus speeding west toward the PCH onramp. The driver sounds his deep horn, swerves slightly, and all the people out walking turn to look. But Sticky's already halfway down the alley behind the big Catholic church. When another anxious glance behind him reveals nobody he slows down, ducks behind a big trash receptacle and bends over, hands on knees. He begs for breath. Salty sweat rushes down his face and neck. It runs into his eyes and ears and mouth and he can't get his wind. He leans his head against the church wall. His hands and knees are shaking. When he thinks about what he's done a wave of panic rushes over him. And then guilt. And then shame. And then incredible excitement. He looks up at the stained-glass windows of the church and prays for a deep breath. Just one good deep breath and he'll figure out what's happened.

Sticky peers over his shoulder again, down the dark alley: nobody. He closes his eyes for a second and tries to swallow. He wipes his nose on his shirt and realizes his entire body is shaking uncontrollably. His teeth are chattering. He can't control any part of himself. Then he notices the steak knife in his hand. He chucks it down the alley and feels a wave of nausea wash over him.

He pulls the wad of money out of his pocket with trembling fingers and slips it out of the money clip. He peeks over his shoulder: nobody. He goes to one knee and quickly counts the twenties in his hands:

Twenty-forty-sixty-eighty-a hundred . . .
twenty-forty-sixty-eighty-two hundred . . .
twenty-forty-sixty-eighty-three hundred . . .
twenty-forty-sixty-eighty-four hundred.

Four hundred bucks, man. Four hundred. It's the most money he's ever seen at once. And it's in his hands. *His* hands. He peeks over his shoulder: nobody. He picks up the four stacks of twenties and counts the money out again:

Twenty-forty-sixty-eighty-a hundred . . .
Twenty-forty-sixty-eighty-two hundred . . .
Twenty-forty-sixty-eighty-three hundred . . .
Twenty-forty-sixty-eighty-four hundred.

He wipes the sweat out of his eyes. The sweat off of his forehead. His shirt is completely soaked through, and his heart is still racing. He peers down the dark alley both ways: nobody. He closes his eyes to try and calm down and pulls in his first deep breath. He tries to think about what he's just done. What it means. Whether or not he's crossed some invisible line he told himself he'd never cross. He doesn't know what to think so he stops thinking and pulls in another deep breath. But his body is still trembling. His heart is still racing. He picks up the four stacks of twenties and counts the money out again:

Twenty-forty-sixty-eighty-a hundred . . .
Twenty-forty-sixty-eighty-two hundred . . .
Twenty-forty-sixty-eighty-three hundred . . .
Twenty-forty-sixty-eighty-four hundred.

All this money. In *his* hands. Four hundred. He could take Anh-thu anywhere she wants to go. Let her order anything she wants to order. He could walk her into Macy's and buy her whatever bracelet she wants. He thinks of Dante. Wonders what he'll say when he hears about this. *You gotta do what you gotta do,* is what he'll say. But then when he runs through it again in his head, the tackle and the knife to the throat and the blow to the back of the head, the panic comes back. The nausea. The uncontrollable feeling of falling. He swallows hard and looks down the dark alley both ways: nobody. *Get out of here!* he tells himself. *Come on! Go!* He looks down the alley again: nobody. Picks up the four stacks of twenties and counts the money out again:

Twenty-forty-sixty-eighty-a hundred . . .

twenty-forty-sixty-eighty-two hundred . . .

twenty-forty-sixty-eighty-three hundred . . .

twenty-forty-sixty-eighty-four hundred.

Four hundred bucks. In his hands. *Get out of here, man! Go find Annie!* He picks up the four stacks of twenties and counts the money out again:

Twenty-forty-sixty-eighty-a hundred . . .

twenty-forty-sixty-eighty-two hundred . . .

twenty-forty-sixty-eighty-three hundred . . .

twenty-forty-sixty-eighty-four hundred.

That's it! he tells himself. But as he stands up to leave, he freezes. He can't move. He hasn't counted right. He hasn't stacked the bills right. He hasn't done anything the way it needs to be done, and his body won't let him move on to the next step. The next stage. And as he stands there cursing himself, fighting with his body, his mind, all these images come crashing down on him at once: stepping in and out of the shower, tucking and retucking his shirt, tying and retying the laces of his shoes, brushing and rebrushing his teeth, washing and rewashing his hands, snapping and resnapping his warm-ups, zipping and rezipping his bag, tossing and retossing change into the bowl with Baby hovering over him, spitting and respitting into the bed of the truck with Baby yelling for him in the background. The cash doesn't feel right in his hands. It's off. He's off. He's leaning to one side, like after you spin around and around on a merry-go-round and then get off and try to walk. Like that.

258

He's counted wrong and now he's off. And he can't move. Can't do anything. He peeks over his shoulder: nobody. He gives in to his body and goes to one knee, starts counting the twenties in his hands again:

Twenty-forty-sixty-eighty-a hundred . . .
twenty-forty-sixty-eighty-two hundred . . .
twenty-forty-sixty-eighty-three hundred . . .
twenty-forty-sixty-eighty-four hundred.
And again:
Twenty-forty-sixty-eighty-a hundred . . .
Twenty-forty-sixty-eighty-two hundred . . .
Twenty-forty-sixty-eighty-three hundred . . .
Twenty-forty-sixty-eighty-four hundred.
And again:
Twenty-forty-sixty-eighty-a hundred . . .
Twenty-forty-sixty-eighty-two hundred . . .
Twenty-forty-sixty-eighty-three hundred . . .
Twenty-forty-sixty-eighty-four hundred.

And before Sticky can pick up the four stacks of twenties and count them out yet again, a dark shadow slinks in from the side and sticks something to the back of his head.

You messed up, buddy, a voice says. Sticky goes to turn around but two taps to the back of the head make him stop short. The voice says: *Just keep on lookin at that wall, buddy. This will be over soon.*

The end of the alley is only twenty yards away and Sticky can hear the sound of a car rushing past on California. He can smell the ocean in the air. But all he can feel is the breath of this man on the back of his neck.

Pick up the money, buddy, and hand it up to me slow. Nice

and easy. Sticky reaches for the cash and slowly brings it up over his head.

That's it.

When the guy takes the handoff, Sticky spins around and knocks the object out of the guy's hand. The gun. It tumbles to the ground. The guy staggers back and loses hold of his money. He catches his balance against the trash receptacle and he and Sticky both stare at the gun lying on the ground between them. Sticky jumps at the guy, tries to smack him with a closed fist, but the guy slips it. He shoves Sticky against the wall and reaches down for his gun, cracks Sticky in the mouth. Sticky puts a hand to his bleeding lip. When he looks up the gun is pointed right at his face. He instinctively lunges to the side and sticks his right hand in front of the barrel.

The gun goes off.

The bullet explodes into Sticky's right hand.

The bullet goes straight through the skin between the thumb and forefinger of his shooting hand, ricochets off the church wall and disappears down the alley.

The guy looks both ways, shoves the gun back in his pants. He reaches down to collect the money and grabs the handle of his briefcase. Then he quickly steps over Sticky and takes off running the other way.

Sticky lays his face down flat against the filthy asphalt. Sweat is streaming down his neck. He rolls over clutching his hand. Rolls back the other way. He opens his mouth wide enough to yell but there's no sound. He opens his eyes, cheek mashed against asphalt, and from this strange angle watches the guy running away. Watches the boots of this man lifting and falling in silence. He rolls over and looks the other way, sees two older dudes looking at him from the edge of the alley. One of them is pointing. Sticky closes his eyes and opens them. He closes and opens them again and settles his stare on one of the filthy trash receptacle wheels. He stares at the wheel and keeps his face completely straight and then he passes out from the pain.

Before Anh-thu leaves Millers, Sergio checks her bag. Like he always does. *OK, birthday girl,* he says, zipping it open, looking in for less than a second and then zipping it back up. *Do your best to forget about this crazy place and go have some fun.*

Bye, Annie, Laura and Dori say in a girl-like harmony. Laura winks. Anh-thu smiles, waves to everybody and then walks out into the quiet mall, alone.

All around her, store doors are being shut and locked for the night. Neon signs are being flipped off. Trash bags are being taken out and tossed. Vendors are breaking down their stands and wheeling them away. Security guards, manning the mall exits, fumble with their keys and nod to all the familiar faces of mall employees who head for the parking garage and the freedom of their cars. Anh-thu smiles at one particular guard, Manny, the old Mexican man she always passes on her way out the Colorado exit.

Outside she looks around for Sticky, but there's no sign of him. She leans against the wall and checks her watch: 9:10. He's late, she thinks. But he's always late. It's possible he's never once been on time in his life. And besides, she thinks, how appropriate that he be late today, after she has just discovered that late is all that she is. Ten days late. Nothing more. There will be no big talk tonight. No discussion about the future. No weighty decision to make. Everything is still the same, and she's relieved. She and Sticky are just two high school kids going together.

All of the nervousness Anh-thu has felt for the past couple days has left her exhausted. She hopes Sticky doesn't want to do anything major. Something that might require her having more energy than she has. Mellow sounds better right about now. Some fish tacos at the park or a hot chocolate on Abbot Kinney Boulevard. Something like that, she thinks. Maybe a slice of pizza on the Santa Monica Pier, where they can sit and watch the tourists spinning around on the Ferris wheel. She'd sit and hear about Sticky's day. About the crazy guys at the gym. Dallas, Dreadlock Man, Old-man Perkins, Dante, New York, Crazy Ray. Sticky always comes back to her with some sort of story involving one of those guys, and she likes listening.

A rattling sound coming from behind Anh-thu makes her turn around quick, but it's only Manny shutting and locking the glass doors to the mall. He waves, and she waves back.

A group of high school guys in a red Mustang stare at Anh-thu while they wait for the light to turn green. One of them points and the rest of them laugh. It's late and Anh-thu's starting to feel a little anxious. It's not the guys, though. Guys like that are everywhere. It's more the dress. For the most part, Anh-thu's a jeans-and-sweatshirt kind of girl. But she decided to wear a dress tonight. For Sticky. She peeks down at her watch again: 9:25. Still no sign of him.

262

There's a cool breeze blowing in from the ocean, and the seaweed smell makes Anh-thu feel calm. She's always loved the smell of the ocean. The breeze kicks up a little and blows her hair into her face. She grabs a rubber band from inside her bag.

Anh-thu looks down at her watch: 9:30. Still no sign of Sticky.

After the Good

Samaritans leave, the two who found Sticky and fired off the 9-1-1 call on a cell phone, followed the ambulance to Emergency in a dinged-up Chevy Cavalier; after the cop leaves, taking his twenty-two unanswered questions with him, his breath like the bottom of a coffee mug; after the tall Indian doctor is out the door, the man who came in holding an X-ray and offering heavily accented words of encouragement, who proceeded to stick needles and tweezer out metal shards and tug and blot and stitch, who disclosed in the breathy voice of a woman that the situation would remarkably be devoid of any long-term complications because of where the bullet entered the hand (this diagnosis meaning absolutely nothing to Sticky); after Georgia hands off the necessary paperwork and runs out the door, having spent her entire fifteen-minute visit listing all the reasons she couldn't stay, never once looking down at her foster boy laid up in a hospital bed; after three different nurses, two ladies and a dude, walk out the door, promising to check back within the hour; after everybody has fled the scene, gone on to other parts of their lives having fulfilled their role in the room, it's just Sticky and Anh-thu left, the two of them sitting under a suffocating silence that has spread through the room like a gas.

Anh-thu sits on the edge of a chair next to Sticky's bed. She has tears in her eyes. Puffy cheeks. A cottony mouth. Every question she could think of to ask she has asked. But Sticky's hand is still a mystery. He's been shot. She knows that. But why? And how? And when? The problem is, Sticky isn't talking. He hasn't said a word since she's arrived. Won't even look anybody in the eye. His face is a blank, like the simple oval outline of a face in some kid's coloring book, precrayons.

Anh-thu is running her fingers through Sticky's hair, but he isn't there. He's absent. He's missing. He's an empty vessel. This is his way of dealing with the hurt, she thinks. It's not personal. This is a defense mechanism. This is shock. This is post-traumatic stress disorder. There's a lump in her throat as she runs through terms learned in psych class, trying to make sense of it all. Today is her sixteenth birthday. It's supposed to be a good day. A rite of passage. How did it end like this? She looks at Sticky again—sitting propped up in his hospital bed, hoop shoes still stuck to his feet, white wife-beater still wet with sweat, right hand wrapped in gauze and set in a sling above his chest—and it seems impossible to her how much she's hurting right along with him.

It's two in the morning. A sterile black and white clock counts the seconds. A small fan spins a subtle breeze through the room from left to right and back again. There are a couple of laminated posters above the door that warn whoever's paying attention about the harmful effects of secondhand smoke.

Anh-thu takes Sticky's good hand, the left one, and lays her head on his forearm. The image of Sticky being held up at gunpoint flashes through her head again, but she manages to push it away this time. No use speculating. He'll explain it all soon enough. She wipes her eyes on Sticky's forearm, picks her head back up and looks in his face, says: *I'll take care of you, Sticky. You know I will.* The words coming out thin and hollow.

When Sticky never showed up at the place they'd planned to meet, Anh-thu panicked and called everybody she could think of to call. She called Sticky's house, her dad's work, her brothers, the high school gym, Lincoln Rec, the police, and finally all the local hospitals. When the new UCLA hospital in Santa Monica confirmed that Sticky had indeed been brought into Emergency, she flagged a cab and told the driver to get her there as fast as he could. When they pulled up she paid the guy, rushed to the front desk, asked for Sticky's room number, sprinted through the halls and up the stairs and around the first corner and pushed through the door, where she found Sticky lying in a hospital bed staring at the ceiling. She wrapped her arms around him and started crying and asked question after question and begged for somebody to tell her what had happened. And even after learning that he would be OK, that he was lucky, that he would make a full recovery, she still felt an overwhelming pain in her chest. She'd never seen Sticky that way. Hurt and helpless. Vulnerable. With a complete emptiness in his eyes. And she lay there on him for quite some time, squeezing his shoulders, trying to ignore the fact that he wasn't talking.

Anh-thu stares at Sticky and recalls the earlier exchange between nurses about the basketball they'd pulled out of his bag. The guy nurse asked what *7 FLOW* stood for. And when Sticky didn't answer, one of the lady nurses who had his file open cited the name of Sticky's old foster care pad: Foster Living of the West. House number seven. She said it must be short for that, and the guy nurse nodded his head in agreement.

Anh-thu's ears perked up when she heard that information. Sticky had told her it was a gift from his mom. Something he found under the Christmas tree way back when he was just a kid. And sitting here now, she wonders how well she even knows Sticky.

It's three in the morning. The TV in the upper corner of the room is on without sound. Sticky's right hand is a constant throbbing pain, one that crawls up his arm and into his shoulder, settles in the base of his neck. On the other side of the curtain, an old man's snoring gets louder and louder until he almost chokes on his own breath and wakes up. The springs in his bed crunch and moan as he rolls over and starts the process again.

A nurse walks into the room and glances at Anh-thu sleeping with her head on Sticky's bed, her hand on his thigh. She smiles at Sticky, tiptoes past his bed and around the other side of the curtain. She pulls the old man out of his snore by telling him something in a soft voice. He answers in a slur. In a few seconds she comes back around the curtain, smiles again and leaves the room.

Sticky listens to Anh-thu's breaths get slower and deeper. Feels her heavy hand slip off his leg.

It's four in the morning and Sticky is completely alone. The entire hospital is asleep. Anh-thu's asleep. The old man on the other side of the curtain is asleep. The TV, having turned into bars of color, is asleep. Sticky finally looks down at his right hand. At this point he has to. Everybody else is out of the picture, and now he can try to figure things out.

He reaches up with his left hand and pokes at the gauze. He traces the outline of his right hand and presses harder. A few sparks of sharp pain shoot up through his arm. It hurts. And he can't even move a finger when he goes to clench a fist. There's nothing.

He looks back at the wall, his tired heart sagging in his chest, and lets his left hand drop back into his lap.

And for the first time, Sticky thinks maybe all that magic in his right-hand fingertips might be gone. Stolen away when he put his shooting hand up to the gun. And if that's the case, maybe his whole life is gone too. Who the hell is he without basketball? He's nobody. Without basketball maybe his life is completely meaningless.

Sticky's head is dancing from the morphine the nurses

have running into his veins. It's tough to focus. The room is fuzzy and dark, aside from the dull shine of the overhead lightbulb. And there's a relentless warm hum inside his head.

For a second he forgets where he is. He's lying on a patch of grass outside Sanwa Bank, and the light above him is the moon. He's dreaming about the guys in the gym and the letter in his bag. He's lying on his back in the park under the sun. He can smell the fruit shampoo in Annie's hair as they drift in and out of sleep. He's walking home late at night and a woman in heels is asking him if he knows how to kiss a woman's hand. He's walking home from the gym after playing ball and it's raining. But it feels nice, like a hundred fingertips touching soft as lips. And he's happy because he played so well. Old-man Perkins told him it was like he was operating at a different speed than everybody else. But he said he was graceful, too, like a dancer. He's parked in Dante's car outside Georgia's house saying his goodbyes and just as he's about to get out Dante reaches for his wrist and tells him: *The only reason I come down on you so hard, Stick, is because I care. I care about you like I do my own sons. My own flesh and blood.* And Sticky's nodding and slapping Dante's hand and walking away, but all the while something's growing inside his chest. Something meaningful, important. This strange sense of belonging that he's spent his entire life without. He's walking toward the house thinking about what that means: Dante caring about him. He doesn't have to. And this makes him feel bigger. Much bigger. He's holding himself completely upright and he feels as big as the biggest big man to ever post somebody up on a Lincoln Rec low block. But then he's curled up along the three-point line on a piece of cardboard, starving. And there's a throbbing pain in his hand. And the humming in his head is the sound of all the other homeless waking up beside him. They're all mumbling street mumbles and he realizes he's mumbling too. He's one of them. And when he looks down at his shooting hand all of his fingers are missing. In fact, his entire hand's been amputated. . . .

He wakes up suddenly and finds his hand in the sling. He remembers where he is. Who he is. He's in a hospital bed cause he messed up. And he's been hurt. And when he remembers everything that has happened his stomach drops and he has to swallow down hard on the lump growing in his throat. He has to squeeze his eyes tight to keep everything inside him locked behind closed doors.

It's five in the morning and Sticky looks down at Anh-thu. Her eyes closed, lips barely apart. Breaths long and drawn out. Heavy. A few strands of her long black hair are in her face. He reaches out with his left hand and moves the hair away. She looks so pretty when she's sleeping, he thinks. He studies her face and notices the contrast—her dark skin against his milky white skin.

When he feels a sharp spasm of pain rip through his right hand, he looks at the gauze and wishes he could take it all back. What he's done. He's made a mistake. He wishes he could go back and erase it. Do it over. He would leave the steak knife in the drawer. He would leave everybody alone. Buy Annie the bear and take her to the pier. That's all she wanted. But when he feels the tears coming he does his best to stop thinking altogether. He swallows down hard on his hurt. Because he can't go back. He swallows it like poison, like he always does, and he stares at the bare wall in front of him.

He has to get away from it.

But this is when all the fragile walls finally come crumbling down around Sticky. He's lying in a hospital bed, his throbbing hand in a sling, and everything splits open. Cracks in two. Tears apart. He can no longer pretend he's someone else. He has to give that up, shed his cool. He lets ten years' worth of pretending he doesn't exist come pouring out of his eyes. Streams of heavy tears rush down his face and he refuses to wipe them away. He's been shot in the hand and he's scared he'll never play ball again.

And right then Annie raises her sleepy head. The second she opens her eyes, though, Sticky closes his. He pretends to be asleep. And she kisses his cheek and shifts around in her chair. When she lays her head back on the bed and falls asleep again, Sticky cries even harder. Everything he's had stored up in his chest comes rushing out through his swollen eyes. Annie is still right here with him. He hasn't said a word to her all night, he won't even look at her, but she refuses to give up on him.

And then Sticky goes back to the moment his whole life changed. When he was in the window spitting into the bed of the truck and his mom was in the bathroom screaming his name. *Sticky!* Something in the way he's crying so hard triggers the images to come flooding back.

He finally pulls himself away from the window. He walks toward the bathroom. He steps through the door and there's his mom. She's slumped over in the tub. Cloudy red water spilling onto the floor and still running. He cups his hands over his ears and stares. His face scrunches up and then goes normal again. It feels like he's choking. He's so small. He's just a boy. He picks Baby's head up, tries to balance it straight on her neck, only to have it slump back forward or to the side. He looks at her wrists. He turns the water off, pulls the plug and watches the red start slowly sucking down the drain. He gets up. Zips around the bathroom: to the sink, the toilet, opens the medicine cabinet and brushes all the prescription bottles off the shelves. Bangs his head against the wall. Races back to the tub and puts a hand on Baby's shoulder. Shakes her. Nothing. Shakes her. Nothing. Shakes her. Nothing. Then he falls to a sitting position in the middle of the broken-up tile next to the tub and rocks himself. Back and forth and back and forth and back and forth and back and forth. He covers his ears with his hands and rocks himself. Back and forth and back and forth.

Two cops bust through the front door, yelling.

Sticky continues rocking himself.

The cops tear around the house, yelling: *Anybody here? Anybody here? A neighbor reported screaming!*

They find their way into the bathroom and swing open the door. *Oh, no,* one cop says under his breath. The other steps over Sticky and reaches for Baby's arm. The water fully drained now. The bottom of the tub pink. They check her for a pulse. Check her neck. They take out special tools and check again.

Other cops show up. One scribbles things down on a pad of paper. *What's your name, son?* he wants to know. *What's your name?*

They pull Baby's naked body out of the tub and lay her on a stretcher.

What's your name, son?

There are five, ten, fifteen blue suits with badges staring down at Sticky. At Baby. They lay a blanket on top of her. They pull the blanket up over her face. They wheel her out of the bathroom. They wheel her away from him.

Sticky holds his ears tight and rocks himself. Back and forth and back and forth and back and forth and back and forth.

A cop lifts a steak knife out of the tub with two fingers and places it in a plastic bag.

What's your name, son?

They take fingerprints from the sink, from the tub, from the broken cabinet. They say things to each other in low voices and then one of them makes a call on his radio.

The cop with the pad reaches down and puts his hand on Sticky's shoulder. *What's your name, son?*

Sticky continues rocking, but he brings up his scrunched-up face. He's crying. He looks up at this cop, this blue suit, this face now burned into his mind and tells him through his tears:

My name's Sticky.

The hospital room is dark. The old guy is snoring on his side of the curtain. The fan is humming. And Sticky's crying. He's crying for the first time since that night, and his entire body is shaking. Baby's gone. But he's starting to feel better too. He's starting to feel like a real person. It actually feels good to cry. It's like he can actually feel himself settling into his own body. He feels the beating of his own heart. He no longer wants to hide, pretend he doesn't exist. He is here. In this hospital bed. Breathing. This is who he is. Sticky Reichard.

Travis Reichard.

He stares through his tears at Anh-thu's blurry fingers and he remembers something the old Mexican director said. That maybe it wasn't his fault that people didn't want to keep him. And he thinks about Baby. His mom. Maybe *that* wasn't his fault either. Maybe she had to go to heaven to get better. And the director said what was special about him wasn't the way he played basketball but that he was a good person. And he thinks that if a girl like Annie cares about him, if she's willing to sit next to him all night even after he's messed up so bad, then maybe the director was right. Maybe he really *is* a good person.

Sticky reaches out and puts his hand on top of Annie's. The tears are still coming and his entire body is trembling, but this feels good to Sticky. Reaching out. Letting go. This feels more than good, it feels like life.

Dreadlock Man

rolls right into Lincoln Rec on his ten-speed, dreads pulled back and wrapped in rope, and holds a hand out for the pass. He coasts onto the court, where Slim and Heavy are shooting free throws, says: *Yo, man, lemme get a shot.*

Slim reluctantly delivers a bounce pass, which Dreadlock Man scoops up on the flyby. He circles around at half-court, heads back toward the bucket and tosses up an awkward one-handed fifteen-footer on the move.

Peanut Butter!

The ball bangs violently off the side of the rim, caroms off toward the homeless court and smacks Crazy Ray in the back of the head. A stunned Ray keeps perfectly still for a few seconds, refusing to turn around, and then cautiously lays his head back down on his piece of cardboard and pulls a blanket over his face.

Dallas, stretching out near the far sideline, springs up off the hardwood and retrieves the loose ball. He tucks it under his arm, taps his dad on the shoulder to see if he's okay. Failing to get any kind of response, he shrugs his shoulders. He races toward the basket on the dribble, slows slightly to time his jump, rises up off one foot and rattles home a questionable dunk. *Still got it,* he says to Slim and Heavy on his way back down to the ground.

Come on, Dallas, Slim says. *That wasn't no dunk. That was a power layup.*

Dreadlock Man bikes back on the court holding his hand out again. *Yo, Dallas,* he says, *let your boy get one more shot.*

Old-man Perkins, walking into the gym with Johnson, yells out, *Yo, man, don't give that cat nothin.*

He says, *Dreadlock, you couldn't score if you was the only man in the gym. What you think you gonna do on a bicycle.*

Johnson laughs, says, *And Dallas, man, you couldn't dunk if Jimmy hooked you up with a pogo stick.*

Trey rolls into the gym with New York. They both sling their bags into the bleachers, pull their hoop shoes out and start lacing up. Big Mac rumbles in sipping a Red Bull. Boo cruises in. Hawk. Rob. It's another Saturday morning and Lincoln Rec is slowly filling up. Everybody's stretching out along the sideline and shooting their mouths back and forth.

Jimmy steps out of his office, folds his arms and shakes

his head, watching Dreadlock Man, who's now riding laps around the perimeter of the gym. Jimmy puts two fingers in his mouth and lets go of a piercing whistle. When Dreadlock Man looks up, spots Jimmy, he quickly hops off his bike and walks it over to the bleachers, where he locks up.

Old-man Perkins yells out: *Let's shoot em up! Get this thing goin!*

Yeah, Johnson says. *Can't be here all day. I got city business to attend to.*

But before anybody can make a move for the free-throw line, Sticky walks through the Lincoln Rec doors with Sin in tow. He has his duct-taped headphones around his neck and a UCLA cap pulled slightly crooked.

It's Sticky's first day back at Lincoln Rec after a mini hiatus. He's fresh off the all-star summer camp circuit—for the last three weeks he's been up and down the West Coast with every other high school hotshot, playing in front of coaches and scouts from every big-time college in the country.

Sticky gives daps to some of the guys, pushes his bag under the bleachers.

Sin quietly follows Sticky's lead.

Dante comes strutting into the gym with his bag on his shoulder and goes right up to Sticky. He reaches for Sticky's right hand and holds it up to get a good look. Sticky's scar looks like a purple spider now, three months after the incident—there's a thick blotch of shiny new tissue growing over his wound with several leg-looking scars underneath. Sticky watches Dante's face as he studies his hand.

Lookin a lot better, boy.

Sticky nods.

You let everybody know you the man at them camps?

I held it down, Sticky says.

That's what I like to hear. Dante turns to the rest of the guys and says, *Let's go, y'all. Let the runs begin.*

A few of the guys head for the free-throw line and shoot for captains. Trey has one go in and out. Slim knocks his shot down. Dreadlock Man barely grazes iron, but Big Mac rattles home a line drive and he and Trey immediately start picking their squads. As usual, Dante is the first to go, but today Sticky is selected second. Secretly listening for his draft position, Sticky smiles inside. He's moving on up the food chain.

While the rest of the teams are picked, Dallas says, *I see you brought your boy with you today, Stick.*

Sticky pulls his cap and headphones off, reaches under the bleachers for his bag. *Yeah, this is my buddy Sin.*

Sin nods his head at the regulars.

Sin? Johnson says.

Yeah, Sin says. *My pops nicknamed me that when—*

S-I-N? Dallas interrupts. He turns to Old-man Perkins, says, *Yo, that shit's kind of blasphemous, ain't it?*

How a youngster expect to be right with the good Lord, Perkins says, *when he walkin around callin himself Sin?*

New York, Hawk and Big Mac join the group now circling around a noticeably nervous Sin.

Nah, first-timer, Old-man Perkins adds, *that shit ain't gonna fly around here.*

It'd be a sin on our part, Johnson points out, *to call the boy Sin.* Everybody nods their head with Johnson's logic.

Sin looks over at Sticky as the guys continue to light into

him about his name. Sticky laughs under his breath. He thinks about how far he's come since *his* first day. How much he's learned. And the guys see him as one of their own now. Dallas said it best just before the end of school. They were all sitting up in the bleachers after a full day's run and out of nowhere he turned to the rest of the guys and said: *Yo, I don't know about y'all, but when I look at Stick now, I don't even see white. I see family.* All the guys nodded their heads when Dallas said that.

Sticky zips open his bag and stashes his headphones and cap inside. He spots the letter from UCLA he received in the mail yesterday and pulls it out. He has the urge to run it over to Dante, tell him: See, D? This is how much I was lettin them know at them camps. But he'll mention it later. When they get a minute alone. Right now all he wants to do is get back on the court. His home court. He wants to run up and down and hear the familiar voices of the guys. Doesn't matter how important all those camps were for his future, there's still nothing that beats a Saturday at Lincoln Rec.

Sticky slips the letter back into his bag and pushes his bag under the bleachers. He pulls the bag out and pushes it under. Does it three more times and then heads out onto the court, where everybody is matching up. Rob motions Dante over to Sticky, tells him, *Yo, you got white boy, D. I ain't feel like chasin his ass around all day.*

Dallas smacks the ball and says over everybody, *Ball's in!* He checks the ball into New York. New York passes to Boo, who immediately swings it over to Sticky on the wing. Sticky holds the ball for a second and stares into Dante's eyes. A hundred possibilities flash through his head. He sees everybody on the court and knows exactly how they'll react to whatever he does. He knows they're watching. Waiting. He jab-steps a couple times. Smiles as Dante goes back on his heels.

Then he makes his move.

Acknowledgments

I'd like to thank the following people for helping make this novel possible: my patient professors, Harold Jaffe and Lydia Yuknavitch; my creative confidants, Spencer Figueroa, Rob Jones, and Brin Hill; my support system, Sean Kim, Melissa Marconi, Tracee Lee, Matt Van Buren, and Dan Hooker; my incredibly talented editor, Krista Marino; my heart, all the de la Peñas; and my best friend in the world, Kristin Foote.